JAMES ROY DALEY'S
INTO HELL

What do you do when the dead open their eyes?

BOOKS of the DEAD

INTO HELL

Copyright 2011 by James Roy Daley

Cover Art by Chuck Hodi
Book Design by James Roy Daley
Cover Design by Cynthia Gould

FIRST EDITION

10 9 8 7 6 5 4 3 2 1

For more information subscribe to: booksofthedead.blogspot.com

For direct sales and inquiries contact:
besthorror@gmail.com

BOOKS of the DEAD

More great titles from
BOOKS OF THE DEAD

As I listened, enchanted,
I suddenly became aware of a change in my
surroundings...

~H.P. Lovecraft ~ The Crawling Chaos

INTO
HELL

CHAPTER ONE:
QUESTIONS & ANSWERS

1

"Tell me what happened!" Officer Lynch barked with his teeth mashed together, the lines in his weathered face growing deeper, and the veins in his neck bulging beneath his skin like he was changing into some obscure form of reptile.

"Or what?" Stephenie screamed, looking helpless and drained. "You going to hit me again?"

In an attempt to defuse the situation, Officer Quill—standing at 5' 7" and weighing 159 pounds on a heavy day—opened his mouth and placed a hand on his partner's shoulder. It didn't last. Lynch pushed him away and Quill snapped his jaws shut; his words became locked in his throat.

Between the two men, Lynch was the dominant one. Always had been, probably always would be. Still, the interview couldn't go on like this.

Quill stepped away from the table; his glasses slid down his nose.

Lynch made a couple noises that sounded like car backfiring. Then his eyes expanded and his nostrils flared. He squeezed his massive hands into fists that looked like a pair of sledgehammers and shouted, "I never touched you!"

"What?" Stephenie whined, holding back a handful of tears. "How can you say you never touched me? Look at my eye! You hit me! Not once, but twice! You fucking prick cop, you hit me right in the face!"

"Your face was like that when we brought you in! Look at you!"

"No it wasn't! My face wasn't like *this!* What kind of bastard are you? Now that there's another pig in the room you deny slapping me around? YOU HIT ME TWICE! You know it and I know it!"

"TELL ME WHAT HAPPENED!"

"FUCK YOU!"

"Stephenie," Quill said meekly, trying to weather the storm of the two opposing standpoints. "If you can just—"

"GET HIM OUT OF HERE!" Stephenie screamed, pointing a finger directly at Lynch. Tears erupted and rolled down her face. "I'LL TELL YOU WHATEVER YOU WANT, JUST GET THIS SQUARE-HEAD ASSHOLE AWAY FROM ME!"

Lynch, brimming with anger now, pushed Stephenie's hand away forcefully. He regretted doing it immediately after and wished he could take it back. He didn't want to make contact with her. Not again, not in front of Quill.

"That's what I get for uncuffing you?" He said, with his voice lowered distastefully. "An accusing finger rammed in my face?"

"You didn't uncuff me," Stephenie said defiantly. "Your partner did."

Lynch poked himself in the chest, raised his shoulders and stuck his chin out. "But I'm the guy that okayed it!"

Stephenie stiffened, but didn't respond.

The tension decompressed as silence infiltrated the interrogation cell.

Lynch walked away from the suspect, rubbed a hand across the back of his tree-trunk neck and cursed. He had little drops of sweat on his brow, beneath his arms, down his back. Looking at his right hand, he could see that his knuckles were red from the pair of jabs he'd given her. In his mind, he pretended the assault didn't happen. But of course, it did. And it wasn't the first time he got physical with a suspect. Probably wouldn't be the last either. Sometimes his hands had a mind of their own. It wasn't something he was proud of, but it was something he learned to live with.

"Officer Lynch," Quill said, struggling to keep his voice steady. "Would you mind standing in the corner for a moment. I'd like a word with the suspect."

Lynch opened his mouth, hesitated, and said nothing.

He didn't like being told what to do, especially by a little runt like Quill. He would have to straighten the man out, maybe not now. But later. Right now he just wanted that fucking psycho-witch to confess to the murders. Not that she had much of a leg to stand on. She didn't. Her goose was cooked and he knew it. Still, a confession would be the icing on the cake.

Lynch moved away from the table. He pulled a chair from the wall, spun it around and sat with its backside in front of him.

Quill reached into his pocket and pulled out a small recording device. He placed it on the table in front of Stephenie and tapped it with his finger.

Sitting down, he said, "Right now you have the luxury of talking to us small town boys, but soon the F.B.I. will be here and I can promise you this: things will deteriorate quickly later if you're not helpful now. Those F.B.I. boys do things with the combined compassion of a scavenging hyena in a chicken coop. And if we tell 'em you were nothing but trouble, things will get worse from there. I guarantee it. So do yourself a favor. Open your mouth, start talking, and don't leave anything out."

Stephenie's face contorted into a mask of revulsion. Her teeth made a brief appearance before she said, "When the F.B.I. arrives I'll be pressing charges against Sgt. Rock, your tough-guy square-head partner that likes beating on women."

Quill didn't want to smile but almost did. *Sgt. Rock*—that was a good one. How a woman like Stephenie Paige knew about Sgt. Rock was a mystery but nevertheless her description hit the bull's eye. Lynch had a haircut you could set an egg timer to and a face like a frying pan. And yes, now that he thought about it, Lynch did look like Sgt. Rock. All he needed was the army uniform, a machine gun, and a battlefield full of Nazis.

Quill swallowed his smirk and said, "It's absolutely within your civil liberties to press charges, if that's what you wish to do. You can lay charges here and now, in this precinct. There's no need to wait for the F.B.I. but you do need to tell us what happened first. Can you do that?"

Stephenie nodded. "I suppose."

"Great. We can't do anything for you until you tell us your side of the story."

From the corner of the room, Lynch mumbled something under his breath. His eyebrows morphed into checkmarks. He didn't like playing good cop/bad cop. If it were up to him he would slide his gun into the woman's mouth and be done with it. But of course, there were rules. There were *always* rules. Every creep from here to hell and back again walked the streets with a bag of crack in one pocket and an Uzi in the other. And why? The answer was simple: the system was flawed. It made Lynch furious. Sometimes he thought about going cowboy and wiping the streets clean of the filth. Sometimes he thought about it *a lot*.

Quill turned towards his partner, narrowing his eyes.

Lynch knew those eyes. Those eyes said: *Don't fuck up, Lynch. You've caused enough trouble; understand?*

And Lynch understood, all right. If they could get the bitch to make a full confession before the lawyers arrived it would be a major accomplishment, even if the confession wouldn't hold up in a courtroom. In a 'worst case scenario' a recorded confession led to added details, a better understanding of what really happened, and a knot of confusion within the suspect's mind. Simply put, a recorded confession was gold.

Lynch mumbled again but kept his thoughts to himself.

He'd play ball... for now.

"Okay," Quill said. "Tell us what happened. From the beginning."

"From the beginning?" Stephenie asked, as if trying to identify the actual moment things began.

"Yes. Just tell us in the best way you can. We're only trying to help." He turned the recorder on.

Stephenie glanced at the recorder. Then her eyes turned mean and she looked at Lynch. There were a lot of things she could say about that 'trying to help' statement. Square-head wasn't trying to help. He was trying to intimidate, with his fists.

Quill waved a hand in front of Stephenie, blocking her view of Lynch. "Please Mrs. Paige. Don't worry about him."

Stephenie bit back her anger. "Okay," she said. "From the beginning."

Quill nodded. "Yes. That would be fine."

2

"It didn't start today," Stephenie said. "Although I'm sure you both think that it did. It started months ago. I was in bed, alone. I thought I was asleep but now… now I don't know. I've been telling myself it was just a dream, nothing more. And until today I was doing an okay job convincing myself it *was* a dream. I'm not well, you see. I've been going to the doctor. I've been taking prescriptions."

Officer Lynch sat back in his chair. He expelled a large mouthful of air, looked at the ceiling and opened his hands as if he was expecting rain. He didn't like where this bullshit story was going. If that bitch was going to plead insanity he was going have to kill her himself. And although his thoughts had traveled this road before, he had never acted upon them. Not yet. But this *bitch*… this bitch was different. There was *no way* she was going to escape her crimes unpunished. Not this time. Not a fucking chance. If he had to become the vigilante he would. Because he had *seen* it, seen it with his own two eyes. He *knew* what she did—the sick fuck. And more than that, *she* knew what she did too.

Insanity? Screw that, lady. Not this time.

"What prescriptions?" Quill asked, ignoring the one-man sideshow playing out behind him.

Stephenie exhaled a deep breath. "You name it, I've probably taken it: Lorazepam, Lithizine, Mesoridazine, Oxazepam, Thorazine… I don't know. There are a few others. Perphenazine, that's one of them. Check with my doctors. They'll tell you what they've prescribed."

Quill said, "I have a cousin with a schizoaffective disorder. I'm pretty sure he takes Lorazepam."

"Probably."

Quill nodded.

Lynch shifted in his chair again, squeezing his hands together. This was such a corpulent load of crap he figured he'd need a pitchfork to dig his way through it.

Stephenie wiped a tear from her eye and sniffed. Then she shifted her stare towards the table and pursed her lips together. She didn't want to look at the officers, especially Square-head. He was ready to blow a gasket and she had no desire to witness it.

In time, she said, "It was late. My daughter and I live alone. She was asleep already so I was pretty much on my own. I was getting ready for bed... going to the bathroom, that sort of thing. I heard something in my bedroom, so I walked across the hall. I still had a toothbrush in my hand—"

Although Quill had been trained to stay quiet while a suspect was talking, he asked, "What's your daughter's name?"

Stephenie looked up. "Huh?"

"Your daughter? What's her name?"

"Oh. Carrie. Her name is Carrie Paige. You know that."

Quill nodded his head again. Yes, he certainly *did* know that. Carrie had presented enough details to give him nightmares for a year and create a hole in his heart that might never go away. But he wanted to hear *her* say it. He wanted to find out if Stephenie even knew her daughter's name at this point. After the things Carrie had said, and the things he had seen, he wondered how psychotic this woman might really be. "Go on."

"There was somebody at the window."

"Which window?"

"The one in my bedroom. But you have to understand something: my bedroom is on the second floor. Our house isn't the biggest one on the block, far from it. But it has two floors and it's almost impossible for someone to be at my window. Still, there was someone there all the same."

"Who?"

"I don't know. It was a woman, I guess. She was naked and pale, clinging to the window like some type of insect. Her hair was dark. Her eyes were large. She put a finger to the glass and tapped it. 'Let me in,' she said. And her voice sounded like she had been dead for a year or more. She smiled a terrible smile, with her eyes shining like dirty silver coins. She wanted me to open the window so I did just that. I walked across the room and I opened the window as wide as it would go. I don't know why I did it, but I did it. My heart sank as she came in. She crawled through the opening, down the wall and onto the floor. Her bones cracked; sounded like pencils snapping. After she scurried around on the floor she stood up… crept up, actually, with her body bending in ways no human body should bend. She looked at me and I thought I might faint. I didn't. Somehow I didn't. I could see her long teeth hiding behind her thin white lips. She had the teeth of a vampire, you know? I could see the bloodless veins in her arms and the dark stomach beneath her translucent skin. I could see the little tuft of hair between her legs and I could smell her. Oh God, I could smell her. She smelled the same as she sounded: like she had been dead for ages. Like she had no business being alive in the first place. She smelled like dirt, like earth. Like rot. And like fire. Yes, she smelled like a fire that burned for days and days and days.

"The dead woman reached out to me with her bony hand, touched my chest with her cold, lifeless fingers and said: '*You… you're the one. The dead will rise for you. It will be the beginning of the end, the beginning of the apocalypse. No one will hear you scream. No one will hear your voice! They won't believe your words no matter how much you try to convince them. They will discredit you and your actions. They will call you names behind your back and say you're the one at fault; you're the one responsible, never once thinking you might be their savior, you might be the one they should fall upon their knees and praise!*' And as she said these things to me—these terrible and confounded things—I knew she spoke the truth. Not the Lord's truth, no. But it was the truth all the same. It was the devil's truth! *THE DEVIL'S CONCUBINE WAS INSIDE MY ROOM THAT NIGHT!* IT WAS THE DEVIL—"

"SHUT UP!" Lynch screamed. "HOLY SHIT CRAZY WOMAN! JUST SHUT THE FUCK UP!"

Quill spun around, lifting a hand to silence his partner. Maybe it was the right thing to do, maybe it was wrong. He didn't know, but he had to do *something*. The last thing he needed was for those two to be at each other's throats again.

Stephenie grabbed her hair and pulled on it like she was trying to rip apart her own skull. "EVEN NOW YOU DIS-CREDIT ME! EVEN NOW YOU TRY—"

Lynch snapped. "WELL YOU'RE MAKING IT PRETTY EASY, DON'T YOU THINK, BITCH?! A DEAD WOMAN CAME TO VISIT YOU? A VAMPIRE?! ARE YOU KID-DING ME? IS THAT WHY YOU KILLED ALL THOSE INNOCENT PEOPLE? BECAUSE A DEAD WOMAN CRAWLED THROUGH YOUR WINDOW LIKE A FUCK-ING INSECT A FEW MONTHS BACK?! PLEASE LADY! WHAT DO I LOOK LIKE, A GODDAMN IDIOT?"

"Officer Lynch," Quill said, thinking only now that it was a mistake to un-cuff the woman. But he did un-cuff her. He did. Oh man, oh man... he un-cuffed her even though it was against the rules and he knew he shouldn't be doing it. What was he thinking? If he didn't get the suspect back into cuffs before the F.B.I. arrived he'd be in the doghouse for sure. "Officer Lynch! Please keep your voice down. This is not helping."

"She's trying to get off on an insanity angle! Don't you see it? Can't you tell? This is bullshit! Complete bullshit!"

"Officer Lynch! *ENOUGH!* She can't get off on anything! This isn't a courtroom!"

Lynch slammed a sledgehammer fist against his knee and his top lip lifted up like it was attached to a string. When they were through with this little interview he was going to have a nice long talk with his halfwit partner Quill. How *dare* he speak with a condescending tone in front of a suspect! Who did that midget think he was? He was nothing. He was just a stupid city boy that got lost in the country, nothing more. And if he couldn't see that this fucking bitch was taking them for a long drive off a short dock, he didn't know shit from shat.

"I'm sorry Mrs. Paige," Quill said. He took his glasses from his face, pulled a small cloth from his pocket and cleaned the lens. "Please, go on."

"It's not Mrs. Paige. Not now. Just Miss, so please stop calling me Mrs."

"Very well. Please continue."

"Quill," Lynch said, trying desperately to control his rage. "Get her to talk about *today*. The crazy shit she dreamt about six months ago isn't fucking relevant, okay? Get her to talk about today!"

Quill closed his eyes and put a hand to his face feeling like he was caught in the middle of a hurricane. Lynch made everything so hard, so *extreme*. Some days the guy seemed more like a character from Wrestlemania than a real live policeman; he acted like he was putting on a show for the whole world to see. But he was right, of course. So far the woman had given them nothing. All she did was reinforce the argument that she was mentally unstable. And who knows. Maybe she *was* unstable. Quill wasn't a shrink. He wasn't even sure about his own sanity half the time.

If you get too close to the inmates, his father sometimes said, *you'll become one yourself.*

Lord have mercy, those words rang true more times than not. He felt close to the breaking point some days. And whose fault would that be? Why, it would be his own damn fault. No doubt about it.

Too close to the inmates, Quill thought. *Dear God, I'm too close to the inmates.*

He pushed the thoughts from his mind and said, "Miss Paige, can you tell us about today?"

"Today?"

"Yes, please. If you don't mind."

Stephenie leaned back in her chair. Her eyes returned to the table. Then she began to reconstruct her day...

CHAPTER TWO:
DRIVE

1

Carrie Paige's favorite duffle bag in the whole wide world had a picture of Kermit the Frog on both sides. The bag was black and cute and it said IT'S NOT EASY BEING GREEN on the strap and Carrie thought it was the greatest thing she had ever seen. She brought her bag into the backyard with her when she was playing with her dolls, and she was planning on showing it off on her first day of school, which was eleven days away. She was excited. *Big kids go to school*, her mother often told her. *Big kids go to school and little kids stay home.* Eleven more sleeps and it would be official; she would be a big kid. She was so excited she could hardly think.

Carrie reached into her Kermit bag and shuffled through her important possessions. This included a flower made of construction paper, playing cards, multicolored rocks, a bag of marbles, a handful of crayons and a plastic horse with a squished head.

The playing cards were *always* in her Kermit bag. If they were out of the bag she had them spread around so she could see every card at once. They were very special to her. She cherished each and every one of them and as a result the cards looked like hell.

Her favorite *boy* card was the one that said READY FREDDIE.

Ready Freddie looked so adorable sitting at the kitchen table with a knife in one hand and a fork in the other that sometimes she kissed the card. Freddie had yellow socks, a green bandana, and his tongue was sticking up from his pencil-line lips suggesting that he couldn't wait another minute to eat.

Her favorite *girl* card was FANCY NANCY.

Fancy Nancy sat on a pink-and-white striped chair. She had a hat on her head and a mirror in her hand and a purse that looked like a teakettle. Carrie imagined Ready Freddie and Fancy Nancy getting married someday and having babies that looked just like them.

Other cards she loved included Jolly Jean, Corny Carl, Lady Luisa, Skinny Minnie, Jumping Jack, Scary Harry and Slim Jim. Then there was the OLD MAID. Nobody liked the Old Maid, and because nobody liked her, Carrie decided she liked the Old Maid just fine. It was only fair. Her mother always said if you can't play fair, you shouldn't play at all.

Carrie pulled a photo album from her bag and put the bag at her feet.

The album had a picture of three Care Bears on the cover: Love-A-Lot Bear, Tenderheart Bear, and Bedtime Bear. Care Bears were *okay*, but they weren't half as good as Kermit and were nothing next to SpongeBob.

SpongeBob SquarePants and his best friend Patrick were amazing. If she were a resident of Bikini Bottom she would eat at The Krusty Krab every day, just to play Old Maid with the pair of them.

She opened the photo album, which held one picture per page. She flipped through the pages slowly; then she lifted her Coke can from the cup holder and sucked a mouthful through her straw like she was in a drinking race. After she put the can back in the holder she said, "I hafta go the bathroom."

Stephenie was thirty years old and looked a whole lot like her daughter. Not so much now, but when she was Carrie's age the resemblance was spooky. Back then she was cute. Today she was beautiful. She had subtle features, a slim nose, and lips that were neither thin nor full. On a day like today she fixed her hair and Carrie's hair the same way: in adorable little pigtails. The twosome looked so delightful it made you want to barf.

Stephenie said, "What's that? You need the bathroom?"

"Yeah."

Stephenie slid a hand along the steering wheel, looked at the gas gauge, and said, "Okay. I need to stop anyhow. I'm almost out of gas." She stuck her tongue out and made a silly face and for a moment, Carrie thought her mother looked like Ready Freddie.

Carrie said, "Really?"

"Yep. The gas gauge is telling me it's time for a fill up."

"Are we going to run out of gas? Madeleine Nyssa said that her daddy ran out of gas when they were going to their grandpa's house and they had to call a doctor to get some help."

Stephenie pinched her smile and tried not to laugh. Sometimes it was impossible not to laugh. Carrie was constantly saying things in ways that only a child would consider appropriate. "Madeleine Nyssa told you *that*, did she?"

"Uh-huh. Yes she did. She also said her mommy got mad at her daddy and they were kissing and then she got a bleeding nose."

"Oh really?"

"Uh-huh."

"Well, I don't think we're going to run out of gas there babe, so don't get too worried about it."

"Okay mommy. I won't get too worried about it. I'll try to keep my nose from getting all bleedy too."

Stephenie smiled. "That sounds good. How bad do you need the washroom, really bad?"

Carrie grabbed her Coke and put the straw to her lips and enjoyed another drink. She put the can down and said, "Yes. I have to go *really* bad. It might come out in my pants a little."

"Well don't do that. If you need to pee I'll stop the car and you can pee at the side of the road. Do you want me to pull over so you can go?"

"No. I can hold it inside my tummy 'til we find a bathroom."

Stephenie put pressure on the gas petal and the car moved a little faster. The highway was pretty much empty so she could drive as fast as she wanted. She didn't need a speeding ticket though, so if worst came to worst she *would* pull over and Carrie could relieve herself at the side of the road whether she thought it was a good idea or not.

She said, "Do me a favor, babe?"

"Yeah?"

"Stop drinking the Coke. It only makes you need the bathroom more."

Carrie eyed the can suspiciously. "Okay, I won't have any more until after I go." She grinned, showing the big hole where a tooth had once been.

"Great. Do you have to go number one or number two?"

"Number one." She held up a single finger so her mother could see.

Stephenie nodded her head and Carrie smiled.

Carrie loved her mommy more than Kermit, the Care Bears, and SpongeBob together. And after watching Stephenie nod her head, she decided to nod her head too.

2

Ten minutes passed.

Stephenie turned on the radio and flipped through the stations. She found a song that wasn't too annoying, might have been *Radiohead*. She turned it low and let it play. Resting an elbow on the open window she looked at the gas gauge again.

She was almost out of gas.

She didn't tell Carrie this information, but she was worried about how much gas was in the tank and how far it would take them. Being stranded at the side of the road was quickly becoming more realistic and today wasn't a great day for that type of adventure. It was hot outside. The late August sun wasn't fighting its way through many clouds and the wind factor was nonexistent. Then again, it was nearly 7:30 pm. The heat was sure to ease soon.

Carrie flipped through the pages of her photo album.

Looking at a photo of her daddy, her face saddened. It had been five months since daddy had gone to heaven and she was finally beginning to accept the fact he wasn't coming back. It wasn't fair. Madeleine Nyssa's daddy didn't have to go to heaven. In fact, none of the kids she played with had daddies that had to go away forever.

She wanted her daddy to come home. Sometimes she asked God to send daddy home and she promised to keep it a secret and not tell anybody. Sometimes she asked God if daddy could drop by for a visit because she missed him, and because she wanted to show him the tooth that fell from her mouth after she wiggled it with her tongue. God didn't respond. She wasn't sure if she liked God. She knew she was supposed to love him and figured that loving him was okay, but she didn't know if she liked him. God didn't play fair. He never responded to her questions, he never dropped by to say hello, and he was keeping her daddy all to himself. Mommy said people that don't like sharing are spoiled brats. Sometimes she thought God was a spoiled brat but she never said anything because she didn't want to say any swears.

Stephenie looked at Carrie; her brow furrowed.

Carrie didn't notice.

Stephenie said, "Do you miss him?"

Carrie turned the page. "Yes."

"It's okay to miss him, you know. I miss him. I think about him every day."

"So do I."

"We'll be okay, babe. We'll get through this. Every day things get a little easier so don't worry. It's okay to miss him but try not to worry."

"Are you going to get us a new daddy?"

Stephenie took a moment to find the right combination of words. "I don't know what to tell you, babe. Right now I'm not looking for a new daddy but I don't want to say there won't ever be one. Do you want me to find a new daddy?"

"No. I want the old one to come back."

"Carrie, you know—"

"Yeah, I know, I know. Daddy is on an elevator for heaven and he can't come back to visit us ever, even if God says it's okay. You don't hafta tell me. I know he's not coming home. God won't let him."

Stephenie didn't say anything. She didn't know what to say. This wasn't a new conversation; they had talked about Hal's death a hundred times or more.

Hal had a terrible accident while he was at work and now he was dead and life goes on, even though it's hard. And it *was* hard. The past five months had been hard for so many reasons. Hal's death was the big reason, of course. But the fact that Stephenie had been in-and-out of therapy and prescribed a handful of drugs wasn't helping anything. She was irritable and irregular and her nightmares had her waking up in tears. The doctors (all four of them) were telling Stephenie that when they found a suitable combination of drugs and dosages, sleep would be easier and her body would function more regularly. Until that time she had to be strong, pay close attention to her body, and let them know what was happening.

Stephenie figured the trip would be good for both of them. Visiting mom and dad was something she didn't do often enough. And besides, a six and a half hour drive wasn't *that* far. It was doable. And it was time.

Hanging from the rearview mirror was a small portrait of Jesus Christ.

Stephenie's mother had given it to her at Hal's funeral. She hung the portrait around the mirror for no real reason, aside from the fact that her mother would notice it and appreciate it being there. Oddly enough, she liked it there too. She wasn't a Catholic or a Christian, but she found comfort in the image. Jesus had eyes that were kind and sad and without a trace of anger. And if the stories were true he had a reason to be angry, *beyond* angry. If the stories were just stories, well then, she supposed there was something worth thinking about inside the message.

Stephenie looked at the gas gauge again.

Empty.

A cold sweat threatened to break out on her forehead.

Carrie said, "Are you okay, mommy?"

Stephenie took her eyes off the road and looked at her daughter. "What's that, babe?"

"I said, are you alright?"

Stephenie was emotionally charged, strung out on meds, and had a reoccurring nightmare where her husband fell eighteen stories and landed on a sign that said DANGER - MEN WORKING. Sometimes Hal screamed as he fell and sometimes he didn't. Sometimes he said things as he dropped. Things like, *I told you I didn't want to go to work today. I told you I wasn't feeling well, right babe? Why did you push me into going to work today, Stephenie? Why didn't you let me stay home? I knew I wasn't feeling well and you said I was being a lazy baby. You said I was making excuses and now I'm dead. Is that what you wanted, Stephenie? Is that what you wanted, babe? Who's going to take care of Carrie now, huh? Who's going to bring home the bacon? Not you, Stephenie. You're falling apart. You're falling apart and I'm just falling. And when I hit the ground I won't make a simple little splat on the sidewalk; oh no. I'll come down on the fence and my body will be severed in half. It will be a closed casket funeral and while you're standing above my remains it will occur to you that I could have been placed in two separate boxes. Whose fault do you think that is, huh babe? Do you have an answer for me? Huh? Do you or not? Do you know what I think? I think it's your fault I was chopped in half at the waist, Stephenie. I think it's ALL YOUR FAULT.*

"Mom?"

"Huh?"

"I said are you alright? You look pale, mom. You look like you're sweating."

Stephenie focused on the road, knowing she could have driven the car straight into a river without knowing it. She said, "I'm okay."

"Are you sure?"

"Yeah. I'm sure."

Carrie put her hand on the Coke can then pulled her hand away as if her fingers had been burned. She squeezed her legs together and snuck a hand in-between them.

She said, "Okay mom. Just checking."

"I love you. Don't worry about me. Things are going to be all right. You just watch."

Up ahead was *something*; Stephenie wasn't sure what the something was, but it looked promising. Less than twenty seconds later everything came into view. There was a gas station with a restaurant attached to it. Carrie could go to the bathroom and she'd be able to fill up the tank. Everything was going to work out just fine.

"Look, babe," Stephenie said. "A place to go to the bathroom."

Carrie looked honestly relieved. "That's good," she said. "I thought I might go pee-pee in my pants even though I said I wouldn't."

"Can you hold it another minute?"

"I think so."

"Well try, babe. Try."

CHAPTER THREE:
KING'S DINER

1

Stephenie pulled off the highway and onto the establishment's asphalted driveway. A large neon sign said KING'S DINER. It looked seventy years old or more. She pulled her car next to a pair of gas pumps that looked as old as the sign, if not older. Above each pump there was a weather-faded notice that read: WE SERVE.

Little Carrie opened her door with a grunt, jumped out of the car, and tossed her photo-album on the seat. The pavement felt hard beneath her feet. The book bounced and fell open on a random page. The page had a photo of Carrie sitting on a swing with Stephenie standing behind her.

"Wait a minute, babe," Stephenie said, reaching for her ignition keys. She thought she heard the words, *Okay, mom.* But then she watched Carrie shaking her head in total disagreement.

"I can't," Carrie shouted. "I've got to go to the bathroom super-duper or I'm going to make an uh-oh in my pants!"

Carrie hustled towards the restaurant like she was in a hurry, leaving the car door wide open. She squeezed her knees together and struggled with the restaurant door, which seemed to weigh a thousand pounds or more. She pulled on the handle with all her might; in the end she managed to wiggle herself inside. Just.

Stephenie turned the car off, unlatched her seatbelt and felt it slide across her waist. She unlocked her door, swung the door open and stepped outside, leaving her keys dangling in the ignition. The sun had begun to set but the temperature was still hot. It was muggy out; the air felt thicker than most days.

Her eyes scanned the parking lot for an attendant. Didn't see one.

Across the road a single bungalow sat before the backdrop of undeveloped land like it had been misplaced. It had dark windows and was made of brick. It had a long driveway on the right hand side. There was no garage, few trees. Thick green grass was growing long. There was no sidewalk in front of the building, no curb either. The grass just shrank away, diminishing into rocks, pebbles, and sand, until it came to the clearly defined edge of the highway, which was old but in good condition, faded but not overly weathered.

She dismissed the house and all the details that defined it. She walked towards the gas pump and looked over each shoulder, once again trying to locate the man in charge. She didn't see him. There was a greased-out gas-shack attached to the restaurant. Maybe he was there? Or perhaps he was picking his ass inside the restaurant, ordering coffee and making time with the waitress. That seemed about right. For a moment she wondered if the attendant might actually be a woman, but for reasons unknown the idea didn't seemed to fit. So, assuming the attendant *was* a man, where the hell was he?

The attendant's hiding place was unknown, a lackluster mystery.

Didn't really matter, she supposed. She knew how to pump gas and if the attendant didn't like it he could suck on a lemon and piss up a rope.

After she unscrewed her car's gas cap, she lifted the nozzle and switched the pump on by lifting an ancient looking metal lever. She stuck the nozzle into her tank and squeezed the trigger. Nothing happened. She opened her fingers, waited a moment, and squeezed the trigger again. Still nothing.

"Huh," she said, with an eyebrow lifted and her tongue peeking out between her teeth.

Stephenie flicked the gas-pump switch on and off a number of times and squeezed the trigger a number of times and still nothing worked. She returned the nozzle to its place and walked around in a circle.

It was a hot day. Nice, but hot.

She waited ten seconds that seemed like ten hours and walked towards the restaurant feeling like a failure.

Between the entrance to the gas station and the restaurant's main door was a patio swing made of wood. The swing could hold three people, two comfortably. Sitting on the swing was a thin girl with dark hair. Her name was Christina Split; she wore an attractive brown dress covered in white polka dots. The dress looked retro. She looked about eighteen. Stephenie noticed her earlier but ignored her because she was clearly not the person in charge.

Christina—who had been quite literally, twiddling her thumbs—lifted a hand from her lap and waved, offering a sad little smile.

Stephenie waved back. She considered saying 'hi' but didn't. Instead she pulled the restaurant door open and stepped inside while nodding her head and making a face that felt comfortable to wear but might have been humorous to see. Bells rang. Not the electric kind, but the old-fashioned, 'bells hanging above the door' kind that made every day seem like Christmas. Carrie didn't open the door with enough gusto to make them cry out, but Stephenie had. Then the ringing faded and the door closed behind her. Stephenie's eyes popped open. Her heart started pounding, her breathing became labored and she thought she might be sick.

The restaurant was a slaughterhouse.

The customers and staff were splattered everywhere. They were slumped over in the booths and in pieces on the floor. Body parts were on the tables and chairs. The walls were soaked with blood. The carnage was nearly immeasurable.

Stephenie stumbled; her mouth became dry.

Spinning, the world was spinning.

She put her hands on her knees and felt her stomach heave. Somehow she held it in. She wasn't sick on the floor but she wanted to be. Not that being sick would fix anything. It wouldn't. And her view wasn't better now that she was crouched over like an umpire at a ball game; it was worse.

She was looking at a corpse.

The corpse wore a yellow waitress uniform that consisted of a loose button shirt, glossy black shoes, and a miniskirt. The dead woman was twenty-five years old, give or take a year. Her nametag said SUSAN; her head was twisted awkwardly towards the door. Her skull had been cracked apart like an egg.

Stephenie could see the woman's brain just as clearly as she could count the bone fragments lying on top of it. And still, she held her nausea at bay. She held it because she didn't want to vomit on the girl. She didn't dare move, fearing her stomach would revolt against such action, leading her into a bought of illness that would last fifteen minutes or more.

She closed her eyes and squeezed them tight.

When she opened them nothing had changed. She was getting a real close look at this waitress named Susan, whose eyes were wide open, shockingly open, dreadfully open. Her face held an expression of terror so absolute she seemed to have died of fright before the killing blow had been able to claim her.

In time, Stephenie lifted herself to an upright position.

There was a puddle of blood around Susan's head and tiny footprints were in it. *Tiny* footprints.

Carrie's footprints.

"Where's Carrie?" she whispered.

Then she closed her eyes, telling herself she was trapped inside a dream, a *terrible* dream—a nightmare, in fact. More than anything else, that's what she wanted to believe. Otherwise she'd need to face the fact that she was standing in a horrific bloodbath and her five-year-old daughter was suddenly gone.

2

The scene was tranquil. Everything was calm. The customers were eating and socializing, the staff were busy working and everyone was happy. There was no blood on the walls, no bodies slumped over in the booths, no body parts lying amputated on the floor. There was nothing out of the ordinary. Nothing disturbing. Nothing to suggest there was a problem big enough to have people shaking their heads in disbelief. It was a diner, just a simple diner with no strings attached. It had stools with red seatcovers, which were bolted to the floor in front of the counter. It had booths with divisional walls that were a little more than waist high, giving privacy but not *too much* privacy. It had cheap paintings on the walls, hanging between the dark windows. Florescent lights buzzed in the ceiling and ceiling fans spun below. It was the type of place that gets labeled a greasy spoon and often times deserves the label. It smelled like coffee, toast, and bacon. The smell alone was enough to get your stomach rumbling and your waistline expanding.

Stephenie felt a tug on her finger. She heard a voice. It was a child's voice, her daughter's voice.

The voice said, "Mom?"

Sitting inside a booth in the center of the diner was a woman named Angela Mezzo. She was a beautiful Italian lady with dark hair and an exotic appearance. Her lips were full and her cheekbones were high. She was roughly the same age as Stephenie, twenty-nine, maybe thirty. But unlike Stephenie her youthful exterior was no longer present. Not in a bad way, in a good way. She had womanly features that weren't restricted to the curves of her body, but on her face too. In contrast, Stephenie's appearance suggested that she might carry her inner-girl around with her until the day she died.

Angela lifted a coffee mug from the table with delicate, manicured hands. She swallowed a sip of coffee without making a sound.

The mug had a yellow happy face painted on the side. It was the same yellow happy face that had been produced and reproduced a hundred million times and can be found on cups and glasses in dollar stores around the world.

Stephenie felt another tug on her finger. She heard the voice again: "Mom?"

Angela sat the mug on the table in front of her. She started to grin, but the grin sat on her face wrong somehow, like it didn't belong there, like it belonged somewhere else.

Stephenie's eyes narrowed. She had seen that smile before but didn't know where.

Angela's grin thickened, growing hard across her features like old gravy left forgotten on the stove.

Now Stephenie knew.

The smile was lifted from her late husband, Hal. It was the same smile he made in her dreams, in her nightmares. Not when he was falling, but the moment before he hit the sign that said DANGER and his body was severed at the waist. But why was Hal's smile on Angela's face? It had to be a coincidence.

Angela began changing. Her eyes turned blacker than oil and her mouth crept open like a squeaky door in a haunted house. Her head tilted; hair swooped in front of her face and her skin became pale. For a moment Stephenie thought she might crumble into dust.

Then came a third tug on her finger.

The tug seemed more urgent this time, but still, it was gentle. A child's hand was wrapped around her finger and Stephenie knew it was Carrie's hand, which was good news indeed because if Carrie was pulling her finger Stephenie knew exactly where the girl was hiding and there would be nothing more to worry about, nothing at all. Nothing except the cold hard fact that a room full of strangers was chopped into a million pieces and somebody was responsible. Strangers don't kill themselves when they step out for a bite to eat—no way, no chance, no how.

But the room *wasn't* filled with dead people. The room was just the way you'd expect it to be: the staff were bustling about and the customers were enjoying their meals.

Except for Angela Mezzo.

Angela was sitting at the table with her happy-face mug in front. Her eyes were black and her mouth hung open like someone had snagged it with a hook and given it a good yank.

Now she was about to say something.

Stephenie didn't want to hear it, not a single word. Once Angela started talking everything would be so bad she'd want to scream.

She felt another tug on her finger. Then the hand slipped away and that was the end of it. The finger tugging was over. If Carrie had been there she was gone now. She was gone to wherever she may be.

Stephenie was alone. Alone in the room with the cheerful people that didn't notice Angela's eyes had turned black and the color was draining from her skin. She was alone in the room with a ghoul that was opening her mouth so horrifically wide that a rat could crawl from her throat with room to spare.

Now Angela did speak. She did. And when she spoke it wasn't a woman's voice that Stephenie heard; it was a child's voice. It was Carrie's voice. Carrie's voice was creeping free of that cavernous void that needed to be shut.

The voice said, "Mom?"

And Stephenie opened her eyes.

3

Angela Mezzo was indeed dead. Her lifeless body was lying awkwardly across the table. Her fingers were wrapped around the coffee mug like she was about to take a drink. The yellow happy face on the mug smiled in spite of the carnage around it.

Stephenie lifted her stare from Angela, but everywhere she looked there was a new horror waiting to be seen. The restaurant was a killing box, simple as that. It was a killing box that had been exhaustively used.

She said, "Carrie?" Her voice sounded weak and shrouded in terror. "Where are you?"

She stepped forward. Her foot brushed against Susan's corpse. A spike of fear and panic gripped her with such strength she thought she'd faint. She turned quickly and reached for the door. Her foot slipped in the blood, not enough to knock her off balance; just enough to let her know what she was standing in. The walls seemed nearer; the ceiling seemed lower.

She pushed on the glass. The door opened, the bells sang a Christmas tune and out she went.

She was outside.

Yes. Outside. Outside was good. The clean air and the open sky eased the claustrophobic feeling that had clutched her so tightly a moment before. She put both hands on her knees and breathed hard, like she had gone running. Her throat felt dry now, the sweat on her neck gave her a little chill.

This was bad, so very bad.

She stood up army-straight and looked over her right shoulder. The swing was empty. Christina was gone. She looked over her left shoulder. Nothing.

The reality of the moment came rushing in, hitting her with enough power to knock her right out of her shoes.

Where is Carrie? Where's my daughter?

At first she didn't know what to do, what to think. The car was empty. The parking lot was empty. So what did that leave?

It left the restaurant; that's what it left. It left that fucking slaughterhouse, the gore-zone, the abattoir. And she didn't want to go in there. She didn't even want to *think* about going in there.

Stephenie stumbled away from the restaurant like she had one too many at the local pub, more anxious now than anything else. She said, "Carrie? Carrie where are you?"

There was no answer.

"Carrie?"

Nothing.

Carrie was in the restaurant. She had to be. There was nowhere else to hide unless she, she—what? Wandered onto the highway? Sprouted wings and flew away? Disappeared into black-hole void like a spacecraft from a science fiction story?

No. She was inside. Goddamn it, she had to be inside somewhere.

Maybe she's dead.

Stephenie spun around quickly, holding a hand at her chest.

Don't think this way, she thought. *Don't think she's dead, not even for a minute. My daughter isn't dead, just misplaced. Whoever's responsible for this mess is long gone, which means there's no danger here. None. So don't start thinking Carrie is in trouble; it'll only make matters worse.*

She eyed the door.

The restaurant's front door looked the way you'd expect an old door to look: big and grimy with a large glass window. The bottom half had little splotches of dirt and mud clinging to the chipped paint. The glass was tinted dark and nearly impossible to see through. Behind the glass, a thin, dirty curtain hung from a cheap gold colored rod. The curtain needed to be cleaned. The rod needed to have its screws tightened, otherwise it would likely fall from the door before the season's end.

Stephenie stepped towards the building and wrapped her fingers around the door handle. The handle felt like trucker sweat and french-fry grease. She tightened her grip; then taking a deep, stabilizing breath, she pulled the door open. Bells rang. The carnage became visible before she even stepped inside.

"Carrie?" she whispered.

The door closed behind her. The room was awful; it was also very quiet. But there was something... a sound of some kind. She wasn't sure what the sound was but it was there, no louder than the buzz of an electric heater. It didn't sound like a heater though. She didn't know what it sounded like. Scratching? Was that it? Did it sound like something scratching the wall?

"Carrie? Are you here? Hello? Anybody? Is anybody... alive?"

No response.

Stephenie's eyes found Angela again, but she didn't want to look at the woman because Angela did one thing very, very well: she made Stephenie nervous—beyond nervous, actually. She made Stephenie feel like she was ready to die of anxiety. So she looked away, looked towards a dead body that was slumped against the counter, because *that* was better. *Sure it was.*

The corpse had a name: Craig Smyth. He was twenty-one, dressed in a nice white shirt. His hands were on his chest. His legs were curled towards his body, suggesting that he recoiled from something terrible in his last moment of life. There was a large wound near Craig's heart; it separated his ribs and caused a giant puddle on the floor around him. His white shirt was drenched in red.

Stephenie turned away. She said, "Carrie? Are you—"

A wet hand slapped the floor, shocking the silence of the room. Stephenie flinched. Her words got caught in her throat as

37

her head snapped towards the corpse once again. She wasn't sure what she expected to see, but she felt like screaming.

Craig's arm had shifted; his hand had fallen from his chest. Now it was lying on the floor, surrounded in blood.

"Don't freak out," she whispered, allowing a little moan to escape. But Stephenie knew she might freak out. Oh yes. Freaking out was right around the bend and becoming more appealing all the time.

She heard the sound again: *scratch, scratch.*

It came from behind the counter. Yes, she was sure of it now.

She moved past Craig, trying not to look at him. And as she rounded the counter's corner she noticed the countertop had a big hack mark in it, like someone had slammed an axe into it. There was blood around this spot, but that wasn't really surprising; there was blood everywhere. She moved ahead. Another corpse came into view, sitting on the floor near the stove, leaning against a cupboard door that was missing a hinge. Another waitress: Jennifer Boyle. The young woman's open eyes stared at nothing. Her legs were spread wide, creating a V, exposing her skimpy pink underwear, exposing her flesh. Her left arm had been severed near the elbow. Now it sat at her side, in a dark red puddle that was easily a quarter of an inch thick. The open hand faced the ceiling like an overturned spider. Blood dribbled from her stump.

Stephenie looked at Jennifer; she looked at the severed arm. She was about to turn away when she heard that sound again: *scratch, scratch.* It sounded like, like... like what, a rat dragging its claws against a door? Maybe. She didn't know. But there was a door beside the corpse, and that's where the sound was coming from.

What was in there, a staff bathroom? Closet? Storage room? *Carrie?*

She walked along the path behind the counter, past a pair of coffee makers, towards Jennifer and the door. She could smell greasy food. She could smell coffee as well. There was heat coming from a stove so Stephenie took a moment to turn the elements off; it seemed like the right thing to do. She placed a foot between Jennifer's open legs, and put a hand on the doorknob. In contrast to the hot stove, the knob felt cold. She turned it quickly and pulled, disregarding the fact that she hated rats. Rats were disgusting.

The door opened, hitting Jennifer in the leg.

Stephenie pulled harder, causing Jennifer's right leg to slide towards her left. The sound of dead skin dragging across the floor was enough to make her stomach churn.

4

The next room, Stephenie discovered, was not very big. Why would it be? It was a storage room; aside from a few cases of bottled water and canned soda there wasn't much to look at. There were a few cardboard boxes and a freezer. There was a homemade shelf that housed a bit of clutter, a box of matches, a jar of pennies, and a flashlight. There was an old rotary phone— black, dirty, and attached to the wall. Above it, a Polaroid photograph of a gothic looking staircase was thumb-tacked into the drywall. And, that was about all.

Stephenie eyed the photo briefly and dismissed it. She lifted the handset and listened. The line was dead. And even after she tapped her fingers on the cradle the line remained dead. But that was okay. Stephenie had a cell phone sitting inside her purse, which (if she remembered correctly) was sitting in the backseat of the car.

Having found no evidence of her daughter in the storage room, she stepped into the area behind the counter once again. The door closed behind her. The restaurant looked the same; there was nobody in it. Nobody alive, anyhow.

Stephenie said, "Carrie? Are you here? Carrie? Carrie?" Her voice was a little louder now, a little more daring and bold. There was still no answer. Carrie wasn't inside, meaning she was out. It was the only thing that made sense.

But what about the scratching sound? What happened to that?

She didn't know.

A rat, she told herself. *It's just a rat, hiding in the walls.*

Stephenie stepped out from behind the counter. The restaurant was eerily quiet; she could hear her footfalls echoing throughout the space.

She stopped, eyeing the area on her right.

From where she stood she could see into the gas station nook of the building. There wasn't a door dividing the two sections, just a little hallway type of thing, home to a couple of vending machines, which sat next to a display of newspapers, maps, pamphlets and brochures.

Carrie wasn't inside the gas station. It looked empty too.

Stephenie noticed a framed painting on one of the walls; it was the image of a man and his two boys. All three subjects were standing by a tree on what appeared to be a beautiful summer day. The boys looked happy; the man looked proud.

Beneath the painting was David Gayle. He was a good looking man with a clean looking haircut. He dressed stylishly, if not slightly feminine. He had a light-pink shirt with a crisp white collar.

David's eyes were closed. His bloodless face was locked into an expression of pain and his body had been chopped apart.

Stephenie looked at the painting; then at David, then she looked away. She didn't want to see another corpse, but it didn't matter where she looked. The carnage seemed to be everywhere.

A man named Lee Courtney was propped against a bathroom door. Blood splashed the booth next to him. And next to Lee there was a body, half in and half out of the ladies bathroom. Based on the shoes and the pantyhose, Stephenie figured the corpse to be female. And there was more. Of course there was more. The bloodshed was everywhere she was stupid enough to look. But Stephenie didn't want to look; she had enough. In fact she had *too* much—much too much. She didn't want to look at Lee or at the motionless legs. She didn't want to look at Jennifer's severed arm or at Craig's wounded chest. She didn't want to look at Angela and her smiling coffee mug, or Susan's broken skull. She didn't want to look at David in his nice pink shirt or the painting that was above him. She only wanted to get out of the restaurant, find Carrie, and get away from the apocalyptic nightmare she was currently standing in.

Stephenie walked past Craig, towards the front door. She caught a glimpse of the nametag that said SUSAN and the little footprints in the blood. Her eyes shifted towards Susan's head as if they had a mind of their own; she cursed herself for looking.

Susan's head, which was cracked open like an egg, looked different somehow. It took a second for Stephenie to realize that she couldn't see the woman's brain. Not now. At first it seemed like a blessing, but then, as she stepped outside, she realized something so fucked up her entire world slipped in and out of focus.

Susan's head was no longer twisted towards the doorway.

It had been twisted towards Stephenie.

5

Outside, Stephenie was saying, "Carrie? Carrie? Where are you?" Her voice was louder now, more worried, more anxious. But she wasn't thinking about her Carrie. She was thinking about Susan and the way she was laying. "Carrie?"

She looked at the swing: still empty. Christina was gone.

She walked towards the gas station, kicking rocks as she peeked through the window. There was nobody in the gas station aside from the attendant Stephenie had been looking for earlier, and he was dead.

Suddenly Stephenie Paige put a hand to her mouth like a megaphone and shouted: "CARRIE? WHERE ARE YOU, BABE? WHERE HAVE YOU GONE?"

There was no answer, nothing. And when she looked to the road there wasn't even a car she could wave down. Not one. Not a bus. Not even a friggin' motorcycle. She was beginning to feel like the last person on earth, or like Will Smith in that stupid movie with the zombies, if that's what they were. But oh Lord, she didn't want to think about that. The last thing she needed to do was reminisce about films that gave her the heebie-jeebies. She walked into that particular hum-dinger thinking it might be fun and came out wondering why a guy as charming as Will Smith would be involved in such a thing. Maybe she was being a baby but Stephenie didn't like anything scarier than Harry Potter.

She walked towards her car feeling frustrated and upset. The passenger door was just the way Carrie left it: wide open.

Carrie wasn't in the car.

And now Stephenie had no choice but to wonder: if Carrie wasn't inside, and she wasn't outside, where on God's green earth could she be? This was getting stupid. Where the hell did her daughter go?

An answer came surprisingly quick: around back.

Carrie must have gone behind the restaurant for some reason—but why, oh why, would she do that?

Gawd, Stephenie thought, *behind the restaurant? Really?*

Finding Carrie behind the restaurant was a long shot, a very long shot. But long shots were the only shots left.

A dry little voice inside Stephenie's head spoke. The voice was new, sounded like an old lady's voice, a witch's voice. The tenor was raspy and the tone was borderline insulting. The voice said: *'Round back? That's not the only place to look. You know where she's at—oh yes ya do. Don't 'tend ya don't know. Carrie was goin' to the baffroom, 'member? 'Member how much she needed to use it? She needed to go pee-pee very bad like. And that's where she at: 'side the baffroom. She's not 'round back dearie; so don't waste ya time lookin'. She's inside... inside the killin' box. Prolly cryin' and screamin' and wantin' her momma real bad like. She's prolly—*

Enough, Stephenie thought.

If Carrie was inside the bathroom Stephenie would have heard her screaming, right? Unless she was... *Don't think it. Don't even think it for a minute.*

DEAD.

Carrie's not dead. She's not dead because whoever did this is long gone.

Stephenie looked at the restaurant. Her choices seemed simple: look inside the restaurant again or look around back.

"I don't want to go inside," she whispered. And with that, it was decided. Her left foot moved forward. Her right foot came next, following along like it didn't know what else to do. She was walking, but really—where was she going? Inside or out?

Inside, she thought. *She's inside the bathroom. Oh fucking, fuck, fuck—Carrie's inside the fucking bathroom.*

As she moved towards the door she thought about the waitress named Susan. *Did her head move?*

No, of course not. That was impossible.

Stephenie felt goosebumps cultivating her arms. She put a hand to her brow and squeezed her eyes shut. She wasn't going inside the restaurant. No way. Not yet. She was going to look behind the building first. If Carrie was missing after she took a quick walk around back, well then, she'd go inside, check the bathroom out. And after that—

And after that, what? What's next? Phone the police?

Yes. That was good, *very* good. She'd phone the police after she looked in the bathroom. Maybe even before. Getting the police here was just what this situation called for. But how long would it take for them to arrive? Ten minutes? Fifteen? Either way, it was too long.

Stephenie walked to the right side of the restaurant, knowing her daughter wouldn't be there.

But she might be, and better safe than sorry, right? Right.

Then I'll call the police.

There was a huge empty field, and when Stephenie looked across it she saw a big white farmhouse and an old wooden barn. She didn't see any animals, but there might have been a few. She wasn't exactly looking for animals. She was just looking.

She turned the corner and walked along the side of the restaurant. She walked past a stack of firewood, approached a door and glanced inside.

From her perspective, she could see into the restaurant from an entirely new angle. Her eyes swept across several bodies and landed on Alan Mezzo, husband to Angela Mezzo, father to Mark Mezzo. He was dead, of course. Looked like he had been chopped a few times with an axe. His face was gone, replaced with gore. The blood surrounding him was shiny and crimson.

Stephenie kept walking.

She walked past a pile of bricks and a hose that had been rolled in a coil. She stepped over an abandoned hubcap that lost its shine but gained an inch of green tinged water. Passing that, she turned the corner. Now she was behind the restaurant and there wasn't much to see. There was a field and a forest. No Carrie, and no reason to believe Carrie had come this way. She walked on. A mouse scurried along the wall. A cricket jumped beneath her feet. After stepping around some type of air ventilation box, she turned the corner again.

Now she was on the parking lot side of the building: still no Carrie.

She could see six cars and a yellow school bus. Leaning against the bus was a woman named Karen Peel. Like the others, she was dead. Her hands were covered in blood. Her jaw had been smashed apart grotesquely. Multiple teeth were missing. Her eyes were open and staring at the sky.

Stephenie shouted, "CARRIE!"

Nothing.

She turned the corner. Once again she was in front of the gas station, and this time she decided to go in. Why not? The gas station was the only place she hadn't looked.

'Cept the baffroom, that haunting voice from inside her mind was quick to point out. *You hafta check da baffroom. Don't forget to lookin there!*

"No," she found herself whispering. "I don't want to go in there."

She opened the door and stepped inside the gas station.

The attendant was lying on the floor, dressed in blue overalls. He had dark hair and dark skin. His head had been split open and a giant amount of fluid had leaked onto the cheap linoleum tiles. One of his eyeballs looked like it had popped, and the juices had leaked across his face. It looked a little bit like apple flavored Jell-O.

Sitting on the counter was another rotary phone.

Stephenie lifted it up and listened.

It was dead. Of course it was dead. Everything was dead. The whole fucking world was dead and at this point, who the hell cared? Not Stephenie. She just wanted to find her daughter and get the fuck out of dodge.

Stephenie stepped outside and approached her car with fast, seemingly angry steps. She slammed Carrie's door shut and screamed—really, really, screamed: "CARRIE!! WHERE ARE YOU!! WHERE ARE YOU CARRIE?! WHERE THE HELL DID YOU GO?!"

Nothing.

"ANSWER ME!"

Again, nothing.

She stormed to her side of the car and whipped her door open. She sat down in the driver's seat, reached into the backseat, and snagged her purse. She unbuckled the buckle, unzipped the zipper and yanked it open. She started rooting around, looking for her phone in a frenzy. It wasn't in there, but it *had* to be in there. She brought her phone everywhere.

"Come on," she bitched. "Where the fuck are you? Where the fuck is my fuck, fuck, fuckin' phone?"

It was gone. It just wasn't there. No matter how much she looked she couldn't find it. It must have been—

"Attached to my fucking charger," she barked. "FUCK!"

She dug through her purse some more and suddenly she had it: her phone. It wasn't connected to her charger. It was right where she left it, inside her purse. She looked at the screen and the battery was full.

"Okay," she whispered. "Stay calm."

She dialed 911 and put the phone to her ear.

Nothing.

She dialed 911 and put the phone to her ear.

Nothing.

She dialed 911 and put the phone to her ear.

Still nothing. It wasn't working. The fucking phone wasn't working—but why? There was no reason in the world for the phone to be out of order. Not one.

"SHIT!"

Furious, she threw the phone into the car's backseat, lifted her purse up and squeezed it like she was trying to extract juice from it. She tossed it into the backseat carelessly. It bounced onto its side and a handful of change fell out of it, along with a lighter, a couple of business cards, and a pair of sunglasses. She was mad now—mad at the asshole that killed the people in the restaurant, mad at Carrie for disappearing, and most of all, she was mad at herself for being in such a dreadful position. This was awful! How did this happen?

Stephenie had *enough*.

It was time to change the situation, time to think outside the box.

She grabbed the keys dangling in the ignition, started the motor, and slammed the car into drive. A moment later she had her foot on the gas pedal, the tires were spinning and the car was racing along the empty highway, chasing its own headlights. Her vision blurred, her chest began quivering and all at once she started to cry.

6

Whacha doing? The voice inside her mind asked, sounding angry and bitchy and not in the least bit amused. *You gonna drive away? Really? You gonna leave ya daughter back at the rest'rant? Have ya no heart? No soul? She needs ya! Don't ya get it? Your daughter needs ya, dearie, now—more than ever. Didn't ya see the blood, the carnage, da bodies on the floor? What do ya think happened to those people? Do you think they's asleepin'? Is that it? Somebody went into King's Diner and chopped 'em apart! You hafta go back! You hafta find your daughter, babe!*

"I CAN'T," Stephenie screamed, thinking: *don't call me 'babe.' That's* my *word, you fucking witch.* "SHE'S NOT BACK THERE!"

For a moment everything seemed quiet. But it wasn't. She could hear the road beneath the tires and the wind coming through the open window. Her breath was coming out loud and labored. The radio was playing a song she didn't recognize, or enjoy. It sounded like pop-punk garbage, a song about life as teenager, written by a middle-aged songwriter.

There were no cars in front of her, none behind. She turned off the radio, making things a little better. She squeezed the steering wheel like she was trying to kill it; then she glanced at the passenger's seat.

The photo album was lying open. The photograph of Carrie sitting on a swing with Stephenie standing beside her was easy to see. Within the image, Carrie's mouth was wide-open and she was having the time of her life. Stephenie also seemed happy. But her facsimile showed a controlled type of happy, a thoughtful kind of happy. Not like Carrie; she was damn near busting at the seams.

Stephenie pulled her eyes away from the photograph.

Carrie's Coke can was sitting in its cup holder, half empty. The straw had little drops of Coke still clinging to its side.

A moment passed. She kept driving.

The voice inside her head returned. It didn't sound angry now. It didn't sound upset or disappointed either. It sounded like a hillbilly psychiatrist, trying to untangle the jumbled clutter inside a client's mind.

It said, *Carrie's not out here ya know. She might not be in the parkin' lot and she might not be behind the rest'rant, but she could be* inside *the rest'rant. You know that. I know you know that.*

There was a pause; it didn't last long.

She said she needed da baffroom and for whatever reason, ya didn't look. Now, I'm not lecturin'. I'm just sayin'. You need to go back and look for ya daughter, Stephenie. You don't have a choice. How do ya think Carrie is goin' feel when she steps outta the baffroom and finds ya missing. She'll never forgive ya. Not ever. When she's your age she'll understand what you did and curse ya fer it forever. Leaving ya daughter 'lone in a place like that? Come now dearie. You're a smarter woman than that. You're a better person than that too. Come now, babe. Stop the car and turn 'round. Go find ya daughter.

Stephenie didn't say anything.

Time passed.

The voice returned, harder this time. Less caring. *Ya gonna run out of gas.*

Stephenie looked at the gas gauge. Empty. It was empty. How much farther until the next station, thirty miles? Fifty miles? If the car died, what would she do? Kick the tires, and then what? Walk towards the restaurant? Goddamn it, that's exactly what she'd do. She's start walking towards that fucking restaurant. It wasn't fair. The entire situation wasn't fair.

Stephenie squished her lips together, hit the brake, and pulled the car to the side of the road. Slowly, she turned herself around. The Jesus portrait swayed back and forth.

The time to return had come.

Lord above, help her; it was time to look in the bathroom.

∞∞∞Θ∞∞∞

The drive seemed shorter somehow, like she returned to the restaurant within seconds. She parked the car carelessly; headlights pointed at the restaurant. And when she shut the car down the sky above was dark.

The car door was flung open and out stepped Stephenie. Her shoulders were slumped; her expression was grave. She slammed the door hard, like she was trying to make a point. After she stuffed her car keys into her pocket, she walked towards the restaurant. Somehow, it loomed. She didn't want to go inside. Seeing those bodies again was the last thing in the world she wanted to do. But here she was, reaching for the door like someone who couldn't get enough of a bad situation.

She stopped; turned around.

Cupping both hands in front of her mouth she tried her luck again, believing in her heart it was pointless. "CARRIE! CARRIE! CAN YOU HEAR ME? ARE YOU THERE? ANSWER ME, BABE! ANSWER ME!"

Nothing.

"Okay," she whispered. "Now I know."

For a moment she looked at the bungalow on the other side of the road. There was a light on inside.

Another option, she thought.

Then she turned towards the restaurant, put her hand on the handle and opened the door. Bells chimed like Christmas.

7

Stephenie stepped inside; the door closed behind her. For a moment she wondered if she was in the right place. The answer was yes; of course she was in the right place. But things were different now. The tables and chairs were in different places, the walls looked dirtier, the light seemed dimmer.

She looked down.

Susan was still there; she hadn't moved.

Oh yes she did, yes she did—she moved her head; remember? She moved it just a little bit before you went for a drive. So don't pretend things are the same when they're not. She moved. You better believe she moved. She moved and that's bad fucking news for you because dead people aren't supposed to move. They're supposed to stay right where they are and not move a fucking muscle. Look at her! Look, and tell me—what do you see?

Stephenie's eyes widened.

The puddle of blood surrounding Susan's head seemed bigger now, and her uniform looked darker. It wasn't even yellow now. It was tan. But how the hell was *that* possible? Simple answer: it wasn't. It must have been tan originally. Or maybe things looked different because the sun had set. Was that a logical reason? No, probably not. But it was the best she could come up with.

Stephenie opened her mouth to speak and discovered her throat was parched. She swallowed, licked her lips, and said, "Carrie, are you here, babe? Please tell me you're here. I've come to take you home. "

No answer. Of course there was no answer.

She stepped over Susan's body. For a moment her thoughts betrayed her. She imagined Susan reaching out and grabbing her by the leg. She imagined the waitress looking up at her with black tar running from her cold and lifeless eyes, a big upside-down grin slapped across her face, and her brains oozing from her skull like they were attached to a pump. She imagined the corpse saying *BRAINS*, or something equally impossible. But that was stupid, right? Of course it was. Dead people don't do that. They don't say *BRAINS* moments before they tear off your head and eat the goop inside. Never have; never will. Only in low budget movies and expensive Hollywood remakes does that sort of thing happen. Not in real life. So what the hell was Stephenie doing? Did she really need to think such crazy thoughts?

She walked towards the booths sitting in the center of the room, looking at Angela's corpse.

Then she looked at Angela's fingers.

The fingers were two inches away from the coffee mug.

Two inches.

That wasn't right. Wasn't she *holding* the coffee mug a few minutes ago? Stephenie could have sworn the woman had been *holding* the mug. Weren't her fingers wrapped around...

Stephenie stopped walking. Her eyes widened and her mouth slinked open. Her left hand trembled and her heart pounded her ribs like it was trying to find its way out of her body.

No, she thought. *I'm wrong. I have to be wrong.*

She was looking at the mug now. Not at Angela Mezzo, and not at fingers that may or may not have been wrapped around the mug's handle. She wasn't looking at the two-inch gap between the fingers and the mug's handle, even though the gap probably hadn't been there before. She wasn't even looking at the big pond of blood sitting on the table, or that terrible look of anguish bolted across Angela's pale and lifeless face.

She was looking at the mug. And it was scaring the shit out of her. More than the waitress that may or may not have shifted her head from one position to another, more than her daughter being gone. The mug. Oh God, the mug. She seriously considered screaming, considered turning around, walking out the door and—

And what? The crazy witch-voice inside her head demanded. *Whatcha gonna do? Drive two miles and run outta gas? Go look in the bloody baffroom Stephenie. Go look, right now!*

But—

She looked at the mug again.

The smiling yellow happy face was gone. The face had changed. It looked neutral now, not happy. Just... flat.

Fuck da mug, the voice insisted. *Walk past it and check the baffroom. For the sake of ya daughter, just go.*

Stephenie pressed her teeth together hard enough to make them hurt and squeezed her face into an expression that articulated how much she disliked the current situation. She walked past Angela and the mug, looking at Lee Courtney.

Lee was in a different position. His legs were fully extended and his hands were sitting in his lap. He wasn't propped up against the bathroom door. Now he was leaning against the booth beside the bathroom door.

And the other bathroom...

The legs, the ones with the pantyhose and the high-heel shoes, they were gone.

What the hell happened? When Stephenie was inside the restaurant the first time, and the second time, a pair of legs were sticking out the doorway, deader than snot. She knew it, one hundred percent for sure. So what happened to them? Did they get up and walk away?

Maybe, the voice suggested. *You didn't see that woman, did ya? No. You didn't. Maybe she wasn't dead. Maybe she was just hurt, or maybe she fainted and passed out on the floor. It's possible; so don't worry about it. There's nothing going on here 'cept a big 'ole case of the heebe-geebees. Now go look in the baffroom, your daughter needs ya.*

Stephenie didn't like it.

Stalling, she said, "Carrie? Are you in there? Answer me?"

No answer.

And now Stephenie was hit with a new terror, a new dread. What if the woman with the pantyhose got up and crawled into the bathroom? What if she was waiting?

That's stupid, she thought.

But was it?

Still, stupid or logical, she didn't want to go into that bathroom. Her instincts had been against checking the bathroom for a while now. So what did it mean?

She was freaking out. That's what it meant. It didn't mean anything except the restaurant was creepy and she wanted to go home.

She decided to look in the men's washroom first, not the ladies. She figured it would be easier, safer. Did it make any sense? No. Probably not, but that was okay with her.

She stepped over Lee's legs, pushed the door open and stepped inside.

The room was dark. It smelled like a mix of cheap all-purpose cleaners and harsh disinfectants.

"Isn't this just great," she whispered.

Stephenie slid her hand along the wall until she found a light switch. She flicked it up and the overhead light came on.

The room wasn't very big. There were three urinals, two stalls and a sink. Both stall doors were open. One was empty; the other wasn't.

Sitting on the toilet with his pants around his ankles and his hands hanging at his sides was a man named Dan Meltzer. Dan was a big man: two-twenty, maybe two-thirty. He had short hair and a white t-shirt. The t-shirt wasn't very white. Not now. A massive amount of blood covered both of his shoulders. It had spread along the back of his shirt, across his chest and onto his sleeves. It wasn't surprising. Dan's head had been cracked open, possibly with a sledgehammer or a mallet. His eyeballs, which no longer sat in the proper position on his face, seemed black. The overhead light may have been responsible. Or perhaps his eyes had so much blood inside of them they turned extra dark.

Stephenie turned away from Dan and noticed something else.

There was a dead boy under the sink, sitting in a pool of blood. The kid had been chopped up pretty good. His name was Mark Mezzo, son of Angela Mezzo. He had black hair and a schoolboy uniform—sort of looked like that kid from the *Omen* movie. And like Dan Meltzer—the big man on the toilet—his eyes were wide open.

Stephenie looked at the boy for a few seconds, and when she turned away she saw something in the corner of her eye.

Blink.

Stephenie's head snapped towards him. But the boy was dead, clearly dead. His face was pale and his chin was smashed apart. The amount of blood that had drained out of him was almost unreasonable.

Stephenie turned away from the child, convincing herself that it was just a trick of the light, deception of the eye. Because that's what it had to be, right? Nothing else made sense. He didn't blink. Dead children don't blink.

She stepped out of the bathroom. Now that she was in the restaurant again, she stepped over Lee's legs, knowing there was nowhere else to look except the one place she didn't want to go.

"Okay," she whispered. "This is it."

She put her hand on the bathroom door marked LADIES, pushed it open, and stepped inside.

8

As Stephenie entered the room she counted the stalls. There were four of them, four stalls and a pair of sinks. Otherwise the room was empty.

All four doors, she realized, were closed. She said, "Carrie? Are you in here?"

There was no answer.

She walked forward, pushed the first door open. Nothing.

She pushed the second door open. Nothing.

She pushed the third door open; there was something sitting on the floor, so she crouched down and picked it up.

It was a nametag.

It said:

–NG'S DINER
– E-ANNE

Looking at the tag, Stephenie said, "King's Diner."

She didn't know about the name on the bottom. Might have been Lee-Anne. Might have been something else. It didn't really matter.

She approached the fourth stall, the *last* stall. Still holding the nametag, she pushed the door open with her knuckles.

It was empty.

Strange, she thought. And it *was* strange. She was sure something would happen in the woman's washroom, and now that nothing did she didn't know what to do. Carrie was still missing and there was nowhere else to look. So where did that leave her?

She's abducted, Stephenie thought.

Immediately Stephenie wished the notion had never come to her mind. She didn't want to think her daughter had been *abducted*, not even for a moment. And besides, when could somebody have done that?

Hello, the voice inside said. Stephenie was starting to hate that voice. It was like a nagging crack-whore stepmother that wouldn't mind her own business. And she wouldn't be silenced. Not today. Not until she said her piece. *You drove 'way; 'member? There was a lotta time to stuff Carrie into the trunk of a car and drive off freely, wouldn't ya think, dearie? They could've broken 'er arms and cut 'er throat in no time at all.*

"Don't say that," Stephenie said, horrified.

But it's true. You know that much; of course ya do. Why do ya think I was protestin'? You left her here; don't ya get it? If your daughter has already been 'ducted, don't come cryin' to me 'bout it. It's your own damn fault.

"Shut up."

It's true.

Stephenie didn't want to hear it. Every time the voice inside her head spoke the words hurt a little more. At first she figured the voice was just a fractured division of her own mind, nothing more, nothing less, but now she wasn't so sure. Now she was gaining a visual to go with the audio, which was making the experience worse.

At first the woman in her head looked cartoonish, like that cackling Witch Hazel from the Bugs Bunny shows she watched as a child. Witch Hazel, with her green skin, her blue dress, and her little black legs that were too small for her body. But as time moved on the image was changing, becoming more real. She was no longer a funny old coot that rode around town on a broom and left hairpins flying in her wake, but rather a twisted whore that died a long ago, in a time of violence and pain, cursing the Lord's name and swearing her revenge as they tied the noose and hung her from a tree.

There's nothing in the bathroom, Stephenie thought.

She opened the bathroom door and stepped into the main room. She looked at David Gayle, the dead man sitting beneath the painting of the two happy boys and their father.

And that's when she saw it: David's eyes rolled open.

Stephenie gasped, putting a hand to her mouth. She desperately wanted to look away from the corpse but didn't. She was afraid—afraid to look away, afraid to close her eyes and afraid to look at the other bodies because she didn't want to see more eyes open.

What do you do when the dead open their eyes?

David Gayle was looking at her, his cold, dead eyes unmoving. But open.

Stephenie returned the glare for a long as she dared, but she didn't want to look at the corpse much longer so she looked up, and gasped again.

The painting was different now. Day had turned to night. The two boys inside the image weren't standing by the tree; they were *hanging* from the tree. They had nooses around their broken necks and tongues that had flopped from their open mouths and the father looked like he was laughing. Laughing like he thought executed children were the greatest gift of all. Inside Stephenie's mind she heard a chuckle. And from somewhere in the room, silverware fell from a table and clanked against the floor.

Stephenie's head snapped away from the painting and towards the fallen silverware. She didn't know what to do, what to think. She stepped forward, cautiously, nervously.

David's eyes shifted in their sockets. He was watching her. Watching her move. A grin touched the corners of his lips and his hands tightened into fists.

She approached Angela's table. Not because she wanted to, but because she was heading for the exit.

She looked at the coffee mug; she couldn't help it.

The mug looked different now. The neutral expression was gone and the face didn't look happy, or neutral.

It looked *mean.*

Stephenie took another step, followed by another.

She approached Susan. Only now the idea of Susan reaching out and grabbing her by the leg didn't seem so crazy. It seemed like it could happen, or *would* happen. And Stephenie didn't want Susan to reach up with her cold dead hand—oh no, she didn't—so she ran past Susan and blasted out the door.

9

There was somebody in her car.

Not Carrie.

It was a woman named Julie Brooks.

Julie's neck was twisted strangely and her head was lying on the steering wheel showcasing the long crack in her skull. Her mouth yawned lifeless towards the open window and her eyes were rolled into the back of her head.

Stephenie slammed on the brakes and said, "Oh my God!"

How did this happen? she wondered. *How was it possible?*

She approached the car apprehensively, snatching quick glimpses of the area around her. She had a terrible feeling the restaurant door was about to bust open and dead bodies would shuffle their way outside like moviegoers after a Halloween night screening of *Dawn of the Dead*. And what, exactly, would the game plan be *then?* Would she run down the road screaming with her fingers clamped against her face or would she pretend that she was a superhero and battle a rot full of zombies?

Looking through the car window, she could see blood dripping from Julie's chin. She reached out, touched the door's handle. She was about to open it when she took one final look at the restaurant.

The restaurant door didn't open. Zombies didn't come bustling out.

But as she was looking at it, Julie shifted. Her eyes changed position. Her mouth closed. Her head tilted and a string of blood dribbled from her nose.

Stephenie turned away from the restaurant. She opened the car door, causing Julie's body to shift again. She didn't notice her eyes watching her with a cold, hateful stare. She didn't notice Julie's hands crumpling into fists. She didn't notice anything really, so she reached out, took the corpse by the shirt and dragged her from the car.

Julie's body swooped into a new position and fell to the ground with a THUD. Her skull cracked off the pavement and blood splashed across Stephenie's feet.

Stephenie crouched, grabbed the corpse by the shoulders and dragged her away from the car. She dropped the body carelessly. Then something across the road caught her attention: the bungalow. She had forgotten about it.

Maybe it's time to give the bungalow a visit, she thought. And with that, it was decided. She stepped over Julie's body, slammed the car door shut and stepped away from the corpse. Walking across the empty highway, she felt like crying.

∞∞∞⊖∞∞∞

Stephenie made her way across the road and up the stone pebble driveway. She walked up the three steps that led to the front porch quickly, and wasted no time ringing the doorbell. There was no answer, so she rang it again. Still nothing. *Third time's a charm*, she had often said, but here and now the third time was no more productive than the first two. She rapped her knuckles against the wood and looked over her shoulder.

She could see Julie's corpse lying next to the car like a sack of smashed tomatoes. She could see the empty pumps, the yellow school bus and Karen Peel's body lying against it. The place was like a ghost town. There were no cars on the highway and nobody around.

"Screw this," she whispered, noticing the name on the mailbox.

It said: JACOB. Might have been a first name, might have been a last. She didn't know, or care.

Stephenie gripped the doorknob and turned it. The door opened. Stepping inside, she said, "Hello? Is there anybody here? Jacob?"

The lights were on, as she knew they would be. But the place seemed empty.

Stephenie stood in a living room; it was decorated with furnishings from the thirties and forties. The walls were dirty and there was a large reclining chair sitting in the center of the room, faced away from the front door.

There might be someone in it, she thought.

She took a step forward, followed by another. "Hello?"

Everything was quiet.

"If somebody's here, I'll have you know I need help. Can you hear me? Hello?"

The chair was empty; her shoulders came down an inch.

She walked past the chair and into the next room, the kitchen. The room was disgusting. The stove was dirty and the counter looked like it hadn't been cleaned in two years or more. There was a fly crawling on the wall and several cockroaches scurrying across the floor. There was a single window that may have been the dirtiest she had ever seen, and a painting on the wall she didn't bother to look at.

A phone rang.

Stephenie turned towards the sound and saw a staircase leading to the basement.

The phone rang again. The sound was coming from below.

On the staircase wall was a light switch. She clicked it on but nothing happened. Somehow it didn't surprise her. Nothing was working; nothing was easy. She took a step down the stairs, wondering if the staircase would collapse. It didn't. She made her way to the basement without incident.

The basement was small and dark, but she could see. There was a television that looked like it belonged inside a museum sitting across from an old couch. In the corner, next to the couch, was an end table. Sitting on the table was a lamp. It was on. Beside the lamp was the phone.

It rang again.

Stephenie crossed the room and lifted the receiver. "Hello?" There was no response so she tried her luck again. "Hello?"

"Mommy? Is that you? Mom? Mom?"

Jesus wept; it was Carrie.

10

Thoughts and emotions hit Stephenie hard and fast, like a snow shovel across the face. The first thought that came was: *Thank God! It's Carrie! Carrie's all right! Everything is going to work out just fine!* Then reality kicked in. How did Carrie know where to phone? And how did she know the phone number? What the hell was going on? Was this *really* her daughter on the phone, or was this some sort of weird twisted prank? Carrie had never even used the phone before, not in her whole entire life, so how could it be her now?

She said, "Carrie? Is that you?"

"Mommy!" The voice sounded like Carrie, all right. Her frightened intonation was unmistakable. "Oh mommy, where are you? Please come get me mommy! Please!"

"I'm here, babe, I'm here!"

"Where's here?"

"I'm in the basement across the—"

Carrie screamed, cutting Stephenie's statement in half.

Stephenie's eyes popped open in shock and her entire body trembled. She needed answers and she needed them immediately. She needed to know why her daughter had screamed and where she was hiding. Was she safe? Was she in danger? What the hell was happening?

She said, "Carrie—"

But Carrie cut her off again, screaming louder than before, screaming like she was in pain. She also sounded terrified, like she was in a boatload of danger, like she was trapped inside a cage with a half-dozen rattlesnakes. With her voice cranked into a high-pitched squeal, she spat: "Oh no! Don't let them get me, mommy! Don't let them get me! You aren't going to leave me here, are you mommy? Are you? You're not going to leave… me—"

The phone went dead.

Stephenie screamed, "NO!" She smacked the phone a couple times with an open hand before flicking the cradle on and off. It was no use. It was dead; the line was dead.

Then it wasn't.

And a voice came on the line she didn't recognize, sounded like a little boy. He sang, *"Girly, girly, what you drinkin'? What the hell have you been thinkin'? Cut your throat. Drink your blood. Bury your corpse in graveyard mud!"*

She heard a gunshot blast. Then the line went dead.

Stephenie looked across the room in a panic. She ran up the stairs. But before she reached the top stair the door slammed in her face. Then the light in the corner turned off. Now it was dark, totally dark. She couldn't see a thing and she was trapped in the fucking basement.

She reached a hand out, searching for the door. She grabbed the knob and gave it a yank. The knob wouldn't turn. It was locked. She shook the doorknob again and again and mumbled something incoherent. Then she slammed both hands against the wood. "Let me out!" she screamed, with a dribble of spit hanging from her lower lip. "Let me out of here! I need to get out of here!"

She stopped pounding on the wood, inhaled a deep breath, and grabbed the knob once again. She rattled it a few seconds and reached for the light switch. It was gone! GONE! How can a light switch be gone?! How can it vanish from the wall?

She slid her hand across the wall several more times, moaning and groaning like she was going to be sick. She kicked her knee against the door and smacked her hand on the wall several times.

Wait, she thought. *Something's different.*

Beneath her fingers she found what she had been looking for: the light switch. Thank heaven; it was the light switch! She flicked it up and down. Nothing. The light switch didn't work.

"Oh no," she said, balling her hands into fists.

Then she heard something, didn't know what. But it was downstairs. Whatever she heard, it was downstairs.

Slapping a hand across her mouth she forced herself to be quiet. She heard it again. A cold and emotionless voice was coming from the basement.

It said, "Mommy. Is that you mommy?" But the voice didn't sound like Carrie. It sounded like a demon trapped in a child's body. "Mommy?"

Stephenie spun around and pressed her back against the door. She still couldn't see anything; it was too dark for that. But she could hear. Oh boy, oh boy, she could hear. And she didn't like the sounds she was listening to. No, not at all.

Footsteps, slowly, one after another, moving towards the staircase. They seemed to take forever, but that *forever* notion was a grave miscalculation. They were nearing the stairs now, one gentle footfall at a time. She could hear the first stair creak, then the second. She imagined Carrie looking the way the others did, with her skull smashed open, her brains oozing from her head, and her eyes locked in an icy cold stare. She felt her stomach contracting. She thought she might scream.

More creaking—

"Mommy?"

Finally Stephenie broke her silence. She said, "Carrie. Is that you?" But even as the words tumbled from her mouth she knew what the answer was. The answer: *NO. Not on your life.*

There was a giggle, but the giggle didn't sound happy.

"Yes mommy," a flat and soulless voice said. "It's me. Why don't you come down the stairs and give me a kiss?"

She heard the third stair creak, or was it the fourth?

Stephenie swallowed back the shriek crawling up her throat, swallowed it and closed her eyes. Not that it mattered. She couldn't see a thing if she tried.

She decided to make conversation. Making conversation seemed like the smartest thing to do. And why? She had no idea.

She said, "No Carrie. I don't want to go down there. Are you coming here? We should get going. Would you like to go home?"

"Oh yes," the thing with the soulless voice said. And it was close now—much, much too close. It was almost on top of her. "I would like to go home with you very much. But you should come to me. I've been a good girl, you know. I've been very good indeed. I want to show you something, mommy. Come down the stairs. Come take a cold hard look at the thing I have for you. You're going to like it."

Another stair creaked.

Then another.

Suddenly there was a noise Stephenie didn't recognize, a chattering sound that reminded her of two bricks being clicked together. The sound grew louder and louder before it stopped.

"Are you coming down?"

Trying hard to be quiet, Stephenie turned around and tried the doorknob again. The door was still locked. She turned again, placing her back against the wood. She was terrified. There was no better way to say it. This was the scariest moment of her whole entire life. She felt her hand quivering and her knees shaking. Her heart was pounding in her chest and eyes were starting to water. She was biting down on her bottom lip hard enough to make it bleed. Oh God, this was bad. This was so bad she thought she might faint. And the thing pretending to be Carrie had to be close now. It just had to be.

She heard a stair creak and it sounded like the one she was standing on.

It was too much. This was all much too much. She wanted to get into her car and drive now. Leaving her daughter behind was a bad thing, a terrible thing, but this was crazy. She couldn't go on this way. And something that wasn't human was creeping up the stairs, coming to get her. She knew it. How long before she felt the icy fingers of death wrap around her neck?

She thought, *the icy fingers of death, what the fuck? Do I have to be so dramatic? Isn't it bad enough I'm trapped in a strange basement with 'God only knows'? Does it have to be the 'icy fingers of death'?*

But yes, that's what it felt like: the icy fingers of death. And they were getting closer, and closer…

She pressed her back against the door as hard as she was able, and then, inside a moment of bravery she reached out.

There was nothing there.

She decided to make more conversation. Right or wrong, she didn't know what else to do. She said, "No babe. I don't want to go downstairs. It's too dark. I don't like it when it's that dark."

The light in the corner of the room clicked on. And to Stephenie's surprise, the staircase was empty.

"Is that better mommy?" The voice asked from somewhere in the basement. "It *is* better, isn't it? Come down here, mommy. I want to show you what we did."

Stephenie didn't know what to do, or what to think. What kind of mind-fuck was going on here? *Something* was on the stairs, right? Or was that just her imagination? She said, "If I come down there, can we go?"

"Oh yes, mommy. Just come down here and we'll do whatever you want."

Stephenie hesitated, pursed her lips together and walked down the first stair. She said, "Okay babe. Here I come."

The voice in the basement giggled again. That strange clicking sounds returned, louder now than before. She heard whispers and the sounds of something scurrying across the floor.

She took another step, followed by another, and another. In a moment she would turn the corner and see all she could see. But she didn't want to—oh shit, she didn't want to see anything at all. And wait a minute. Did the fake-Carrie say *we*? How many creatures were down there? Two? Five? Twenty?

"Come to us," the voice mimicking Carrie cackled.

And Stephenie did as she was told.

Oh God, she thought. *I'm stepping into madness.*

And then she did.

11

She turned the corner, imagining Carrie standing in the center of the room with snakes for hair, an upside-down cross in her hand, and Satan on his throne behind her.

Didn't happen.

The room was empty… well, almost empty.

There was a huge splash of blood on the wall, and beneath the blood several body parts were scattered randomly: a leg, a hand, a piles of bones, a few scattered teeth and a rope of intestines. There was no way she missed seeing these things earlier. This was new. Impossible—perhaps, but that didn't change anything. The blood was still dripping from the bones.

Suddenly the television clicked on; the screen showed nothing but static.

Stephenie looked at the blood on the wall, at the gore lying on the floor and the static blanketing the screen. She heard another giggle and quickly spun around, but the room was empty, *still* empty.

What is this place? She thought.

Then it came to her: *I'm in a haunted house.*

Maybe she was right. Or maybe it wasn't the house that was haunted, but the entire area. Was it possible? Could it be? At this point, the area being haunted seemed like a reasonable solution, perhaps the *only* solution. Things didn't make sense now, not in a traditional sort of way. Things had become ugly. So, assuming you swallowed the concept of a haunting, did any other explanation seem half as likely?

Stephenie walked up the stairs. She put her hand on the knob and with a turn of her wrist, the door opened.

Haunted, she thought. *My God, the place is haunted.*

As she stepped into the kitchen she heard a voice coming from the basement. "Mommy?"

Stephenie turned around; goosebumps crawled along her back. "You're not my daughter," she said, even though the voice was perfect. And it *was* perfect. Somehow Carrie's voice was coming from the basement. "You're a ghost or something. I don't want to talk to you."

"Yes," the thing that sounded like Carrie said. "I'm a ghost. I'm dead. You know that, right mommy? I died but I didn't take an elevator to heaven. I came here instead. I could tell you where my body is buried, if you'd like to see it."

"You're a liar."

"Oh no I'm not. Please, don't be mad at me. I didn't mean to get kilt. Did you see the farmhouse, the one sitting down the street from the restaurant? My corpse is in there. There's a bad man inside the farmhouse, mommy. He kilt the people in the restaurant and he kilt me too. He cut my neck whiff a steak knife. He did it as soon as I gots through the door. I didn't even get a chance to go pee-pee, which I needed to do very badly."

"I don't believe you," Stephenie said. But she wasn't too sure what she believed. "My daughter's not dead."

"But it's true," the voice said, almost pouting. "I *am* dead. *I am.* There's a secret passage going from the farmhouse to the restaurant. Did you know that mommy? It's scary in there. I should know. Now that I'm kilt I can see it in my mind. The man who made me all bleedy snuck through the passage and kilt the people while they were eating. His name is Blair."

"I don't want to talk to you."

"That's because you don't want to believe me, mommy. But everything I'm saying is the truth. Go to the farmhouse. What's left of my body is there. Maybe after you see it you'll believe me better; then we can be friends again, 'cause I love you mommy, and I'm scart. I don't wanna be here all alone whiffout any friends to play whiff. I don't like being dead and scart. It's not fair."

"You're not scaring me. I don't know why you're doing this, but it's not working. It's not…"

There was a glass on the kitchen table, tinted yellow and filled with water. It slid along the wood, and when it reached the edge it tumbled off and smashed on the floor. Little chunks of glass mixed with water vomited across the tiles. At the same moment, a painting of an old man fell from the wall. It landed with a CLANK, and when Stephenie looked at the painting the man's painted image was looking right at her.

Stephenie didn't say a thing.

She backed across the room, keeping an eye on the open basement door, trying to erase the painting from her mind. But it was hard. She didn't want to look at the painting or *think* about the painting for a number of reasons, including the fact that the old man in the painting looked like her grandfather. And she didn't like her grandfather. The guy was crazy. At the age of eighty-five he killed his wife with a baseball bat and committed suicide by throwing himself in front of a motorcycle.

Stephenie's eyes betrayed her. They shifted towards the painting.

The image didn't *look* like her grandfather; it *was* him. Grandpa Ray, the old man's name was. Grandpa Ray, on her father's side. He had a flat nose, small lips and a scar that started at his chin and went all the way to his ear. His teeth were small and sharp. He had a nest of white hair bunched on top of his head like Albert Einstein. She knew the man in the painting very well. Oh yes she did.

He was a madman; he was her grandpa.

She turned slowly, walking away from the painting and the voice of her daughter.

The big chair in the living room startled her. Upon seeing it, she thought somebody was there. Thankfully she was wrong.

She walked past the empty chair. When she reached the door she had a terrible feeling it would be locked. It wasn't. She opened the door without a lick of trouble and stepped outside freely. The air smelled clean, like a pleasant fragrance, like freedom, if such a smell existed.

She closed the door with a CLICK. Then her head snapped towards the front yard, and the fresh corpse that was lying on it.

12

The corpse on the grass had a name: Denise Renton. Her skull was caved in and her eyes stared aimlessly towards the house. With her arms and her legs spread apart, she almost looked like a snow-angel.

There was a growl.

Stephenie turned towards it.

Then she got a feeling (this terrible, terrible feeling) that something was coming towards her. Something big and awful, something she couldn't see. She heard the growl again and this time it sounded closer, close enough to make her raise a hand in self-defense. She needed to get away from this thing, whatever it was. She needed to run because if the invisible thing got hold of her she wouldn't know what to do. But it was coming. Holy green-eggs and ham sandwiches, it was moving towards the porch. Soon it would be coming up the stairs!

She took a step back.

It was too late to run into the yard. The thing, this huge and terrible thing, whatever it was—it was right there, almost on top of her. She could practically taste it now, and if she didn't do something quick it was going to be knocking her over and ripping her body into pieces.

Stephenie whirled around and grabbed the doorknob.

Now it would be locked. Of course it would be! Now that she *needed* it open, the door would be locked for sure.

She turned her wrist and pulled on the door as hard as she was able. But of course, the door wouldn't open. She pulled and pulled and pulled. She cursed once, and she was getting ready to scream, but then she pushed on the door and the door opened just fine. She had to *push it*, not pull it. How could she be so stupid?

Stephenie plowed her way inside, bewildered and relieved. She slammed the door shut and rammed her back against the wood. Her eyes were wide and her heart was racing. Her knees were threatening to knock together.

The big chair in the center of the room was facing her now. And it wasn't empty; it was full, more than full. There was a man sitting in the chair that weighed five hundred pounds or more. Must be Jacob.

He was dead.

But wasn't.

The enormous man was shirtless and pale; his skin was decaying, his teeth were glistening and his beady little eyes sat deep within the dark sockets of his head. His shoulder blades stuck through his skin like ugly white fins. Bugs crawled across his belly thick enough to cause pile-ups. One hand sat on the arm of the chair, with fingernails long and black. The other hung off the side.

Stephenie looked at the hand hanging off the side.

Her mouth slinked open.

Jacob's fat-knuckled finger's gripped something that Stephenie didn't want to see. Oh god—oh sweet, merciful god—it was a girl. He was holding a young girl by the hair in a way that could only mean trouble. She was lying on her stomach with her hair hanging in her face wearing nothing more than a pair of worn-out blue jeans. She couldn't have been much older than twelve, thirteen at the most.

Stephenie whispered, "Oh Lord."

Then she heard that strange clicking sound again, the sound from the basement. She turned towards the noise, looking into a dark corner, afraid of what she might find.

She couldn't see much, just a shadow.

The shadow moved.

Stephenie's eyes widened and she started babbling.

"Oh I'm sorry. I shouldn't be here. I was looking for my daughter and I knocked on the door but there was no answer so I came inside because I needed to use the phone but I didn't touch anything. I'm looking for my daughter and I didn't mean to disturb you so please don't hurt me. I'll go now. I'll leave you alone and I won't tell anyone about this so you don't need to worry about me. Does that sound okay? I'll just go. I'm sorry to have disturbed you. Oh God I'm sorry, I'm so, so sorry. Please God don't kill me."

The girl on the floor lifted her head.

"Help me," she said with a voice that was barely a whisper.

Stephenie looked at the girl just in time to see Jacob yank her head into the air and smash her face into the hardwood.

The girl screamed.

And Jacob smashed her face against the floor again. Teeth crunched. Blood splashed.

The thing hiding in the corner stepped from the shadows and Stephenie got a real good look.

But that's not human, she thought. And she was right. It wasn't.

The thing didn't have skin or hair. There were no sexual appendages, no organs of any kind. Just bones. Oddly shaped bones that were connected together and twisted into strange and unlikely shapes. They were as thick and white as bones could be. The creature had giant eye-sockets. And inside those giant eye-sockets, long square teeth opened and closed very quickly, creating the clicking sound she had heard earlier. Perhaps the eye sockets were equipped with jaws, she considered, not knowing if it was at all possible.

But its very existence was impossible, wasn't it?

Stephenie cringed.

She looked at the creature's face, at the ribcage freeway that sat in a mangled nest above the stalk-like legs. She looked at the creature's hands: eight bony digits on each. And inside one was a knife that gleamed in the shadow like a sliver of terrible sunshine.

The girl gurgled and whispered, "Save me."

And Jacob smashed her head against the floor a third time, harder now than before.

Her skull cracked.

Stephenie had seen enough.

She spun around, grabbed the doorknob and yanked the door open. She had to get the hell away from Jacob and the impossible framework of bones. She couldn't save Mary. How could she possibly do that? She didn't have a weapon, assistance, or a plan. She didn't have anything. And even if she *did* have a weapon, what could she do against them? The answer seemed simple enough: nothing. The answer was nothing. Jacob was huge and the skeleton creature wasn't even human and there was nothing that Stephenie could do.

Outside will be better than inside, she thought.

And the very concept seemed like a logical one. But she was wrong. Outside was worse—much, much worse.

The real terror was just about to begin.

CHAPTER FOUR:
SPILLING BLOOD

1

Stephenie ran down the stairs and across the bungalow's front yard.

Denise Renton—the corpse lying in the grass—lifted her crushed head and grabbed Stephenie by the ankle as she flew by.

Stephenie didn't feel any pain, but she was thrown off balance. She slipped and tumbled onto the soft grass like a kid in a schoolyard. And when she lifted herself up she was facing the bungalow, and looking at the corpse. And it *was* a corpse. There is no other way to describe it. Denise Renton's shattered head looked like a cantaloupe that had been smashed open with a boot heel. One eye hung free of its socket.

The corpse grinned and pointed a bloody finger, and moaned, "You've been bad." The phlegm-soaked voice sounded trapped inside her throat, trapped—like Denise's corpse didn't have enough, if any, breath to push the words from her lungs. And the words didn't really sound like *You've been bad*. They sounded more like, *Quoove beanbade*.

Stephenie felt a cold shiver roll down her spine.

The big growl came again, not from the mouth of the zombie but from the invisible monster she could not see. She didn't have a clue what the creature was, but figured it was more powerful than everything else she encountered. And it scared her. It scared her in a way nothing else could, for it was nameless and faceless, something that defied all physical boundaries.

Denise Renton's corpse grinned.

Stephenie forced herself to her feet and ran. She ran onto the driveway and across the road, aiming straight for her car. That was the destination now: the car. She was leaving this screwed up place behind. More than that, she was leaving her daughter behind too. Right or wrong, that was the plan. She couldn't do this any longer, and she couldn't do it alone—couldn't *handle* it alone. And she *was* alone. At this point, it was a fact.

She didn't slow down crossing the highway, but she did look in both directions. For a moment she thought she might get lucky. She thought a car might drift down the road and she'd be able to snag a ride, but no, of course not. The road was empty, completely empty. She could see an outline of trees at the side of the highway sitting near a farmhouse that was at least a half-mile away. She could see the moon in the sky, a handful of stars, the gas station and restaurant. Nothing more.

Her feet moved her across the road and onto the parking lot; her heart pounded in her chest.

She noticed something as she ran. Something was different; something was out of place. She wasn't sure what it was and she didn't have time to analyze.

She reached her car, grabbed the door handle and pulled the door open. Then the information she was seeking emerged: it was Julie Brooks. Once again, Julie's corpse was sitting inside the car, in the driver's seat. Her head was leaning on the steering wheel; her eyes were closed. Blood dribbled from her chin in thick shimmering strings.

Stephenie mumbled, "But how?"

The corpse opened her flat, cold eyes and lifted a hand.

Stephenie stepped back startled; then she looked across the parking lot nervously. There was nothing to see, but that didn't mean much. That thing—that big, nameless, invisible thing that seemed as heavy as train and as deadly as a great white shark at dinnertime—it was coming. She didn't understand how she knew this, or why, but she did. The ethereal matter was coming straight at her. Soon it would arrive and tear her in half like a rag doll.

Her eyes shifted towards the bungalow.

Denise Renton shuffled around on the bungalow lawn. She had bits of brain clinging to her hair and an eyeball swinging back and forth like a yo-yo 'rocking the cradle.' She lifted her pale hand and pointed a thin finger across the road.

Stephenie could almost hear the zombie's words in her mind…

Quoove beanbade.

Stephenie stumbled away from Julie Brooks, the corpse in the car.

The restaurant next to her was looming, enticing her with a notion of safety and security it couldn't possibly provide. But at this point her choices were simple: inside or out. She needed to make a decision and she needed to do it now.

"Shit," she said. And the decision was made.

Inside.

Even before she opened the door she knew it was a bad idea. If the corpse in the car—Julie's corpse—had come back to life, what terrors were creeping around inside the building? As she reached for the handle she realized it was a mathematical equation: how many bodies did she see? Ten? Twenty? She didn't know. But entering the restaurant was a bad idea, a very bad idea. It was a shame hanging around the parking lot felt like suicide.

She swung the door open and bolted inside.

Christmas bells chimed.

There was a waitress standing at the door. Blood covered her arms and chest and it dripped from her mouth in generous proportions. Her name was Dee-Anne Adkins. A broken nametag hung from her shirt. It was cut in half, split down the middle.

Stephenie raised a hand defensively. "Don't," she said, noticing Dee-Anne's broken nametag.

At the same moment Dee-Anne grabbed Stephenie by the throat. She opened her bleeding mouth really wide and leaned in.

Stephenie tried to step away, only to discover she couldn't do it. Something had gripped her leg, anchoring her to the floor in a most unforgiving way. She looked down, somehow more shocked now than she was before.

Susan Trigg was lying on the floor, holding onto Stephenie's leg like a football player aiming to tackle. She was holding on as tight as she was able, despite the fact that her brains were oozing from her skull. She looked evil, hungry, and alive—yes alive, very much alive. Her eyes were bright and knowing; not filled with understanding really, but filled with something nonetheless.

Stephenie wanted to voice a complaint, a concern, a protest. She wanted to say, *'Let go of me you crazy zombie bitch! Can't you see I'm busy here?'*

She didn't.

She pushed Dee-Anne.

Dee-Anne's feet shuffled like she might step away, but her fingers continued to squeeze Stephenie's throat.

Then Susan Trigg—the zombie on the floor—lifted her hand.

And Stephenie caught a glimpse of the future.

2

Susan Trigg gripped Stephenie's leg with one arm while raising the other arm in the air. Her hand wasn't empty. Oh no. The living corpse was holding a long pencil. The pencil was yellow and dull. It had thin blue lines that ran from the eraser to the sharpened end where the graphite poked free of the wood. It had the words: *EMPIRE PENCIL CORP* on one side and 2 HB on the other. And when Stephenie saw it hoisted into the air she knew what was about to happen.

She watched a movie when she was a kid; couldn't recall the name of the movie but she remembered somebody getting stabbed in the ankle with a pencil. At the time she wondered how much it would hurt in real life, because in that fucking movie it seemed to hurt like hell. What was the movie again? The Exorcist? The Shining? She couldn't remember and the fact was, it didn't matter. The only thing that mattered was her personal safety. Oh sure, you could argue that Carrie's safety mattered too. Sure you could, and why wouldn't you? But the truth of the issue was this: Carrie's wellbeing was getting forced into a lower position on the priority line because shit was getting ugly.

Stephenie shouted, "NO!"

Dee-Anne's teeth snapped the air next to her face. Spittle speckled Stephenie's skin, causing her to flinch and pull away as much as she was able.

Then the worst thing ever happened: life imitated art.

Susan stabbed the dull pencil directly into Stephenie's ankle. The wooden spear plunged halfway through her limb before it snapped in two.

Blood spilled out in a hurry. Stephenie's eyes blasted open and she screamed; the word 'NO' became "NOOOOOO-UUUUUUUUOOOOOOOOOO-oooo!!" Then she was dropping to the floor and away from Dee-Anne.

Stephenie slammed against the tiles and felt the wind get punched out of her. And that was bad, but not half as bad as the pain in her ankle. Hot sweltering agony blistered up her leg and into her thigh. Her toes were aflame. Her muscles were contracting. Her body became clammy and moist all over, and for the second time in however many minutes she thought she was going to be sick.

Dee-Anne looked down at Stephenie with anger and hatred embedded into her features like a jail cell tattoo. A little string of blood hung from her chin, swaying back and forth like a pendulum. It fell free and landed on Stephenie's knee.

Dee-Anne's hands became fists. She lowered into a crouching position.

She was hungry.

Susan grabbed the broken pencil hanging from Stephenie's ankle and wrenched it back and forth, causing bones to crunch and muscles to split.

Still on the floor, Stephenie screamed, and squeezed her face into a ball as she kicked Susan away. She didn't have time to cry or beg. She didn't have time to complain about her ankle or wonder how the hell the doctor would be able to fix it. She had to escape the monsters before they tore her apart. It could happen. No, strike that. It *would* happen, and it would happen soon if she didn't get her ass in gear in a hurry.

She flipped onto her hands and knees and crawled away from them. Looking up, she could see another corpse shuffling from a booth.

His name was Eric Wilde. He was thirty-three years old and wore a cheap, blue suit that made him look like a used car salesman. His tattered arm hung unresponsively at his side, broken in several places. Blood dripped from his fingers like cherry raindrops.

Craig Smyth, the man leaning against the counter with his chest torn apart, opened his mouth and leaned forward. Blood poured from the massive hole in his front, landing on his lap in a wave.

Dee-Anne staggered towards the counter.

Stephenie couldn't believe it. She was surrounded by zombies, the living dead, animated corpses—what were the odds?

She figured the odds to be hovering right around the zero percent mark, maybe even negative one. Of course, she didn't have time to figure percentages; she only had time to crawl around Craig before he blocked her path, which is what she did. Craig didn't seem to be moving too quickly so she scrambled past him and made her way behind the counter and towards the corpse formally know as Jennifer Boyle. She tried not to look at Jennifer's severed arm or at the puddle of blood it was sitting in. Not to suggest that the severed arm was worse than any of the other things her eyes were falling upon. It wasn't. Things were bad all over.

Zombie-Craig tried to stand, but was having a hard time managing it.

Zombie-Jennifer, still sitting behind the counter, opened and closed her mouth like she was chewing on her tongue.

Stephenie forced herself to her feet. The pain in her foot was still blistering, making her wince and squeal, making her want to cry, *'why me Lord?'* But she only had time to pull her ass off the floor, which she did. She needed to see what she was up against. It was the only way she'd survive.

Angela Mezzo, the carcass with the happy face mug, began slidding out of her seat. And she wasn't the only one. Everybody in the restaurant was getting animated, each and every one of them. Blood dribbled and bones creaked. Teeth snapped and eyes rolled in their sockets. Drooling zombies turned and moaned and lifted their arms hauntingly.

Stephenie reached for the storage room door and slapped her hand on the knob. She thought the door would be locked, and maybe—she had to admit—it would be for the best. Just what kind of plan are you working with when you lock yourself inside a closet? And there was another thing to consider: *could* she lock herself in the closet? Did the door have a lock? Or would she be in there, holding the knob with her hands as blood streamed from her foot?

Hiding in the storage room was bad idea, another one of many. But Stephenie had painted herself into a corner. She had nowhere else to go.

On the floor, Jennifer reached out and grabbed Stephenie's wounded leg, but thankfully not the ankle.

Stephenie turned the knob; it wasn't locked.

Jennifer pulled on Stephenie's limb, trying to bite her knee.

Stephenie didn't allow it. She kicked the attacker away and screamed in pain. She slid her body through the doorway and slammed the door shut. Tears were in her eyes and her mouth hung half open.

She looked at the door.

There was a hook-lock hanging from the wood. Why it was there, she did not know. Or care. The lock wasn't great but it was better than nothing. It was the first bit of luck she had and for that, she was grateful. She grabbed the thin piece of metal and clicked the male end and the female end together.

That's when the phone rang.

3

Stephenie grabbed the phone without thinking. It felt warm and greasy in her hand. She said, "Hello?" Her voice was close to tears.

"Mommy? Is that you?" It was Carrie.

"Babe?"

"Yes mommy, it's me! It's me! Don't let them get me again mommy! Please don't let them get me!"

Stephenie didn't know what to say or think. Things were happening too fast, way too fast. Was this really Carrie on the phone, or another imposter? How did Carrie get the phone number? And why was the phone in the storage room suddenly working?

She looked down.

She was wearing a comfortable pair of slingback shoes and pants that were snug around the ankle. She could see the broken pencil quite clearly. Its yellow painted wood was sticking out of her skin between her shoe strap and her pant cuff; she wore no socks. There was an expanding trickle of blood on the floor now, and more running from her wound. It was leaking onto her shoe and in-between her toes. Her ankle had already started to darken and bloat.

"Mommy?"

Stephenie didn't respond. She was thinking about her foot rather than the phone call. She couldn't help it. The pencil was sticking out of her foot like a candle in a birthday cake.

"Mommy? Are you there? Talk to me!"

"It's me, Carrie," Stephenie said, snapping her eyes away from her wound. "It's me! I'm here! Is that really you?"

Carrie began crying and crying.

Yes, Stephenie decided. She was talking with Carrie on the phone. But oh, there were questions, so many questions. She had an ever-growing list of them that couldn't possibly be answered in a simple phone call.

She said, "Carrie, are you alright? Are you hurt?"

The answer she received wasn't what she anticipated, or wanted. For some reason, she expected good news. She thought Carrie would say she was doing just fine but would like to get going now. She expected Carrie to explain that she was a little afraid but everything was going to be okey-dokey because after all, she was just a little kid and things are supposed to be great for children. She wanted to enjoy a laugh or two with her daughter, followed by a cute little statement that would make Stephenie grin from her to ear.

It didn't happen.

Instead, Carrie screamed, "They cut off my fingers!"

"What?"

"They cut off my fingers, mommy! Please come save me! Please come and save me from Blair mommy! My fingers are all bleedy and Blair is coming back soon and I don't want to see him again! I don't want to see Blair anymore mommy!"

"Where are you baby? Where are you?"

"I'm at the farmhouse! Oh no, mommy! HE'S COMING! OH NO HE'S COMING! PLEASE DON'T! HE'S COMING AT ME—"

The line went dead.

Stephenie screamed, "NOOOOO!" But that didn't change a thing.

She looked at the phone in her hand, the blood running out of her ankle and the flashlight sitting on the shelf. She looked at the bottles of water, the cases of cola and the hook-lock on the door. She needed to do something, but what? What do people do in situations like this?

When the hell are people *in* situations like this? Never! That's when. Never!

What was going on? Why were those people murdered? Why on God's green earth did the dead rise up and attack? And excuse me? What did Carrie just say? *They cut off her fingers?!* That wasn't right! They cut off Carrie's *fingers?!* Really?

This is a big bag of shit! Complete shit! Who would do such a thing to a child?

Stephenie hung up the phone and put her hands to her face.

"Okay," she whispered. "I've got to get out of here. I've got to get over to the farmhouse and save Carrie. Then we've got to get going. We can't stay here. Staying here is suicide. This place is bad, so, so bad."

There was a single BANG on the door and Stephenie jumped.

"WHAT DO YOU WANT FROM ME?" She screamed.

She was losing it now, really losing it. It was easy to see. Her face was sticky and clammy and her eyes were completely glossed over. Her knees were shaking and her hands were trembling. She had sweat along her neck and spine.

There was another loud BANG at the door, followed by moaning, growling and scratching.

The dead had risen, and now they were bunched up on the other side of the door, trying to get inside, trying to get at her, trying to eat her mother-fucking brains like something straight from the script of some shitty horror movie—because *that* made sense! Oh mighty, mighty fuck-balls with brown sugar on top— that made *total* sense!

Shifting her weight, Stephenie felt a sharp pain knifing its way up her leg. She bit down on her lower lip and tried not to cry.

Okay, she thought. *Enough is enough.*

She needed a plan, which meant finding a weapon of some kind. But before she did that she needed to deal with priority number one: her ankle. She couldn't go on like this; the pain in her ankle was too much. Pulling the pencil free was her main concern, and then what? *Concealing the wound?* Bingo! Concealing the wound.

Carrie would have to wait. It sucked, but it was true. Carrie needed to deal with the nightmare she was facing alone, with blood dripping from the places her fingers used to be.

Oh Gawd. This was bad. Everything was *sooooo* bad.

Stephenie put her back against the door and cringed. She lifted her wounded leg an inch off the ground and slid downward, along the smooth surface of the door until she was sitting on the floor. She removed her shirt. It was a thin, blue dress shirt. Now she was dressed in a wife-beater undershirt. Using her teeth, she tore a sleeve from the dress shirt. She dropped the shredded garment on the ground and carefully put her fingers on the pencil. The very act of touching the wood was enough to make her suck air through her teeth, wince, and shy away from her thoughts of bravery. But shying away from bravery meant what? Cracking a can of Pepsi and singing a tune? No, that wouldn't do. Bravery or no bravery, she needed to deal with her ankle.

Knowing how much pain she was about to feel, she crunched the shirtsleeve into a ball and stuffed it in her mouth. Then, before she had a chance to over-think the situation, she grabbed the pencil and pulled.

4

Her teeth clamped down. The pain was enormous; like having your hand slammed in a car door, like having your fingernails pulled from your digits with heavy pliers.

A line of blood squirted across the small room and splashed the wall.

But here's the bitch of it: the pencil wasn't out. It didn't want to come out; it was wedged inside her body really good.

Stephenie would have to try again.

She tugged the wood back and forth, trying desperately to jerk it free. The pencil was stubborn. It didn't want to come free. Her face turned pale and her eyes widened. Goosebumps cropped across her arms and legs in patters and blotches; sweat rolled down her forehead. She could hear her bones grinding and cartilage cracking. The pain was blazing hot now—searing, scalding. It was way beyond any sensation she had prepared herself for.

But she hadn't prepared herself for *anything*. She stuffed a rag in her mouth and grabbed the wood before she had a chance to think. The result? There was juice bubbling from the hole in her ankle and blood on the wall. Her skin had turned pale and her eyes were the size of hockey pucks. Plus the wooden pencil was still in there.

It wasn't coming out!

Stephenie screamed into the shirtsleeve rag while biting it as hard as she was able. She looked at her hand through blurry eyes, surprised to find her fingers working diligently. The hand seemed foreign now, like it didn't belong to Stephenie any longer. Had it become its own boss, busy with its own agenda? Apparently so. As Stephenie swayed back and forth, screaming and biting back the pain as drool dribbled from her lips, she began asking the hand to stop, if only in her mind.

Please stop, she thought. *Oh please, please stop.*

But the hand didn't listen. Once her hand stopped pulling, the pencil would be in there for good. It was now or never. The hand seemed to know it, which meant Stephenie was to endure the agony.

She closed her eyes, wishing her mind would be somewhere else, anywhere else. She needed to escape reality, mind over matter, right? And maybe she could do it. Maybe if she tried really, really hard she could pretend she was somewhere else, somewhere better, somewhere new—at least for now, until the misery had ended.

A vision came, and that was good. Anything was better than suffering through wood and graphite grinding against cartilage and bone.

Whatever the vision might be, she'd take it.

Her vision—

Stephenie's could see herself lying on a table. Her arms and legs were tied down, her head was wedged into a large vice; she could feel it pressing against her skull. Her lips were pulled apart with barbed chicken wire, exposing her teeth. And although she couldn't move her head she *could* move her eyes and she could see a man standing beside her. He had a slim nose, greasy black hair, and was dressed in a white coat. Looked like a doctor. He had a hammer in his right hand, but it was small, just a toy, really. No good on a construction site but okay for driving a nail into drywall.

He said, "This is going to hurt."

Stephenie couldn't say anything, not while her lips were pulled apart and her teeth were exposed. So she tried to struggle; she tried to move. Unfortunately she couldn't. Her body was secure.

The man tapped her teeth with the hammer. Tap. Tap. Tap. He stroked his chin and then he tapped harder. TAP. TAP. TAP. Teeth didn't break, so he hit them hard. THUMP. THUMP. THUMP. One tooth cracked, which made the man smile. Enjoying himself, he put some muscle into it. SMACK. SMACK. SMACK. His smile became a grin, then: CRACK. CRACK. CRACK. A chunk of tooth broke free. He hit her harder still, with his grin becoming a sickle. He pounded the little hammer (*which was just a toy, really, hardly useful at all*) with all his might. The tool started missing the mark. He smashed her in the gums and lips; he hit her in the chin and in the eye. Blood splashed. Teeth broke into pieces of jagged wreckage. CRUNCH. CRUNCH. CRUNCH. Drops of red speckled his white coat. Her lips were becoming chopped sausage; her gums, chewed steak. The man laughed and screamed. It was too much, much too much. She began choking. Tooth splinters and bone fragments filled her throat like chunky stew.

Stephenie wanted the man in her fantasy to stop, just like she wanted her hand to stop pulling at that fucking pencil. But the pencil was stubborn. It was really wedged in there good and apparently that was okay because her fingers were stubborn too; they just wouldn't quit. There was blood pouring out of her foot now. It was running into her shoe and all over the floor. Her fingers were red, her hand was red and her leg was shaking. Her face had turned white and her ankle was swelling, getting larger by the moment. The pain was scorching. It seemed to never end, only get worse.

Please stop, her mind screamed. And the man with the white coat did, he really did. He stopped what he was doing and lifted her from the table like a baby. He walked her towards an open window and before she had a chance to thank the man for easing his insane surgical procedure he tossed her outside, never saying a word.

Now Stephenie was falling.

She was falling and falling, and when she held her hands in front of her eyes she saw the strangest thing: they weren't her hands at all. They were somebody else's hands, a man's hands—*Hal's* hands.

Hal's hands were held out in front of her and the wind was pressing against her body so hard that when she opened her mouth she felt like she was drowning. Air was rushing in, her lungs were expanding to the point of agony and nothing was coming out. She was drowning in nitrogen and oxygen instead of hydrogen and oxygen but that didn't make the experience much different. She was trying to breathe and couldn't do it. Perhaps it was because she was terrified. Perhaps it was because she knew that nobody tumbles off an extra tall building and lives to tell the tale. Or maybe it was the fact that she had a chunk of pencil rammed into her ankle and she couldn't pull it free.

The ground grew nearer. People that looked like raisins became the size of plums. The matchstick sidewalk grew as wide as a ruler and as the seconds rolled past it only got bigger. Now she could see the fence. Oh boy, it was coming right at her.

Her body started turning, rolling forward. Hair danced and clothing fluttered. Feet kicked and arms waved. She wasn't going to land on her feet, but she *was* going to land on the fence; there was no escaping it.

Plum-sized people became the size of pumpkins; several watched and screamed. A boy Carrie's age slapped his fingers over his eyes and started to bawl. A lady dressed in blue jeans and a white bikini top wrapped her arms around her head like it was a baby.

Stephenie hit the fence.

Skin, organs and muscle were demolished. The pelvic bone and vertebrae destroyed. One body became two separate pieces and with that, she heard Hal's voice inside her head, clearer than it had ever been.

He said, "*Why did you send me to work today, Stephenie? Why? Were you mad because I talked to my old girlfriend? Is that why you sent* *me off to be killed, because I sat down for a cup of coffee with a girl I hadn't seen in eight years? Is that the reason I'm being ripped in half by this industrial-strength portable fence, because you're jealous about a coffee and a conversation? That's not fair Stephenie! It's not fair and you know it! And you know what else Stephenie? I wanted to stay home and you made me go! You made me, Stephenie! You forced me out the door with your thoughts and your words and that terrible streak of cruelty you unleash at random. Why are you like that? Why are you so selfish and uncaring? How can you be the nicest girl I've ever known one day, and queen of the bitches another? Why do you love me and hate me at the same time? This accident isn't my fault; it's **your** fault. Everything is **your** fault Stephenie! IT'S ALL YOUR FAULT!"*

Now Stephenie was screaming. She was screaming like she wasn't capable of doing anything else. And...

POP!

Just like that, the man with the hammer was gone; the falling was over.

The pencil had come free.

5

There was a period of time that *drifted* by, and 'drifted' would likely be the best word to use. Once the pencil slid from her body, the intensity of the moment dropped significantly. The storm had passed. Of course, she was still stepping into the heart of the storm, all things considered, but she didn't know that.

She rested. Mentally and physically, she rested. Not for long, and not enough, but that's what she did. And when her thoughts cleared as much as they were able, she remembered the swarm on the far side of the door.

Zombies. Was that really the situation? Really?

No offence, she thought, *but how impossible is this?*

She allowed her thoughts to drift, just like the time. Blood drained from her body. She faded in and out of consciousness, trying to find a Zen moment, a moment of peace and tranquility, a little taste of serenity, because once she opened that door... yikes. It was bad news on top of bad news.

Her ankle throbbed.

She ignored it the best she could, and listened.

She heard scratching, knocking, growling and moaning.

Carrie.

She thought about Carrie and her missing fingers. How many were missing anyhow? Two? Five? Eight? Had they been cut off with a knife? With scissors? Hedge clippers? Were they cut off at the knuckle, near the fingertip? Or were they snipped somewhere near the center of the bone? One hand or both? Did she lose toes? Was she losing toes now? Assuming a man was responsible, what did he look like? Was he big, small? Was he enjoying himself? Did he sexually abuse her too?

"Stop thinking about it," she whispered. But she couldn't stop thinking about it. Having a child abducted and abused was a mother's worst nightmare.

She was awake. Oh God, she was awake.

The moment of tranquility had passed. And yes, her ankle hurt, but it was time to stand up and take it. Time to ignore the pain, if possible.

The rag that had been stuffed into her mouth was lying on her lap. She held it in front of her. The rag was too small to be useful so she tossed it aside. She lifted her shirt off the floor and tore another strip free. This strip was longer than the first. She tied it around her ankle in an attempt to stop the bleeding but by the time she hauled herself to her feet the rag was drenched with blood.

Standing made her dizzy; she hoped it would pass.

She looked at the doorknob, looked at the door. Beads of sweat gleamed on her forehead. Looking at the hook-lock, she wondered what would happen once she unlatched it.

Things were about to get bad, real bad.

She put a small amount of weight on her wounded leg and felt the pain ignite her nerves like fire. Was she ready? The question almost caused a smile. No, she most certainly was not ready; she could barely stand. Did her physical dilemma matter? No, probably not. She had to do what she had to do.

She put a hand against the door and slowly unhooked the lock. Then she put that same hand on the doorknob and took a deep breath, wondering how to open the door—fast or slow?

Fast, she decided. Yes, fast. Fast was the way to go. Do it like a band-aid, one quick pull and it's over.

Stephenie nodded, confirming the idea to herself.

But it *wouldn't* be over, that was the problem. Once she opened the door things would just be getting starting.

She told herself it didn't matter. She told herself to be brave. She was going to open the door quickly and be done with it. Carrie needed her.

On the count of three, she thought. *One. Two. Three!*

She didn't open the door—of course not. Opening the door was suicide and she knew it. How many of those things were out there? Twenty? Thirty? And what about her ankle? That bitch in the restaurant stabbed her pretty damn good. Did she really think she could fight a room filled with zombies now?

The odds were clearly stacked against her.

"Fuck," she whispered.

Then she opened the door.

6

Stephenie only opened the door an inch and peeked through the opening. She didn't see any zombies, so she opened the door a little wider.

Jennifer was sitting on the floor with her arm lying beside her. The arm didn't look pale; it looked shriveled white, excluding the smudges of bright red blood.

Stephenie closed the door quietly, re-evaluating the situation.

They're not swarming the door, she thought. *So now what?*

Go back to the original plan. Do it quick, swing the door open and make a run for it. But run where, to the farmhouse to save Carrie? How?

Assuming she was able to scoot past a couple dozen brain-eating zombies...

Stephenie's thoughts hit a snag.

Brain-eating? Who said anything about brain-eating? Where am I getting this stuff? First it was: THE ICY FINGERS OF DEATH, and now this?

Get it together Steph. Please.

Stephenie put a hand to her temple and exhaled a deep breath. "Where was I?" she whispered. "Oh yeah. Saving Carrie. Do it fast, do it now. Right now. Just go, don't think about it; go. They're chopping off her fingers."

With a grimace and a moan, Stephenie threw open the door.

Jennifer looked up, groaning. She lifted her arm off the floor and squeezed it. Blood dribbled from its end.

Stephenie stepped past Jen's legs, wincing as she put pressure on her ankle, wondering what her next move would be.

Craig stood at the end of the counter, blocking her path. He lifted a hand; blood bubbled from his chest.

Stephenie stumbled, moving sideways, almost like a crab. She opened both of her hands and pushed zombie-Craig as hard as she was able.

Craig went tumbling back with his arms pinwheeling and his mouth open. He fumbled into an oversized plant and pushed over a chair as he fell down.

Using the countertop as leverage, Stephenie continued on. The agony in her ankle was bringing a fresh batch of tears to her eyes but she didn't let that stop her from trying to escape. This was her moment. As the saying goes: it was now or never.

She noticed a pair of corpses she hadn't seen before.

Wayne Auburn had long sideburns and a round potbelly. He wore a red-checkered shirt that looked like a tablecloth and jeans that were two sizes too tight. His skull was opened up like a Venus flytrap and his brain was wedged into the gap between his eyes. Looked about fifty-five.

Wayne stood next to a man named Gary Wright. Gary was lying on the floor wearing a cook's uniform that was covered in ten years of food stains and five minutes of bloodshed. He had a gold tooth near the front of his mouth that shined in the florescent light. His hair was short, his nose was long and both of his legs had been chopped off at the knee. There was a trail of blood behind him four feet wide.

Behind Gary was Dee-Anne, the waitress with the broken nametag.

And behind Dee-Anne, zombie-Susan was still holding a broken pencil in her hand like a knife. Stephenie wondered if she wanted to play another round of 'ram the pencil in the ankle.' It seemed as though she did.

Zombies were doing a good job of blocking the main exit, so Stephenie moved away from them. She remembered the restaurant had a side door, and when she looked across the room she spotted it near the woman's washroom.

She hobbled nearly six feet before she suffered her next attack. She knew it was coming. Lee Courtney, David Gayle and Alan Mezzo were all—in one way or another—blocking her newest plan for escape.

Lee grabbed her first. Lee, whose neck looked like it had been chopped with a full-sized axe, grabbed her by the shoulders. He had strong hands and a firm grip.

She tried to push him back but was unable. She tried to pull his hands away but it seemed to be impossible. They staggered towards the bathroom doors together, zombie and woman, Stephenie screaming in pain now, screaming—not because of the hold he had on her but rather the inferno inside her ankle. The pain she felt was horrendous, incalculable. Like she had one foot burning in Dante's Inferno, the outer ring of the seventh circle. The pain, she feared, may be her undoing.

She looked over Lee's shoulder and saw David Gayle less than three feet away. He was dressed in a nice looking suit and walked like a man with a shattered spine, with his weight lumped on one side. An arm dangled uselessly. It looked like a fish on a line.

Beside David was Alan. Blood boiled from the huge, clam-shaped hole in his face.

Lee slammed Stephenie against a bathroom door.

She felt it give, and a moment of inspiration came. She dropped her arms to her sides, slapped her hands together, raised them in front of her face and pulled her arms apart.

Lee's fingernails scratched her skin as they were forced away from her. And now she had a moment, a single moment.

She pushed Lee. Hard.

Lee tumbled, staggered and growled, but he did not fall.

But Stephenie was in a better position now. She had enough time to slip into the woman's bathroom without having a zombie clinging to her like dirt on a rock. And that's what she did. She slipped into the bathroom.

7

Stephenie saw the blur of the restaurant, the zombies, a ceiling fan turning in a slow moving circle and the door's casing. The wall inside the bathroom came next, looking oily and off-white. She turned herself around and put a hand on the door. It made a BANG when she rammed it closed. Another sound came when she slammed her back against the wood. She screamed a little, but then her voice trickled off and her scream became something that resembled a cry. She breathed heavily, worried heavily, thinking the living dead would force their way into the room and tear her limb to limb. She pressed her back against the wood with the bulk of her strength, and braced her undamaged foot against the floor. Squeezing her teeth together, she lifted her wounded foot off the floor. It swayed left and right gently, dribbling blood.

Nothing happened.

She inhaled a deep breath. The smell of all-purpose cleaners and disinfectants remained strong, but now it was mixed with something she couldn't quite recognize, something bad.

She thought about the zombies and the door that separated her from them. It was the door keeping her safe. And praise God, it didn't move—not a little, not a lot. Nothing was fighting its way in yet. But still, how long could it be?

Maybe they forgot about me, she thought.

But no, that idea was ridiculous. Soon enough, those fuckers would push their way inside, and what would happen next? They'd rip the meat from her bones, suck her eyes from her head and gobble up her intestines like a home cooked meal. And with *that,* she'd die, she supposed—unless she could escape somehow, but how?

She looked across the washroom, hoping to find a window. And there it was, sitting in the far wall between the stalls and the sinks, taunting her.

A joke, that's what it was. The window was the size of a goddamn shoebox. She'd have a hard time wedging her head through the opening; forget the shoulders. And that was assuming she'd be able to pull the prison-style screen from the window's casing. That alone would take an hour. She wondered what kind of asshole designed such a thing. If there was a fire, the bathroom was a textbook deathtrap.

Waiting.

Waiting.

The door never moved.

Her suspended foot continued to sway.

Blood continued dribbling.

Maybe the door isn't going to move, she thought. *Maybe I'm safe.*

She wondered if her thoughts were logical or if she was caught up in a bout of wishful thinking? *Wishful thinking,* she decided. But still, she couldn't help but wonder.

A thought: if the dead were mentally slow, which they seemed to be, maybe they forgot she entered the bathroom. Perhaps they had no memory at all, and were surviving on instincts alone. Was it possible? Yes, of course it was. But was it likely?

Stephenie tried to think logically, despite the illogical situation.

She almost didn't want to admit it but—yes, perhaps it *was* likely. Maybe the zombies forgot about her. That would explain why they didn't attack the door to the storage room, wouldn't it? Out of sight, out of mind. Could it be that easy?

Stephenie pulled her back away from the door, testing the situation, balancing on one foot. She counted to five, and when nothing happened she felt satisfied. She leaned against the door again just to be safe.

Better safe than sorry, her late husband Hal sometimes said.

Don't think about him.

She closed her eyes and organized her thoughts. She was trying to find a solution, trying to remember those old zombie movies she watched as a child. She had only seen two or three, had no idea what they were called. *Night of the Zombies? Night of the Dead?* Something like that. *Zombies of the Dead...* maybe?

"You have to kill their brain," she whispered, hunting through the filing cabinet in her mind for information that might be helpful.

Then stall-door number three rolled opened, making a sound that could straighten the whiskers of an alley cat.

CREEEEAAAAAAAAAKKKKK—

Stephenie froze. Her eyes ballooned to the size of pint coasters and she bit her bottom lip hard. She wanted to say, *who's there?* But didn't need to. She could see who was creeping into view and she didn't like what she could see.

Angela Mezzo.

Angela stepped from the stall with her back twisted awkwardly. Her white dress shirt was red with blood, especially on her right side where the torn fabric was still drenched. She wore a black miniskirt, which sat high upon her legs. The skirt might have looked nice given a different set of circumstances—a lunch date, a business meeting, something like that. But here and now it only added to the obscurity of the moment. When the dead woman smiled, or grinned, or did whatever it was she was trying to do with her teeth, the blood rolled off her bottom lip in a stream. Above her blank, dark eyes—eyes that seemed to be bulging from her skull—her hair was pasted against her forehead in a shape that resembled a lightning bolt. Her skin seemed to be changing, turning moldy and grey right in front of Stephenie's big round eyes. Angela was rotting. That was it. She was rotting and little pieces of withered flesh were peeling away, falling from her body like thick wet snowflakes.

"Do you like this?" The corpse woman said, pushing her chest out. "Do you?"

Her tone was soft and lustful, yet the syllables she forged were fraying at seams. The words 'Do you like this' sounded like *Doquo lietis*. Stephenie couldn't understand why she understood the woman at all.

And as she spoke those words, those lustful, awful, implausible words, her hands cupped her breasts. She pushed her bloody shirt against her tainted skin. Fingers that became more skeletal with each passing moment slid along the fabric, touching her top button. She unfastened it and slid her fingers to the next.

"Oh my God," Stephenie said, pressing her back against the door harder now than before, like she wanted to become one with the wood. She couldn't believe what she was seeing. Angela was more ghoul than girl, unsettling on several levels, none of which were good.

"You *do* like this," Angela mocked, sounding the way that she did, answering her own question with a nod and a grin. She licked her top lip suggestively, unfastened a third button, and then a forth. She wore no bra. "You like *this* and you like me. I can see it in your eyes."

"Get away from me," Stephenie said, forcing her words out in a whisper. Her mouth felt dry. "Leave me alone."

Angela unhooked her final button, pulled the shirt from her body and dropped it to the floor. It landed with a wet sounding *FHWAP* that sent little dots of red soaring.

Stephenie shuddered.

Angela's body was twisted strangely; her rotting breasts were exposed. Her right shoulder had obviously suffered a terrible blow, Stephenie could see; it looked like someone had chopped it with an axe. There was a thick flap of meat dangling near her ribcage and a broken blade of bone sticking through her shoulder.

Angela moved closer, decomposing quickly now. Her eyes were falling into her head and her hair was dropping to the floor in light, feathery clumps. Her lips, which had once seemed beautiful, were withering into twisted worms.

If Stephenie could disappear, she would. She didn't want to see this, not *any* of this. This was horrendous. This was insane.

"You like me?" Angela asked. Her voice was soft and lustful, but she was gurgling little chunks of tissue. She slid a hand between her legs and lifted her skirt up high, exposing the putrid flesh beneath.

Stephenie's eyes shifted and turned away. She thought she might be sick. "What are you doing?"

"Do you wanna touch me, touch it?"

"Oh God," Stephenie cried. "No!"

"Do you wanna kiss me, or lick me down there?" She moved a little closer, then a little closer still.

"No!"

"Please Stephenie, taste me. I taste good, I promise you. Fall to your knees and put your lips to my lips. Taste the meat of yesterday."

Stephenie closed her eyes, but only for a moment. She had to get away from this woman, this nightmare, this... *thing*.

Of course, that meant entering the restaurant again, which she didn't want to do. But her priorities were changing; she felt that she had no choice. She couldn't stay in the bathroom much longer, could she? No, of course not. And besides, Carrie was waiting; they were cutting off her fingers.

"FUCK!" Stephenie screamed.

She lifted her hands, spread her fingers apart (*which were in perfect condition, adequately manicured and all accounted for—thank you very much*) and pushed Angela Mezzo as hard as she could.

Angela went flying towards the far side of the bathroom with her arms extended and little pieces of flesh falling from her body. For a brief moment she looked like the reversed version of Dracula rising from the grave, then her feet got tangled and she crashed against the wall hard.

A *SNAP* was heard, might have been Angela's back. Or neck.

As it happened, Stephenie staggered forward, shrieking in pain as her ankle shot daggers of agony up her leg.

She caught an unexpected glimpse into the first stall.

Angela's son, Mark Mezzo, was sitting on the back of the toilet with one knee at his chest and his arms wrapped around it. He looked the same as before: like the boy in the *Omen* movie, only dead. And as Stephenie stumbled into a stable stance, he lifted something up and flaunted it proudly as it dangled from his fingers. He said, "Baby Jesus loves all the little boys and girls."

Stephenie looked at the child before she eyed the item in his hand.

It was the portrait of Jesus—the one from inside her car, the gift from her mother that had been hanging from the rearview mirror.

Impulsively, she said, "What?"

Mark giggled.

And that's when the bathroom door blasted open.

8

Lee came charging in unthinkingly, arms out, fingers extended, snarling like a dog with a bad case of the fuck-offs. Stephenie spun around quickly and gave his left shoulder a shove. Lee's body twirled one-hundred-and-eighty degrees and before she knew what she was doing, Stephenie had wrapped an arm around Lee's neck and was pushing him forward like a gangster with a hostage. She yelled something. Inside her mind it was something like 'GET BACK', 'LOOK OUT' or maybe even 'OUT OF MY WAY ASSHOLES', but all that came from her mouth was "YARRRRRREEEEHHAAA!"

At the same moment Alan shuffled into the bathroom, slumping to one side like a poor-man's Quasimodo. Drool hung from his mouth in a fat red string.

Stephenie wasted no time slamming the two zombies together.

Zombie-Lee, meet Zombie-Alan.

Zombie-Alan, meet Zombie-Lee.

Lee, who was a little taller than Alan, slammed his chin against Alan's forehead.

Alan staggered out of the bathroom backwards, grabbing at nothing as he fell. He fumbled into David, knocking him down in the process.

Now, with two zombies sprawled on the floor and one being used a human shield, Stephenie was in the best position she could hope for. She held Lee tighter now, ignoring the fact he was shrieking, and groaning, and an all around pain-in-the-ass to hold onto. She moved him towards the dinning area and made for the restaurant's side door, screaming in pain and screaming for the sake of screaming.

Craig stepped into her path. Blood poured from his chest in comical proportions. He had one hand over his head and one hand held low. He looked like a zombie bear trap.

Stephenie slammed Lee into Craig and hoped for the best.

Craig stumbled and moaned but unlike Alan, he did not fall.

Lee, on the other hand, unexpectedly did.

He growled, spat, and fell hard, slipping from Stephenie's grasp. A CRACK was heard as he shattered his left knee. Blood smeared across the floor; almost looked like a magic trick.

As Lee went down, Stephenie tripped. She knocked Lee on his face and released a new batch of screams as her ankle endured more pressure. Once she was done screaming she looked up.

They were coming: Jennifer Boyle, Susan Trigg, Eric Wilde, Wayne Auburn (with his Venus flytrap head), and whoever else was hungry for action.

Stephenie scrambled across the floor like an iguana, with her head waving left and right. She grabbed a chair and used it to pull herself to her feet, cursing when it slipped forward an inch.

Lee, still on the floor, reached a hand out; his fingers briefly tickled the side of Stephenie's foot. She stepped away from him, only to have Craig Smyth lunge forward. His hands wrapped around her neck and a moment later he was squeezing her, choking her, making her vision blur.

Ignoring his assault the best she could, Stephenie pushed towards the door. Once she arrived she opened it up and stumbled outside, into the dark, into the unknown.

Zombie-Craig clung to her and a half dozen more were close behind.

Shadows were long; night had fallen.

Outside now, outside and tumbling towards the long unkempt grass at the side of the restaurant and whatever lay waiting. Stephenie felt fingers at her neck tightening as her knees buckled from under her.

She wondered if the end was upon her.

9

When Stephenie hit the ground she had her arms extended; a cry escaped her lips.

Craig fell in the opposite direction with teeth snapping in the air. He landed on his side, flipped onto his belly, slammed his face into the earth and bit the lawn. When he lifted his head he had dirt rolling from his mouth.

Stephenie shuffled away from him, watching his besotted display as she moved. She opened up her mouth and out popped another scream. She screamed in pain, yeah sure, but mostly she screamed because of the nonsense she was witnessing. How do you fight against something like this? How do you fight against something that bites the lawn?

The restaurant door closed, only to be swung open once again.

The Alan Mezzo zombie bumped into the doorframe twice; then he staggered outside like the town drunk on welfare day.

Craig slammed a fist against the earth. A second later he bit his knuckles.

Stephenie pulled herself to her feet. And with a great amount of effort she started to run. Every time her wounded foot hit the ground she allowed another shriek, another cry, another wail. Tears exploded from her eyes. Running. Running. Out of the short cut grass and into the field. Grass, knee high, made her journey more challenging. Screaming in pain as she looked over her shoulder. Running.

Three zombies now. Not two, but three. Alan Mezzo, Craig Smyth, and Lee Courtney. Yes, Lee was back, looking for more action, more blood. The zombies were coming, oh yes. As sure as a longhaired dog has shit beneath the tail, they were coming, but they were none too quick about it. They were sluggish and senseless, moving with no grace whatsoever. Feet shuffled, knees knocked together and arms flapped around like slow-moving chicken wings. At one point Lee grabbed himself by the face and hauled himself to the ground.

Stephenie stopped running.

They were coming, yes, yes. But she had time, and her foot was crying out to her, pleading with her, begging her to rest. She stumbled, almost lost her balance.

"What am I doing?" She whispered between breaths. Followed by, "Carrie. Oh God Carrie, she's at the farmhouse."

She turned away from the zombies and limped on, looking at the farmhouse.

It was big and white, framed between several large trees. It had wood panel siding and open shutters on the windows. It looked like it belonged on that old forgotten TV show, *The Waltons*. The driveway was long and it looped around in a J, so from Stephenie's point of view she was headed towards the front door. There were no cars in the driveway. No motorcycles, bicycles, or trailers either. There was a barn, a big red one, two and a half stories tall; it seemed to double as a garage. The driveway ran from the barn's giant doors to the highway, which remained as empty a politician's campaign promises.

Stephenie looked over her shoulder once again. When she felt confident the zombies were none too close, she stopped walking and turned around.

There were six of them, six walking dead. Two were heading in her direction, two fighting each other, one was crawling along the ground on his belly, and one was standing still, staring at the sky.

Looking at them now—with a little buffer of space to help ease her worries—Stephenie decided that yes, they were definitely mindless. Whether or not they were 'brain-eaters' was still undecided. Hopefully she'd never find out.

She crouched in the long grass, brown in some spots, green in others. She put a hand on her ankle and fell into a sitting position. The rag was completely red. Her ankle was wet; it felt like mush. Plus it was sore, swollen. She wondered if it would ever mend.

After a few seconds rolled by she stood up, feeling guilty on top of everything else. She needed to find Carrie and every moment she wasted Carrie would suffer. It wasn't fair. She needed to continue her journey.

Limp by limp, she pressed on.

Then she heard it: the growl.

She spun around.

What was it? *Where* was it? She didn't know—but then she did.

It was that *thing*, the thing she couldn't see. It pressed down on her. Invisible, yes—but that didn't make it harmless. She imagined it squashing her like a bug beneath an open hand. She imagined it creeping inside her belly somehow; causing her body to explode. She was afraid. Oh golly, Miss Molly, was she ever. The fear was real. Justified. She couldn't see the demon causing it, not yet anyhow, but she knew it was there, getting closer, getting ready to strike.

She stumbled towards the house faster now, wearing the pain on her face—enduring it, not liking it. Hating it. As the front door grew near she noticed the stairs that needed climbing: two of them. They were going to hurt, unless she slowed herself down and took them one at a time. But she wasn't going to do that; couldn't do that. The big invisible monster was almost on top of her now, getting ready to crush the life from her body. She knew this like she knew her own name.

Still limping towards the house, she looked away from the stairs and eyed the door.

It had a long handle and a latch for your thumb. But what if the latch was locked? What would she do then? She didn't have time to knock, or did she? Could she wait that long? Would she survive?

Soon, but not soon enough, she found herself in shorter grass. Then she was at the J shaped driveway. Rocks crunched beneath her feet. For a brief moment she wondered how (and perhaps why) they managed to get all of the stones in the driveway to be white. Then she followed a path that led to the front door, leaving drops in her wake.

Slapping her wounded foot onto the first concrete step, she pushed herself up. Something inside her ankle squished in a way that made her knees tremble and another scream blasted from her throat.

The invisible monster was near.

She reached out. The door handle was in her hand and the latch was beneath her thumb. She squeezed it. Oh God she squeezed it, hoping for the best, praying for a miracle, praying the door wasn't locked.

CHAPTER FIVE:
THE SPLIT FAMILY

1

Blair Split, father of Christina, husband of Anne, owner of the farmhouse that looked like it belonged to the Waltons, sat in his favorite chair, reading a newspaper that bore a date of a time long since past. He had short dark hair and beady little eyes that sat low and wide on his slender face. His arms and legs were thin but strong. His chest muscles, which seemed neither large nor small, were well hidden behind his black dress shirt. The shirt itself was simple in design and looked like something a gun-fighter would wear to a brawl that ended in killing.

Blair looked up, dropped the paper on his lap and eyed the front entrance.

"What's that?" he said; his voice was rough and intended for nobody but himself. But he knew what was happening on the far side of the door; somehow he knew.

The door flew open and Stephenie plowed her way inside.

With a wild sweep of her arm Stephenie slammed the door shut. Eyes bulged from her head. Ignoring Blair, she hunted the door's lock. And it was there. Thank God it was there. She clicked the latch with shaky fingers—fingers now red with someone else's blood, not to mention her own. She tested the door, pulled on it, tried to get it to open. The lock was a strong one. It would hold. She hoped. She thumped her back against the wood, much like she had in the restaurant bathroom. Two seconds later she looked at Blair for the first time, panting and shaken.

Blair stood up slowly, irritably.

He was none too happy, that much was obvious, maybe even understandable. But his lack of happiness was quickly becoming the type of anger that seemed ready, willing and able, to bubble its way right into the realms avid fury. Stephenie could see this clearly; she could see it just by looking at him.

He tossed his paper aside and with a stern voice he said, "What the hell is going on?"

"There's something out there!" Stephenie offered; she had her wounded foot elevated and both of her hands flush against the door.

Blair hesitated; his eyes became slits.

Then a woman stepped into the room: Anne, Blair's wife.

Anne looked like she had been caught in a time machine, sent straight from the summer of 1968. Her brown hair had little wings on both sides, sort of looked like the brunette version of Florence Henderson, mother on the Brady Bunch. She wore a green frilly apron, and if that wasn't enough, she wore it over banana-yellow dress that was shaped like the fat end of a bugle.

Following Anne into the room was a girl.

Stephenie recognized her at once.

It was Christina, the teenager that had been sitting on the patio swing, twiddling her thumbs. And now that Stephenie got a better look at her, she too was dressed in a questionable manner. Her cute little brown dress covered in white polka dots suddenly seemed very odd. When was the last time a mother and daughter team shared a nostalgic type of fashion sense that most people on the planet wasn't ready to embrace? When was the most recent—

Blair cleared his throat, flashed his teeth and said, "What are you doing in *my* house?"

Stephenie, who was looking at Christina, turned towards Blair once again. Lines of fear seemed etched in her skin. She said, "Huh?"

"You heard me."

Stephenie's face contorted into an array of expressions: confusion, pain, turmoil, aggravation, stress—it was all there. She bundled her thoughts together the best that she was able and blurted out: "You don't understand!"

"Maybe I don't *want* to understand," Blair proclaimed. "Maybe I just want you out of my house!"

"But there's something out there! Something's outside!" Stephenie slapped a hand against the door twice; then before the sound even dissipated she wished she hadn't been so bold. What if that *thing*, drawn by the noise, blasted its way into the house and killed them all. Whose fault would *that* be, huh? It would be her fault! Easy.

Christina stepped next to her father. Wagging a finger judgmentally, she said, "I know you. You were at the restaurant. What happened to you? You're bleeding now. You look bad."

Anne joined the conversation. "What's your name, darlin'?"

Stephenie eyes shifted from Blair to Christina, then landed on Anne. She thought about her daughter Carrie.

Was Carrie inside the house somewhere, tied down and bleeding with her fingers chopped off? It seemed unlikely.

Blair said, "I'm going to ask you one last time you stupid bitch, what are you doing in my house?"

Anne swatted Blair with the back of her hand. She didn't do it hard, but she let him know she was there. "Oh Blair," she said.

Stephenie heard the name Blair and her eyes widened. So this was Blair…

Anne continued. "Don't be like that now. Are you blind? Can't you see the girl's been cryin'? And look! She's got blood all over her. What happened girly-girl? You get in an accident? Come on now, you can tell me." She patted her hand on her chest. "My name is Anne. This is my daughter Christina. And

117

don't let my husband upset you none, either. Blair's just a big ole bear with no sense in his head, that's what he is. Come to the couch and rest yer feet darlin'. I'll take care of ya. I'll fix ya right up."

"But what if… " Stephenie trailed off.

"No," Blair said, lifting a hand. "I may be a *big ole bear*, but I want to know who you are, and what makes you think you can enter this house—*my* house—without knocking. We have rules in these here parts, missy, and before you even said 'hello' you started breakin' em in bunches."

Stephenie's chin began shaking, doing a little foxtrot right there on her face. She was about to cry; it was easy to see. She said, "I'm looking for my daughter."

"Your daughter?" Blair seemed to consider things on a different level. He rubbed a hand against his knuckles and said, "Very well then. I'll get the axe."

2

Blair turned away from Stephenie, nodded his head and walked out of the room. Inside the kitchen, he opened a drawer and retrieved a flashlight. He clicked it on. The flashlight worked fine. On the far side of the room was a door. He placed his hand on the knob and opened it. A moment later he was outside, behind his home, walking towards the big red barn, following the beam of light the flashlight was creating.

Next to the barn's two giant-size doors was a smaller door. Blair opened it, stepped into the barn, clicked on an overhead light and kept walking.

Shadows cut the room into sections.

He walked past three old cars, one of which sat on concrete blocks without any tires. It was a 1957, two-door, four-cylinder, Metropolitan convertible. In its prime it was beautiful—white along the bottom, yellow on the hood and fins. Now it was a rust-bucket with no place to go and no way to get there.

At the back of the barn there was a homemade tool bench. He approached it, eyeing the stuff that hung from the wall above it. There were lots of things to look at; he had plenty of tools. But it was the hatchets he was interested in, and he had two of them: a large one and a small one. He pulled the large one from a hook on the wall; it was quite a bit smaller than a full sized axe and it would be easy to handle; figured it was exactly what the girl needed.

He returned to the house—flashlight in his left hand, hatchet in his right. He stepped inside, clicked the flashlight off and plunked it in the open drawer. He was about to slam the drawer shut when he changed his mind. He snagged the flashlight and entered the living room once again.

Stephenie was sitting on the couch now, Carrie on one side, Anne on the other. She had a glass of water in her hand, which was trembling noticeably.

Blair approached, holding the flashlight between his arm and his ribcage. He pulled the water away from Stephenie and sat it on a nearby shelf.

He said, "Here." Looking into Stephenie's sad face, he handed her the hatchet. "You can have this too." He dropped the flashlight on her lap.

"What's this for?" Stephenie asked, looking up at him with teary eyes.

"You may need them."

"Yes dear," Anne said, supporting her husband. "You *will* need them. I'm quite sure of it."

"I don't understand."

Stepping back a foot, Blair said, "*Don't understand?* What are you talking about? I'm giving these to you. What's not to understand?"

"But what about my daughter?"

"She's not here."

Stephenie huffed. "But I talked to her on the phone. She said she was here. She said… " Stephenie's eyes squinted. She didn't want to finish that sentence. She didn't want to say her daughter had been crying and screaming, saying her fingers were getting cut off by a man named Blair. She didn't even want to think it.

Anne said, "We don't know where your daughter is, Stephenie."

Blair followed that statement with: "It's time for you to go."

Christina, who had been rather quiet, said, "You don't want to be here, Stephenie. Trust me."

"How do you know my name?" Stephenie's head shifted from Christina to Anne. "I didn't tell you guys my name. How do you know what my name is?"

Anne said, "It's time to go."

Christina agreed. "Yes, it's time to go."

Anne and Christina stood up. Now Stephenie was sitting on the couch and all three of the family members were standing. They were looking down at her. From her angle, they seemed tall and intimidating.

Stephenie started to feel a little bit like Rosemary having a baby, like her friends and acquaintances were plotting against her. "But I didn't tell you my name," she said. "It's impossible for you to know who I am! How do you know, huh? How do you know what my name is?!"

Blair crouched down and put his hand on Stephenie's knee. His eyes were very cold, impassionate. In some ways he looked like a reptile. He said, "There are two ways we can do this Stephenie Paige of Martinsville, daughter of Richard and Cynthia Brownell, widow to Hal Paige, who died on the job on a day he didn't want to go to work, who died because you forced him to go. Stephenie Paige, born on a cold September afternoon—September 22nd, 1979, to be exact. Stephenie Paige, a simple girl on too many medications, who didn't finish high school all those years ago because she didn't think she needed to, figured her good looks would land her a husband that would bring home the bacon. I know more than you think I do Stephenie, five-foot eight, one-hundred-and-twenty-two pounds. You can either take the hatchet and go, or I'll take the hatchet... to you. I'll chop your fucking arms off."

Stephenie gasped. They didn't simply know her first name; they knew her last name and everything else about her too. And worse than that, she had been threatened, right? Did that really just happen? Blair was going to chop her apart with the hatchet unless she, she—what? Went outside? Was that the game plan? She had to go outside and face the zombies and that big invisible thing that wanted to squash her like a bug? Oh God, did she have to go back outside? Really?

"You don't want to be in the basement, girly-girl." Anne said. "It's not very nice down there."

Christina nodded with agreement. "Bad things happen."

"Very bad things."

"This doesn't make any sense," Stephenie said.

Blair stood up. With a firm voice he said, "Carrie's not here."

"Yes she is," Stephenie challenged. "I never told you my daughter's name is Carrie! I never told you *her* name, or *my name*. That means she's here! That means that, that… she must have told you those things! Right?"

But even as Stephenie barked out her dispute, she knew those pieces didn't fit her puzzle very well. Carrie didn't know half the things had Blair said. She didn't know the year Stephenie was born, or the fact that Hal didn't want to go to work on the day he died. Aside from her, nobody knew *that* little nugget of information, nobody except Hal. And Hal was D-E-A-D.

Blair's attitude was unflinching. "Get out of my house Stephenie," he said. "Now, before I lose my temper."

Reluctantly, Stephenie stood up. The flashlight was in one hand; the hatchet was in the other. She gripped the hatchet tight. "What if I don't want to go?"

Blair's nostrils flared and his eyes widened. Suddenly he was grabbing Stephenie by the arm and squeezing it. He yanked her away from the couch and dragged her towards the door like a pissed off mother with her spoiled brat child, not being polite or courteous in any way.

Stephenie shrieked in pain, not because of the way he grabbed her but because of her ankle. She was walking on it wrong and it hurt like hell. She said, "I don't want to go outside! It's dangerous outside!"

"You don't want to be lost in the basement, do you Stephenie?" Anne said, looking psychotic now in her green frilly apron and her yellow bugle dress.

Christina agreed. "It's bad in the basement. Terrible things happen."

"Yes," Anne said. "Terrible things indeed!"

Blair said, "It's time to go!" He unlocked the door and swung it open.

Stephenie, favoring her wounded ankle, resisted valiantly. "Please! Don't put me outside! I want my daughter! Tell me, where's my daughter?"

"She's not here, Stephenie!" Blair said with a smile that sat on his face dishonestly.

"But—"

"But nothing!" Blair pushed her through the door forcefully and out she went, easy as pie. The hatchet fell one way; it landed by the door. The flashlight slipped from her hand and fell the other way; it rolled into the garden.

Stephenie stumbled and grabbed onto a handrail before she found herself tumbling down the stairs. She landed funny, but did not fall. Then she looked into the house.

Christina stepped into view. She said, "She's not here, Stephenie! Carrie's not here!" She sounded completely crazy.

Anne poked her head into Stephenie line of vision. In a different set of circumstances she would have looked hilarious. "You don't want to go to the basement, Stephenie! Nothing good happens in the basement!"

"No," Christina agreed. "The basement's bad!"

Stephenie, holding the handrail for balance, was desperate for help. She begged, "Well... can I use the phone?"

"Oh gosh-golly, girly-girl," Anne said, tilting her head to one side. "We don't have a phone!"

Christina grinned. "Bye, bye. And good luck."

And with that, Blair slammed the door.

CHAPTER SIX:
THE NIGHTMARE CONTINUES

1

Stephenie banged on the door three times with her fist before she spun around and cursed out loud. Her knuckles throbbed slightly as they turned red, not that she noticed, or cared. She was too busy being worried for her wellbeing, and it was more than safe to say she didn't like being outside *at all*, so she banged on the door one last time with the palm of her hand.

Nobody answered her call, which she had to admit wasn't surprising.

Looking down, she saw the hatchet sitting by her feet, lying on the porch like a premonition.

"Oh God," she whispered.

The very notion of picking the object up was a *statement*.

She wasn't about to chop wood, was she? No, of course not. So picking the object up meant what, exactly? *Oh, she knew.* It made her stomach churn but *she knew*. Picking the axe off the ground meant using it defensively, as a weapon. Could she do it? Could she hack her way through a bunch of zombies if they attacked? Could she slice somebody's face open or bludgeon the back of some guy's head? Was that her future? Did she have a choice?

She looked across the grassy field, eyeing the restaurant meticulously. The field seemed to be empty now. There were no zombies coming this way or that, no zombies hanging around the restaurant door either.

This was good, she recognized. Her spirits lifted slightly.

She could see the sign that said KING'S DINER overlooking the parking lot and the gas pumps. She could see her car sitting alone; the headlights were off, the doors were closed. It looked far away; everything seemed far away. Getting to her car by foot was going to hurt, but what other options did she have? None. Unless she considered banging on the door for the next ten minutes an option, which needless to say wasn't the case. Looking at the bright side of things, not getting attacked by zombies made the moment undeniably better. It also made the task of arming herself easier to handle. At least she wasn't grabbing the axe and using it, which seemed like a real possibility when Blair was tossing her out the front door like a bag of yesterday's garbage.

She turned partway around, ring finger between her teeth, eyebrows lopsided. She looked at the door one final time, cursing under her breath. Blair and his asshole family weren't going to open it for her; that much was obvious. And if they did open the door they wouldn't treat her nicely. Where that left her, she did not know.

And where was Carrie? Was she in the farmhouse? Yes or no?

The answer was inconclusive.

With a squint of her eyes, Stephenie pulled her finger away from her mouth and crouched down. She picked the hatchet off the porch and gripped it firmly, trying to make it feel comfortable in her hand. It didn't. The hatchet felt as foreign and unfamiliar as it possibly could. Chopping wood (or anything else for that matter) wasn't something she did often. In fact, she couldn't recall doing it once in her whole entire life.

She ran a finger along the blade. She wasn't sure why. Just checking, she supposed. The blade was sharp; it sliced her skin open before she knew it would happen. Surprised by her self-inflicted wound, she pulled her hand away from the hatchet. A drop of blood fell from her thumb, landing on her foot.

Damn thing's sharp enough to split hairs.

She made her way down the steps with her thumb in her mouth, tasting blood on her tongue. She lifted the flashlight from the garden and stood there, looking around with her eyes wide and face washed in fear, like a child separated from the grown-ups at the mall, like a puppy tied to a pole on a busy street corner, looking for its master. After a moment she limped towards the stone pebble driveway, clicked the light on and sniffed back the liquid that was threatening to leak from her nose.

The light worked just fine. Again, for this she was thankful.

She walked, fighting through the pain, following the beam of light that illuminated her way. The pain in her ankle wasn't a searing hot poker scorching her bones. It was a slow roasting agony slugging along inside her flesh. It was an ugly brand of misery that didn't let up. In time, standing on her wounded foot felt no different than *not* standing on it. Her senses didn't grow numb exactly, but the pain was becoming a throbbing constant that seemed as endless and relentless as the sky, the sky above the sky, and everything else that came after that. Across the short grass and into the field she went, holding the flashlight tight and the hatchet tighter. Her eyes shifted left and right nervously. The grass swayed in slow moving waves. Some of the grass was still green, but the August sun had baked much of the grass until it had turned dry and brown. She half-expected a zombie to jump out of the field screaming *GOTCHA* as it waved its hands over its head and made stupid faces. Wouldn't happen though. Even she knew *that*. Still, she felt nervous. And not having a plan wasn't helping her frame of mind in the slightest.

So, what is the plan? she wondered.

Stephenie released a sharp squeal as she stepped on a ridge of dirt awkwardly. Her face pinched into a ball. Her eyes squeezed tight.

She kept moving.

The plan, she supposed, was to retreat. She needed to return to her car and start driving. Obviously she didn't want to leave her daughter, but she didn't know where else to look, or what else to do. And it was dangerous here, too dangerous to leave Carrie—yeah, sure. But it was also too dangerous to keep up this one-person rescue mission she found herself submerged in. She needed help, lots of it. The sooner she got it the better. Was she scared? Yes, of course she was. But fear wasn't the only emotion pushing her buttons. Carrie wasn't in the restaurant, or in the bungalow across the street. As far as Stephenie could tell Carrie wasn't inside the farmhouse either. And if she *was* inside the farmhouse, Blair, Anne, and Christina, weren't about to give her the opportunity to search the place—that much was for damn sure. Hell, Carrie wasn't even in the *baffroom*, as that crazy witch-voice inside her mind was suggesting. And where the hell did that voice come from anyways? She didn't recognize *that* voice. So what was the deal there?

Another mystery, she supposed, another, in a long line of mysteries.

Halfway to the restaurant, Stephenie tucked the flashlight beneath her arm. She checked her left pocket. No keys. She shuffled the hatchet from one hand to the other and checked the right pocket.

No keys again.

"Oh no," she whispered.

Stephenie looked over both shoulders slowly, quietly. There was nothing in front of her, nothing behind her. Feeling reasonably sure she wasn't about to be attacked, she sat the hatchet and the flashlight at her feet and checked her pockets more thoroughly—front and back.

She didn't have them. Her keys were gone.

Instead of screaming in frustration—which Lord knows, she wanted to do—she tapped her fingertips against her forehead, fluttered her eyelashes and tried not to cry. Her breath was unsteady; her bottom lip found its way between her teeth.

What was she going to do? That was the question that needed answering. Without her car keys she wasn't going anywhere quickly. Without her keys, she was fucked.

She looked into the parking lot.

Still no sign of zombies. For the time being she was safe.

She looked at the highway, still no cars. Not one. Not even a friggin' motorcycle to wave down. Her luck was unbelievable.

The keys must be in my purse, she thought as her eyes shifted towards her car. But where was her purse? Did she leave it in the car? Maybe. No, not *maybe*. *Yes*—now that she thought about it—*—yes*, her purse was in her car, sitting on the backseat. But it didn't matter. Her keys weren't in her purse, she put them into her pocket; she knew it. That meant they were now lost.

Damn.

She checked her pockets one final time, nothing of course—nothing but a small amount of pocket-change, a little bit of lint, a half-empty pack of matches, and a stick of gum with a loose wrapper.

She crouched down, lifted the flashlight and the hatchet and kept walking.

Her ankle squished; her teeth squeezed together.

Looking at her car, she wondered if the Julie-zombie was waiting inside of it, grinning like a manic with her head smashed apart and blood dripping from her chin. She hoped not. God, she really, really, hoped not—but if Julie was there, what then? She couldn't run; she couldn't fight.

Stephenie looked at the hatchet, tightening her grip as she eyed the blade.

Although she had never been in a battle before, not a real one anyhow, maybe she *could* fight. Yes, yes. That was an intriguing thought now, wasn't it? It would be a whole lot different than the hair pulling, face slapping, shin kicking spats she found herself engaged in back in grades four, five and six. But the basic concept was the same: defend yourself while manufacturing an offensive strike.

Walking, limping. She arrived at the parking lot limping, always limping.

Still no zombies...

She approached her car and turned off the flashlight.

The car was empty. The doors, she soon discovered, were locked. And on the backseat was her purse. It was right where she left it: lying on its side with its contents spilled across the seat.

After a few moments of having her face smooched against the glass, she stepped away from the car and looked across the road, eyeing the bungalow. The corpse in the bungalow's front yard was gone now. Everything was quiet. The wind hardly blew at all. And as strange as it may seem, it was then—in her moment of serenity—that something terrible occurred to her. Today was the day she might actually die.

2

A crow flew overhead, circled the parking lot, and landed on the gas pump. It cawed, shuffled from on end of the pump to the other and flew off. Stephenie watched it go as she approached the restaurant, which seemed to have the insanity drained out of it. All things considered, this was a good thing, a great thing—perhaps the best news of the day.

Looking through the restaurant's big windows, Stephenie came to the conclusion that the building was empty; the zombies were gone. The idea of stepping inside the building seemed ridiculous, of course. *(Cyanide, anyone? It's free!)* But the idea hanging around the front of the restaurant seemed equally as bad.

Out of the frying pan and into the fire was the expression that came to mind. If she only knew which was which, the decisions may have come easier.

Where were her keys?

That was a question that felt all too important. Keys meant choices; no keys meant: no choices.

If they were inside her purse, she might as well smash a car window and get on with it. But the fact was, she didn't think they were there. She didn't remember tossing her keys into her purse; she remembered cramming them into her pocket, and figured they were lost during a battle.

Maybe near the restaurant's side door?

She walked to the side of the building. Upon arriving, she clicked the flashlight on once again. Shining the flashlight into the grass, she inched ahead, leaving a little trail of blood where it fell. She couldn't see anything. No. That wasn't right. She could see a fair amount of blood, little pieces of flesh and a tattered piece of clothing, but no keys. She kept looking; still, she found nothing. So what did it mean? Were the keys in one of the bathrooms, or in that little closet behind the counter?

Maybe. Truth was, she didn't know.

This isn't fun anymore, she thought. But it was a stupid thought, a preposterous thought. There hadn't been a moment of fun since before she parked the car.

In her mind's eye she visualized the way she'd been sitting inside the storage room. Did her keys fall from her pocket while she was sprawled out on the floor?

Again, she didn't know. But maybe.

Stephenie returned to the front of the building, leaning against the building's wall for support. She looked through the big windows. Then, shaking her head in disgust, she shuffled to the front door. Yes, the idea of limping towards the highway and either A) waiting for a car, or B) walking to - *wherever* - occurred to her. But she couldn't walk much farther and she hadn't seen a car driving along that road since she arrived so, right or wrong, she made her way to the door. And opened it.

And stepped inside.

Overhead, the bells chimed, making Stephenie cringe. She had forgotten about them completely. Hearing them now didn't remind her of Christmas; they reminded her of a dinner bell, as in: *SOUP'S ON! COME AND GET IT!*

It was a shame she felt like the main course.

The restaurant was empty. No screaming zombies. No dead bodies. Nothing. Well no, not *nothing*—there was still blood on the floor, the walls, the tables, chairs, and everywhere else she looked. Plus the room looked different: the walls were darker, the tables and chairs were darker, the air felt heavier and tasted sour.

That was *something* wasn't it?

She made her way to the counter, being careful where she stepped, not wanting to slip in the blood. She remembered the impossible things that happened the last time she entered the restaurant, and pushed her thoughts away. She placed her knuckles on the countertop; then using it as a crutch, she hobbled past the sink and the stoves, towards the storage room door. Her hand touched something that gleamed. It was a knife, a butter-knife. She picked it up and stuck it in her back pocket without hesitation, just in case. And yes, even then she knew she could find a sharper tool if she took a moment to look, but she wasn't going to. Did she expect to *use* the knife? No, of course not. Why would she? She had a hatchet sharper than a scalpel, so the butter knife was for backup. If she got desperate enough, she might even use it.

Stephenie tucked her flashlight beneath her arm while approaching the storage room. She took a deep breath, placed her hand on the doorknob, opened the door, and looked inside.

"Oh shit," she whispered into the mouth of madness. "This can't be here. This can't be happening!"

But it was happening.

It really was.

3

At first, she thought she was seeing it wrong. Because, well… because seeing it wrong was the only thing that made a lick of sense. But after rubbing her forehead with her fingers and thumb, like someone stressed beyond repair, she opened her eyes real wide and knew—beyond a shadow of a doubt—that she *wasn't* seeing it wrong. She was seeing it the only way she *could* see it.

She took a step forward, followed by another. She flicked the overhead light on and limped another foot.

Her fingers found her throat, which suddenly seemed very dry.

There was a staircase, a big wooden one that descended into darkness. It looked like something you'd find inside a haunted house (she couldn't help thinking how well the description fit the situation). The storage room had a staircase, on loan from Dracula's castle. Awesome.

You don't want to go to the basement Stephenie. Nothing good happens in the basement. The basement's bad. You know that, right girly-girl? Sure you do.

Everybody knows the basement is bad news.

Was the staircase there before?

No, it wasn't.

Could she have missed it somehow? Lord, no. It was huge, took up the whole room. It had two big Victorian handrails curving away from each other, leading into a gloom that seemed to have no end. Each stair was at least four feet wide. The wood looked like oak, maybe mahogany. There was no dust on the staircase, no bloody footprints or body parts strewn across it either. It was just a staircase, a simple and impossible staircase that shouldn't have been there.

As Stephenie was sizing it up, the storage room door, which was now behind her, creaked. It slammed shut with a TWHACK, rattling in its casing as the little hook-lock danced around freely.

She screamed, spinning quickly as her eyes bulged from her head. The flashlight dropped to the floor and rolled to the edge of the staircase, almost tumbled down the stairs. The hatchet knocked against her knee.

Oh God, she was locked in. She knew it!

She banged her fists against the wood. *BANG, BANG, BANG, BANG.* She grabbed the doorknob and gave it a turn. It never occurred to try the knob *before* pounding on the wood, which was the logical thing to do. It also never occurred to her that opening the door might have been a big mistake, not that it mattered. The door was locked, as she knew it would be. The knob wouldn't turn; there was nothing she could do about it. Or was there? She had a hatchet. Maybe she could chop the fucker down.

"Shit!" She screamed.

Then, with the curse still touching her lips, the phone rang, causing her to yelp.

She looked at the phone with her eyes wide and her muscles tense.

It was hanging off the wall the same way it had been for the past fifty years or more. It was an old black thing, greasy and forgotten, in need of being replaced—or more accurately, thrown away.

It rang a second time, and Stephenie didn't hesitate to lift the receiver. When she put it to her ear she heard a voice that sounded like it belonged to Blair. "Don't go in the basement, Stephenie. Don't even think it. Bad things happen in the basement. And when bad girls like *you* go into places they shouldn't be, they get what they deserve."

A question snuck out: "What did you say?"

"You heard me, you fucking psycho cunt. You heard every last word."

CLICK. The line went dead.

Then a new voice came, not from the phone. Oh no, the line was dead and nothing was coming from there, no more statements, no more questions, accusations or insults, not even the dial tone. No, this voice was coming from the basement. It was a child's voice, a girl's voice—recognizable in every possible way.

It belonged to Carrie.

"Mom?"

Stephenie hung the phone on the cradle and turned around slowly, oh so slowly, like she was in a daze inside a dream. The locked door was forgotten now. The phone call was forgotten too. She looked down the stairs—those big oak/mahogany stairs that weren't suppose to be there yet somehow were. She felt her guts churn inside of her. She took a step forward, followed by another. And as she stepped down the first of 'Lord only knew' how many stairs, she felt a tear roll from her eye and onto her cheek.

Heaven help her, with that one single word from her daughter's mouth it was decided: she was going into the basement. The warnings she received had been cast aside without a moment's delay.

4

"Carrie?" she asked, with a voice both quiet and meek.

There was no answer.

She took a step, followed by two more. She snagged the flashlight off the floor and pointed it down the stairs. Then, with a hand squeezing the hatchet and an elbow on the handrail, she paused. She thought about the *other* basement—the bungalow— the way it looked, the way it felt. *Like holding hands with a rotting corpse*, she thought; her body trembled soon after. Carrie had been calling her name from the belly of *that* beast too, as she *not so fondly* remembered. And how did that story end?

Stephenie didn't care how that story ended. She didn't care because it didn't matter. The only thing that mattered was rescuing her daughter, and the only thing that worried her was the concept of failure.

The voice came again, cutting her thoughts short. "Mom?"

Stephenie felt her mouth twitch. She didn't grin exactly, but she almost did.

The voice in the basement belonged to her daughter; she knew it. That was the difference this time around, Stephenie promised herself. This time the crestfallen voice belonged to her daughter for *sure*.

So why was this little adventure starting to feel like Ground-hog Day?

She took another step, allowing a fair amount of weight to fall upon the handrail. The stair creaked. The handrail creaked too; she hoped it wouldn't break. The beam from the flashlight showcased nothing but darkness.

"Carrie? Is that you?" She took another step, wondering if the staircase would fall apart from the weight of her.

"Yes Mom." The voice sounded quiet, far away, nervous. Above all, the voice sounded real.

"Where are you?" Stephenie asked, then a thought came. What if she found her daughter safe and sound and they left this haunted place together, and what if it happened soon, like in the next few minutes? (And yes, at this point there was no denying it: the place was haunted, or something that wasn't too far from haunted at the very least.) Escaping the nightmare, wouldn't that be nice?

"Carrie? Can you hear me?"

No answer.

Stephenie hunted the dark corners of the room she was stepping into, shining the light where it seemed most suited. But she couldn't see *anything*. Not a wall, not the floor. Nothing—unless she turned around, of course. When she turned, she could see the light from the storage room revealing the area behind her.

Still descending the staircase, she pointed the flashlight in front of her feet. Yes, the stairs were there, easy to see and impossible to miss. She followed the beam at her feet, shining the light before her.

She said, "Carrie?"

Still no answer.

After another dozen stairs or so she came to the floor. She stepped onto it, heard the rail creak one final time. Then, as her shoes touched the concrete, her heart rate increased. She swallowed back the urge to turn around and run up the stairs, which she definitely wanted to do. She was afraid now, very afraid. The room was too dark and creepy, too unknown. Plus she had been fooled once already so her confidence in this particular situation wasn't exactly soaring.

She coughed, tried to say something but found she couldn't. The words were chained to her gullet.

She took a step ahead, followed by another. And another.

The room seemed blacker than night, blacker than death. So she closed her eyes and for a moment she thought she might actually die of fear, right then and there. When she opened her eyes once again nothing had changed. Her night-vision wasn't going to become active, not with the flashlight on and she wasn't about to turn it off.

"Carrie!" she finally said, louder than before. "Carrie, where are you?"

No reply.

"CARRIE!"

"I'm here Mom," the voice said.

"Where?" Stephenie stepped deeper into the room, trying to find her child inside a darkness that was wrapping around her like fingers. But the voice sounded further away now. Was it just the acoustics of the room, or was Carrie drifting out of reach?

A splinter of light appeared.

Stephenie's eyes snapped towards it.

On the far side of the darkness a door was opening. It seemed to be a mile away or more; the door looked so small.

The door opened wider, then wider still; the sliver of light increased in size.

Stephenie realized the door didn't look small; it *was* small. It was probably less than two feet tall and a foot wide.

The slice of light continued to thicken.

Carrie appeared at the door, in the light. She was on her hands and knees (all the room she had been granted in such a place) and her face looked pale and frightened. Her eyes were like saucers. She opened her mouth to speak; then she looked over her shoulder and quickly shuffled back, evading Stephenie's view.

Stephenie screamed, "Carrie!"

Something happened, she thought.

She began running. Well, not *running* exactly. She couldn't run, but she could try. And she did. Fighting back tears of pain and screams of agony she charged towards the door. Her left arm spun wildly, still gripping the weapon with a blade sharp enough to split hairs. She tried to hold the flashlight steady but it didn't work. The light bounced up and down, illuminating shadows at random.

Carrie was gone from view. Oh shit, she was gone.

"CARRIE!" she screamed.

Then Stephenie found herself at a door that only came to her waist, huffing and panting, her face masked in pain. Reaching down, she found a handle. She grabbed it with the same hand that held the hatchet, using her ring finger to grip. She pulled the door open and dropped to her knees.

5

Behind the door, a little round tunnel went straight into the earth; looked like it had been dug with a hammer. The walls were made of rock, clay and dirt. A string of lights were attached to the ceiling, though Stephenie couldn't quite figure out how. The tunnel went on for about twenty feet before it came to its first juncture.

From Stephenie's point of view, she couldn't tell if the tunnel turned left or right at that juncture. She wouldn't have cared one way or another if Carrie had been in view, but she wasn't. Carrie was gone.

For a brief moment Stephenie thought about her favorite movie, *The Shawshank Redemption*. More specifically, she thought about a scene near the climax of the film where the story's hero, Andy Dufresne, is declared missing from his jail cell and his best friend Red finds himself standing with the prison's warden plus a guard or two, looking into the mouth of a hole that looked very much like the one Stephenie was looking at now. She figured she might even be wearing the same expression that Morgan Freeman's character Red had wore. Lord knows, a hammer-dug tunnel wasn't what she expected to find.

"Carrie?" she said, too quietly for anyone to hear.

But then the response came, echoing off the tunnel's wall: "I'm in here mommy! Come get me, please!"

Stephenie looked over her shoulder, first the one on her right, then the one on her left.

Nothing.

Nothing but darkness.

The darkness made her skin crawl, and she could feel it weighing down on her—not just around her body but in her heart, too. This child-thing calling her name, maybe it wasn't Carrie. She wished with all her soul that it was, but what if it wasn't? It was a terrible thought but it was true. Still, she had come this far, why not a little farther? Why not another step? Or two? Why not place her neck upon the guillotine and have it over with? She couldn't turn back. She couldn't turn away. Where would she run? Upstairs? The door leading into the restaurant was locked, and even if it *wasn't* locked, even if the troubled spirits running this nightmare decided to throw her a bone and unlock the door, what else had they decided? What other horrors lie waiting on the far side of that door if she was fool enough to open it? And worse than that—worse, but somehow more important, more real—what if she walked through the door at the top of the staircase alone, without Carrie? What then? What was her next move? Would she stumble onto the road and wait for a car that may never come? Would it be time to look for her keys again? Time to visit Blair or make another trip to that fucked up bungalow on the far side of the highway? No. She was a mother and her child needed her. She would do what she had to do. She would extend her neck across the chopping block if need be. Wonder why? The answer was a simple one.

What if Carrie *was* calling her name?

Stephenie was traveling a one-way street, and she intended on driving its corroded pavement 'til the end because that's what a good mother does. Darkness sat in her heart like a lump of coal because her heart was empty, and without her one-and-only daughter—without *Carrie*—her heart would stay that way until it broke or dried up and she felt nothing. And Stephenie didn't want to feel nothing. She wanted to feel whole again. She wanted to put things in place. The cupboards in her heart were empty; she needed Carrie to fill them up.

"Carrie!" she said, not like a question but like a statement. Her voice was stern and strong. "I'm coming to get you!"

She pushed herself into the hole, into the earth, into the unknown void that would have a character from her favorite movie hang his mouth open in an expression of awe, because she was forging ahead. God help her, with a flashlight in one hand, a hatchet in the other, and an ankle swelled up like a balloon, she was forging ahead. And as she shuffled along with her arms and knees scraping against the floor, breathing hard with tears rolling from her eyes, she couldn't help thinking that this was it, the moment everything would end. And maybe it was. Maybe the end was exactly what she needed. Maybe it would be for the best.

"Carrie," she said. "Hold on, babe. Hold on."

Behind her, the door closed without making a sound, locking her inside; the hinges were slicker than grease.

6

Stephenie crawled forward, knocking her head against the hanging lights twice. The air tasted damp and stale, filled with an earthy, wormy aroma that wasn't pleasant in any way. She crawled to the place where the tunnel changed its course. It didn't turn left or right; the tunnel did both. It was shaped like a 'T'.

This new section of the tunnel was slightly smaller than the first, but not too much smaller. She would be able to move easily enough, but the claustrophobia factor would increase.

Stephenie looked left.

A string of hanging lights continued along the path, but most of them were out. Light shone upon the empty floor in three separate places. Then the path either changed course or continued without light. She didn't know; it was too dark for her to make it out.

She swiveled her head from left to right.

Along the path on her right a solitary light was shining, illuminating the floor in a single place. And at the edge of that place, where the light and the darkness met, a twenty-two inch rat watched her movements with its little black eyes. It had brown fur, a twitching nose and a bloated belly. It had pink hands, pink ears and fingers that looked strong enough to play the piano. Its long dark tail tapped the floor periodically, almost rhythmically.

Seeing the creature, Stephenie cringed.

She didn't like rats. She didn't like mice much either, but rats were worse. They were big and brave and the thought of being touched by one made her stomach turn and the little hairs on the back of her neck stand on end. Cockroaches she could handle. Rats, not so much.

She heard it squeaking. Or was there a different rat doing the squeaking? Yes, now that she listened she could hear quite clearly; there was more than one rat creeping around with her. Squeaks and squeals and the pitter-patter of feet were coming from both ends of the tunnel.

Stephenie turned left, away from the rat sitting at the edge of the light.

She said, "Carrie? Where are you?"

No response.

Crawling along this new path, she wondered if her journey would be easier if she dropped the hatchet. She couldn't use it, not in a place so small. And it was starting to be a pain in the ass. She wondered if hauling it around was worth the bother.

She saw a rat run off from a dark corner, hobbling on what seemed like a sore hind leg.

She decided to keep the hatchet. Better safe than sorry.

Beneath the glow of a light, she paused. There was nothing to see, just the floor, the walls and the occasional rodent. But something was different. Something was off. She felt like she was being watched, but was she?

After moving ahead another couple feet the answer arrived.

She *was* being watched.

"Hello, Stephenie." It was a voice—male, ugly, terrifying. It sounded like it belonged to a corpse.

Stephenie bolted into kneeling position, banging her head off the ceiling. Her flashlight fell from her hand and rolled forward until it was out of reach.

"Who's there?" she said, holding the hatchet near her chest. She wondered if she should grab the flashlight. It was only a foot or two away. Afraid to move, she decided against it—for now. She didn't want to budge until she figured out what was happening and who was in the tunnel with her.

144

Her eyes strained, defining shapes inside the shadows.

The voice came again. It sounded closer this time, maybe fifteen or twenty feet away. "You know me, right?"

Stephenie responded without a moments delay. "No, I don't. I can't see anything; I don't know who you are."

There was a shift in the darkness, the sound of something getting dragged across the floor. A fresh wave of stink came wafting through the tunnel, and Stephenie found herself leaning away from it.

"You don't recognize my voice?"

"I'm afraid not. Should I?"

"I would think so. You know me. You know me very well. Oh yes. You know me very well indeed."

"Well," Stephenie said, keeping her voice steady (or at least attempting it) while she watched the figure in the darkness shift. "I don't know your voice," she offered. But there was something in the voice she *did* recognize, something that seemed familiar, but what?

"Come on. Take a guess."

"I don't want to guess. I don't want to play games. Step into the light where I can see you."

"Oh, that's no fun. And it's a little tight in here for stepping, don't you think?" A chuckle came, cold as a dead fish. The sound of something dragging across the floor continued.

"Look, I don't want trouble. I'm trying to find my daughter and I don't have time for this."

Her reasoning sounded good, at least in Stephenie's ears; too bad she was full of shit. The problem wasn't that she was in a hurry. The problem was that she didn't want to have a discussion with some unknown *thing* in the bowels of crazy town.

"Here," the voice in the dark said. "I'll give you a hint."

Suddenly there was a flash in the shadows and something came soaring towards her, something small, cutting through the air in a straight line.

Stephenie lifted a hand from her hatchet, raising it in front of her face in a protective posture. The projectile, wherever it was, spun up and around like it hardly weighed a gram. It was a card——a baseball card or a playing card. And when it fell to the ground it landed face up.

Stephenie recognized it at once.

The face on the card was Ready Freddie, from the *Old Maid* deck.

Freddie was sitting at the kitchen table with a knife in one hand and a fork in the other. He had yellow socks and a green bandana. His tongue was sticking up from his pencil-line lips like he couldn't wait another minute to eat. The image was adorable. It was Carrie's favorite card.

"Where did you get that?" Stephenie asked, trying to sound demanding. But she didn't want to know the answer, not really, not deep down. And she wasn't in any position to fake authority and get away with it. She was out of her element and clearly *not* in charge of the current situation.

"Do you want me to tell you? Do you really want to know where the card came from? Think about it Stephenie, think really hard. I know you can do it, *babe*." The voice sounded closer now; it was moving towards her.

Stephenie inched back; then a rat ripped past her, followed by two more. They were squeaking and squealing, scurrying close to the wall. They dashed over the flashlight and away they went.

Stephenie released a helpless little yelp. She didn't like rats. More than that, she didn't want to 'think *really hard*'. She just wanted out. *Again.*

Praise the Lord and shame the devil, as her mother would sometimes say, she stepped into another trap. And she knew better. At this point, she really did.

Why didn't I just—

But that's where her thinking came to a rushing halt. Why didn't she just *what*? What was she supposed to do in a situation like this, knock her heels together three times and transport into a chocolate fantasyland? Sprout wings and fly away? Her choices weren't bad, they were non-existent, and there was a new problem, one that was about to have her crying like a baby in no time at all.

She knew that voice. Oh yes she did.

It belonged to her late husband Hal.

7

Hal's voice had become hard to recognize. The best way to describe it might be by saying he sounded half human, half cement mixer cooking up a fresh batch of mud. But as soon as he said the word *babe*—a term he picked up from Stephenie and used many times before, she knew who was hiding in the shadows, like some terrible beast from a monster movie. There was no two ways about it, she knew.

Hal, the living corpse-thing, plunked a hand into the light; his fingers were bony and thin. Several fingernails were missing. Knuckles gleamed white. Skin and muscle had morphed into one another, becoming knots of soft, mushy paste covered with insipid, writhing worms. Several worms dropped from his hand in a small bunch; others squirmed deeper into his flesh.

Hal shifted forward again, bringing a half-dozen flies with him.

Now Stephenie could see his arm, long and wilted and stinking like last year's garbage. Forearm muscles hung from his ulna bone, bugs scurried on the furry mold.

She put a hand to her mouth, to her lips. Her eyes expanded, her stomach clenched and her heart pounded hard inside her chest.

She didn't want to see any more; she wanted that *thing* to stop moving.

And no, it was not *Hal. It was a thing. Oh please, oh please—it couldn't be Hal because Hal would never turn into something like that, right? He wouldn't turn into a bundle of rotting meat, tattered limbs, and mold. Tell me it isn't so; tell me I'm imagining things...*

Hal put his other hand into the light, the one with the wedding ring on it. The ring shifted; it no longer fit. The finger—bony and withered and decayed beyond reason, black in some places and green in others—had grown thin.

Stephenie forced herself to move towards the creature, not away. She had to know, had to see. She reached out, placed a hand on the flashlight and pulled it towards her. With a trembling grip she squeezed it between her fingers and lifted it.

She pointed the flashlight at the corpse.

The beam cut the darkness.

Just then, as the light beam hit its mark, Hal gripped the floor and pulled himself forward again. Flies buzzed. Now his face was beneath the hanging light; his features were well lit.

Stephenie didn't need the flashlight to see the horrors before her. Not now. She could see much—too much in fact, and she didn't need the flashlight to help her see anything more.

Yes. It was Hal.

His hair fell to the ground in singles and in small clumps. His eyes had recessed deep into his skull, which was cracked open at both sides. Mounds of festering brains had pushed through the split above his ears. His teeth, smashed apart and pointing in all directions, sat together in his mouth horrifically wrong. His jawbone had been dislocated and flattened. His nose was gone now; there was nothing left but a hole and a memory. Maggots clung to withered lips, which were thinner than shoelaces and tougher than leather. His black tongue was boated, fattening his words as he spoke them.

"Stephenie," he said, sounding strangely arrogant.

Stephenie dropped the flashlight in front of her and looked away from his face, but her eyes were none too kind. They fell to the floor for less than a moment before returning to his chest, causing her to see more, rather than less.

The expensive white dress shirt Hal had been married and buried in was wet and sticky—brown, green, and red. The collar was lopsided, the buttons undone. Something was living inside his chest now; Stephenie could see it moving behind his shredded muscles and broken bones. It was clearly visible, bigger than the maggots and worms. Was it the size of a man's fist? Was it bigger? Stephenie thought that it was. She considered two possibilities. Either Hal's heart had become a living thing that was trying to crawl free, or a rat had chewed its way inside him.

The corpse pulled closer. He—or perhaps *it*—grinned a terrible grin, with a mouth so rotten and fractured that nothing shy of a miracle could have possibly made it right.

"Stephenie," he said again, with his tongue pressed against his broken teeth. He crawled closer still. A maggot dropped from his chin. And then, with something that might have been a smile, he said that word again: "*babe*."

"Don't," Stephenie replied.

The single remark seemed to say it all: don't come near me, don't be real, don't touch me; don't exist.

"What's wrong?"

Stephenie didn't respond.

Hal shifted closer, not once, but twice quickly. His terrible face became lost in shadow and for Stephenie that was okay, because for a moment it seemed like someone else was hiding behind his terrible and somehow ancient and primitive eyes, which looked foreign and not at all from this world.

Stephenie pinched another look.

Hal was only half there. Oh God, he was severed at the waist. Black and red entrails hung from his belly, stretched out behind him like pasta. He almost looked like a snail, crawling the way he did—a snail with arms maybe, a snail from another world.

Stephenie, astonished, fell back, breaking free from her kneeing pose. Her legs found their way in front of her. One leg banged off the flashlight making it roll towards the wall. Stephenie looked at it; then she eyed the hatchet still gripped tightly in her fingers.

Hal shifted closer, clearly swimming with larva.

Then it hit her: he was only a couple feet away. If she didn't do something Hal would be close enough to touch her and she didn't want that. She didn't want his decomposing digits wrapping around her leg. She didn't want his stink pressed against her.

Hal shifted, moving closer still. Then he reached out with both hands and allowed himself to fall forward. His guts squished. He grabbed her foot—her *wounded* foot—and gave it a good squeeze.

Stephenie shrieked in equal portions of surprise and pain.

She lifted the hatchet, wondering if she'd be brave enough to use it. She felt her muscles tingle, like they were getting ready for battle, ready to fight. This monster, which was crawling with worms and maggots and insects of all sizes, needed to be dealt with. This wasn't her late husband Hal, who she loved more than she could possibly express. This was an abomination wrapped in Hal's discarded flesh for reasons she couldn't possibly comprehend. She didn't want him touching her skin. She didn't want—

Her thoughts were severed.

Hal screamed something incomprehensible and dug his fingers deep into her wound.

Stephenie fell onto her back with her eyes bulging. Pain, gigantic and unforgiving, dominated everything. The hatchet fell from her hand. Her meat was being ripped at, torn open, shredded apart. Blood splashed. Her hands gripped the sides of her head and her fingernails dug into her skin. She screamed, letting it all out. And with that—as if she had summoned them with her shrieks—the rats came.

Not dozens, not hundreds, but hundreds and hundreds and hundreds.

She was covered.

8

Stephenie yanked her foot away and flipped onto her belly just as the rats arrived. One of the critters, a fat black rodent with long white teeth and eyes that seemed to sit on top of its head, managed to find its way beneath her chest before she turned all the way over. She landed on it and felt it struggling beneath her. The rest of the vermin scurried across her head, back, and limbs, sometimes stopping, sometimes not. This all happened very fast, causing Stephenie to release another scream. And the rats screamed with her. Squeals came from every direction, echoing off the walls and assaulting her senses.

Suddenly she had four hungry animals in her face, trying to bit her lips, nose, ears and eyes. They seemed to fancy her eyes the most, but they weren't opposed to biting her everywhere they could. A pair of rodents chewed on her hair. Several more gnawed her legs and neck. The smell of dirty animal fur was tremendous. She was getting pinched, nipped and nibbled overwhelmingly.

Then she felt something different. Something *not* rats.

Hal's fingers were circling her ankle like a snake. And as she felt his tombstone grip tighten, he cackled insanely, with a voice that rose above the squeal of the rodents. It was a dry and evil sounding snicker, not unlike wood crackling in a campfire.

More rats came—crawling, biting and squealing.

She kicked Hal's hand away the best she could, which is to say she tried. But Stephenie was covered with vermin and the kicking didn't come easy. She was covered head to foot, swimming in them, submerged. Of course, Hal was submerged too, but that didn't stop *him* from playing his little games. Nothing would stop him, for Hal was dead and the dead are not easily swayed.

She screamed a second time, a third time, a fourth time. She kicked her legs and waved her arms wildly.

Hal held on with all his strength, still laughing, still amused.

Stephenie felt a claw in her eye, tasted blood in her mouth. And fur. My God, she tasted fur—she was biting one of the rat's head off.

More screaming came, followed by more yelling, more chaos, and more insanity.

A block of time passed, might have been thirty seconds or longer. And in that time, as she kicked and punched and bit down where she was able, her thoughts, feelings, and fears, became too much to handle. Her mind shifted gears, becoming nothing more than a swirl of black and red. And when she arrived on the far side of this moment, which came none too soon, nothing had changed. She was being picked, clawed, and nipped relentlessly. Blood ran from her wounds without restraint. She was still kicking her legs, waving her arms and screaming madly. But at least she was thinking again, and that meant a lot.

A rat bit her nose and tore a piece of it clean off.

Stephenie punched it twice, breaking its back. Then an image came: Carrie. Oh shit, what about Carrie?

If Carrie was waiting around the corner she was covered in rats too, which was the worst thought of them all.

Stephenie couldn't dwell on what might be happening, *wouldn't* dwell on what might be happening. Not now. Thoughts of Carrie needed to be put on hold, otherwise the rats would eat her alive in no time. She pushed herself onto her hands and knees and pulled free of Hal's cold-blooded grip easier than expected. Rats scurried beneath her. Some were as large as housecats; others were small like mice. They found their way into her shirt and started biting her belly and chest. Her face was exposed now, and the bastards seemed to know it. One managed to cling onto her chin for a handful of seconds before she was able to shake it free.

Crawl, she thought. *Go Stephenie, go!*

And with that, she began to move. With her head lowered, her hands and knees shuffled forward. She was constantly landing on something that squirmed, clawed and chewed what it could find. She paid no mind to the critters and their attack. She leaned a shoulder against the wall, closed her eyes and crawled as fast as she was able. And when the wall fell away from her shoulder she knew she found her exit. She turned the corner and suddenly there were fewer rats to content with. She opened her eyes and saw a living blanket of fur beneath her, running like wildfire in all directions.

She wanted to scream but managed to hold it inside.

Her arms and legs moved rapidly, trampling what they would. Surely the exit wouldn't be much further. And it wasn't. Without warning, her head slammed against something solid. Stars appeared before her eyes.

She reached out. Dizzy now—dizzy, and on the verge of fainting. She touched something solid with her bleeding fingers and suddenly a dreadful comprehension came crashing in.

Kicking rats with her feet, she said, "Dear God, I'm locked inside."

And she was right; the door was locked tight.

She was trapped.

9

For a moment Stephenie seemed to be falling; that was the only way to describe it. She pushed on the pint-sized door, realized it wouldn't open and her mind just snapped. Colors zipped past. Things (rats mostly) morphed in and out of focus like she was caught in a time warp. She felt her stomach flip and for a time she thought she'd faint.

A rat the size of a small beaver chomped on her left nipple hard enough to draw blood and she sat up, turned herself around and rammed her back against the door. Blood poured down her chest in a stream. The rat that bit her found itself trapped beneath her ass and she knew it, so she shifted her weigh forcefully and felt something snap inside the pest.

It twitched; it died.

Good riddance, she thought, but she felt far from victorious. Rats scurried everywhere. They were on her legs, biting her shoes, clawing her legs.

What am I going to do? she wondered, still bleeding from the chest, among other places. Truth was, she didn't know.

In desperation she placed her hands on the floor and pressed all of her weight against the door, praying it would open, praying for a miracle.

The miracle didn't come. The door never budged.

A rat jumped onto her chest. She lifted a hand off the floor and smacked the critter towards her feet.

She felt like crying and feared she would, but she wouldn't. She needed to get tough, think offensively, not defensively. She needed to attack these little fuckers if she wanted to see the light of day. But could she do it?

Could she fight an endless army of rats?

The rodents were plentiful and they could smell blood, *her* blood. It was making them aggressive, hungry and insistent. They wanted to eat her alive and they'd do just that if she let them.

A rat bit a chunk from her knee and she slapped it away with the back of her hand. She looked at her hands, both of them. They were empty. The hatchet was gone; the flashlight was gone too. It was almost funny but holy shit, it wasn't funny at all.

How, she thought, with her eyes watering and her hands beginning to tremble, *how am I going to escape this?*

"I need to be strong," she said out loud, tasting rat's blood on her lips. Her voice didn't sound strong. It sounded defeated and weak. So she raised her voice higher, made it sound stronger, thinking she could scare them away if she sounded mean.

Pushing out her chest, she said, "Get the hell away from me, rats!"

But the rats didn't seem to notice her voice, or care about what she was saying, so she swung her hand across her waist and sent several of the creatures flying. Physical assaults seemed to be the only thing that made a difference.

Just then, a rat with pink eyes and large hands started clawing at her wounded ankle.

She kicked it away screaming, "FUCK OFF!"

But screaming at them wasn't going to change anything and she knew it. She needed to block them out, or kill them with something. And she didn't have anything to block them out with, so what did that leave?

The knife!

Stephenie's eyes sprang open and her shoulders lifted. The butter-knife! She had forgotten about it!

She reached into her back pocket feeling hopeful, but was suddenly struck with a terrible thought: the knife would be gone. After all, that's the way her luck had turned, was it not? Yes it was, but the knife *wasn't* gone. It was right where she left it: in her back pocket, right-hand side.

She held the knife in front of her with her right hand, eyeing it like Excalibur with a magic sword.

She looked at the rats.

They were crawling along her legs again, nipping her where they dared.

"Fuck you," she whispered, grinning a little now. The smile was anything but happy; she looked insane.

Stephenie opened her legs spread eagle and picked out her first victim. It was a sixteen-inch rat with black fur, a fat belly, small ears, and pink hands. She lifted the knife high and licked the blood from her teeth.

And with that, the battle had begun.

10

Stephenie's muscles tightened as she slammed the knife into the creature's back, impaling it. She lifted the weapon in front of her eyes and using her fingers, she cleaned the rat off the blade like a mechanic wiping oil from a dipstick. The rodent squealed and twitched as she washed it away.

A grin bullied its way onto her lips.

She had to admit: killing the little bastard was fast, easy and a whole lot like fun.

She picked out her next victim and plunged the knife into its neck. The rodent's back-legs twitched madly and a little squirt of blood shot into the air. She wiped the creature off the knife and moved onto the next. It was a black rat, twenty-one inches long. She stabbed it near the tail and when she lifted the knife the rat stayed on the floor, squealing wildly. She stabbed it again. Bull's-eye. Got it right in the heart. She wiped it away and plunged the knife into another. It cried out; she wiped it away and repeated the motion.

Just like that, there were fewer rats around her.

Stephenie pulled her legs in, shifted her position and sat upon her knees, crouching.

Two rats came running between the twitching bodies and she stabbed them both without having time to clean the blade. The first one ended up impaled on the handle, trying to bite her wrist. The second one fell from the knife and landed on its side. Its mouth opened and closed franticly, like it couldn't get enough air. She wiped the first rat away, pushing it off her weapon from the handle end.

Seven rats were dead or dying. Her victims were piling up.

Behind the fallen, a hundred more were in view. They scurried and scuttled and did what they pleased.

An energetic rat came zipping along the wall, bobbing and weaving.

Stephenie rammed the knife into its face, and when she raised her hand the rat slipped from the blade and flopped onto its side. Its back legs kicked, recoiled, and kicked again. A moment later she held the creature in her fingers. She threw it into the crowd and more rats arrived, giving her little time to react. A black rat scrambled onto her arm and she knocked it against the wall. A thin brown rat, looking a little bit like a weasel, bit her neck and she screamed.

She swatted rats away and stabbed wildly. She had no time for cleaning the blade. Not now. The floor had become a living blanket once again.

She heard herself cursing, and that wasn't a good sign.

Her arm moved up and down quickly—again and again and again. Rats screeched. Blood splashed. Little limbs were severed from the bodies. Guts flew everywhere. A severed head rolled across the floor with a string of gore clumped against it. At one point she looked at her blade and found three rats, all flattened and wedged together like a rodent-kebab. She wiped them away in a single motion and killed the next in line. Sometimes she stabbed dead rodents just to keep up the momentum. And when it looked like she was running out of victims, she crawled forward. Crawling and stabbing, crawling and stabbing—that's what she was doing now, crawling through the cave, stabbing everything that moved.

She found herself at the juncture and she decided to turn right, leaving the trail of bloody rat-corpses in her wake. There were lots of rodents in front of her; lots behind her too. The further she crawled, the more rats she found. Her weapon hand never stopped moving; it never stopped killing. At one point two rats crawled onto her back and she screamed, not in pain or in fear but in battle.

She felt like a gladiator, fighting an incessant multitude of enemies.

It was becoming obvious to Stephenie that it would take a long time for the rats to overpower her completely. She was losing blood by the thimbleful, not the gallon. It was maddening and terrifying, frustrating and painful, but so far the rats were not a single-minded army, hell-bent on bringing her down; they were individuals, reacting to the smell of blood and the excitement of their brethren. They didn't attack in waves. They attacked often, but at random, biting, scratching and clawing, lost in terror as much as anything else.

Stephenie killed indiscriminately, without mercy or hesitation. In time she was bleeding from her arms and legs, her chest and stomach, her face and hands, her feet and neck. She was bleeding everywhere.

She sat upon her sticky knees and pounded the rats with both fists. Sure, she only had one knife, but she didn't care. She was beyond caring.

This was a war she didn't plan on losing.

She forged ahead, grinning and killing. Right, left. Right, left. Blood splashed and guts spewed. She could feel them on her skin and taste them on her tongue. The air stank of rodent. She slapped a rat from her hair with an open hand. One crawled inside her shirt and she crammed it against her body and pinched its neck with her fingers.

"Oh God!" She roared, with a voice that came from deep inside her belly.

For a moment she considered giving up but she didn't; the butchery continued. Her battle went on for fifteen minutes or more. She wasn't thinking about the carnage she unleashed. She didn't have time to think; she only had time to act.

Crawling over the bodies of the dead and dying, she edged her way through obscurity, out of the light and into the darkness.

She felt them twitching and nipping at her knees as she trampled them. Now she was killing blindly, stabbing her way along the trail.

The rats had to come from somewhere, right?

Of course they did. And with that morsel of logic swirling inside her mind, she continued on, lost in the art of conflict.

The vermin lessened in volume, until the war seemed manageable. She pushed on, crawling through the darkness and the gloom and further into the regions of the unknown.

After a few minutes she saw something new.

It shimmered.

She moved towards it, no longer lost in battle but in something that seemed a lot like hope. And when she placed a hand upon what she now recognized as a door, it opened with ease. Light spilled into her face, bright and alluring. There were no rats in this new place. The air tasted clean and pure.

CHAPTER SEVEN:
TWISTED VERACITY

1

Stephenie shuffled through the tiny door, spun herself on her knees and looked into the cave. She wasn't surprised to find a dozen rats scurrying around in front of her face, but she was surprised to find none of them willing to step into the light. One came close, but then it fled in the opposite direction with its tail high and its head low.

She closed the door, blocking the rodents from view. Their twitching noses and black bubble eyes were gone now, and Stephenie felt comforted by the sound of the latch clicking shut. A moment later she was sitting on the floor with her legs extended, the butter knife gone, her arms at her sides and her back against the door. She was practically *shocked* by her abrupt change of scenery, but for the first time in a while the shock seemed like a good thing.

The new surrounding was pleasant and sterile. The ceiling was high, the lights were bright and the air tasted clean. If she had to guess where she ended up, she'd say she was in a change room in a fitness center. *Bally* and *Goodlife* came to mind. Of course, she didn't *really* think she was in a place like that, but that's where the room seemed to belong.

There were benches attached to two of the four walls, which had that 'painted concrete block' look, made famous in public places everywhere. Three showers sat together in a corner, each with its own little cubicle. Two toilets sat inside two separate stalls. Both stall doors were open. The stalls were clean and empty. There were no windows in the room, only a single door. The door was big and normal looking. There was a sink area and a shelf loaded with clean towels. Sitting next to the shelf was a small table, and on that table a slim vase had a single fresh-cut flower propped inside. She didn't know too much about flowers, but to her, this one looked like a bellflower. It was purple and blue with oddly shaped petals. Sitting next to the flower in the vase, a glass bowl was filled with an assortment of chocolates wrapped in foil. They looked delicious, yes they did. But delicious or not, Stephenie wasn't brave enough or hungry enough to plop one into her mouth and find out for sure.

Stephenie said, "Huh." And that seemed about right.

Huh indeed, she thought.

She looked across the room; then she looked across the room again. Dare she say it: she felt safer than she had for a while.

Her eyes shifted from the chocolates to the showers to the only thing concerning her: the door on the far side of the room.

What if it opened?

Looking at the door with a touch more scrutiny, she noticed a bolt lock attached to the wood, just above the doorknob. All she had to do was make her way across the room, slide the bolt over and she'd be secure. But what about the little door she had come through? Was it safe? Was it secure?

She thought, *Yes, perhaps it is.*

Enhancing her personal safety was worth a moment's discomfort, so she forced herself to her feet before her body grew lethargic.

She limped slowly. She was bleeding from many places, too many to make health assessments with any amount of accuracy.

163

For the time being, this was okay. It wasn't time for assessments; it was time to create security.

With her hand on the lock she considered opening the door. She was curious to see what was on the other side. In the end, she didn't do it. She'd seen enough and needed a moment's peace. With little effort the bolt slid into place. Now she was safe and secure. Or so she hoped.

With a grunt and a whimper she made her way to the nearest bench and plunked herself down. The wild and nasty scent of the rodents was strong. It came from her clothing, hair and skin. It was inside her pores too.

Disgusted by her own stench, she pulled her wife-beater shirt over her head and dropped it on the bench in a wrinkled ball. It looked like a rag. The idea of wearing it again was disgusting. It stank. Everything she had stank. And the shirt wasn't white. Not now. Now it was black, brown and red.

Stephenie wasn't wearing a bra. If she had been, she'd have taken *that* off too.

Looking at her belly, chest and arms, she counted more than twenty separate rat bites. Some were just little nips. Some were gouges. If she had to guess, she'd say she'd been bitten over seventy times.

Two minutes passed.

Stephenie lifted herself to her feet, releasing a groan.

She made her way to the shower, turned both faucets on and held her shirt beneath the running water. Her plan was to wash it and put it back on, nothing more. But after a few seconds she accepted the fact that *she* needed water as much as the shirt did. Maybe more. Yes, she needed to find Carrie, she really did. But she was bleeding and dirty, covered in rat bites and rat shit. She couldn't go on this way; she needed five minutes to clean her wounds before they became infected.

The shirt slipped from her fingers. It fell to the tiled floor beneath the stream.

Stephenie made her way to the nearest bench and sat down like a woman in great pain, which she was. She removed her shoes. She removed her pants and her underwear next. Lastly, she removed the shredded cloth that was wrapped around her wounded ankle. It felt heavy, sticky and wet. She tossed it on the floor and assessed the damage.

The injury was considerable.

Her ankle was bloated and swollen in ways she didn't know was possible. It had turned black and red and the oval abrasion was oozing white colored puss. The skin was pushed into strange bulges. There was dirt on top of dirt. To say it didn't look good was like saying Tiger Woods knew how to play golf. And when she ran her finger along the soft lumpy flesh that was shielding her bones, her skin felt numb.

She stood up, pulled the elastics from her hair and dropped them on the bench. She approached the shower, placed a hand on the faucet, and adjusted the water's temperature. She stood beneath the flow.

The water felt good, maybe even great.

For the next seven minutes she justified her actions with ease. After all, her wounds needed to be cleaned, especially the one in her foot. She didn't want seventy-plus infections; it was bad enough she might have rabies.

Images of Hal crawling on his wormy hands, and dragging his guts behind him like a dead octopus, threatened to dominate Stephenie's thinking. She didn't allow it. This was her time and she planned on taking it, for good or bad, right or wrong. And if Hal opened that little door and came creeping in like a human snail, so be it. She couldn't control the monsters, only her own actions.

The water fell, washing the filth from her body.

And when she was finished cleaning herself she lifted the shirt from the floor beneath her feet and rinsed it out as much as possible. After that, justifying her actions became a harder sell. Adequately clean wounds and a rinsed out shirt meant it was time to move on, time to find Carrie. Of this there was no denying.

She turned the water off, squeezed the liquid from her shirt and stepped out of the shower. She picked a towel from the shelf and dried her body. The towel became marked with little spots of red. After she rang out her shirt a couple more times she pulled it over her skin. It was still wet but it was in better shape than before; it didn't make her want to be sick.

She slipped into her underwear and pants. The pants were beyond dirty; wearing them over her clean skin felt counterproductive, but washing them and wearing them wet wasn't something she wanted to do. She put on her shoes, wincing in pain. She lifted her hair elastics from the bench, rinsed them off and tied her hair into a ponytail. She looked at the bowl of chocolates, thinking they might be okay.

She lifted one, unwrapped it, smelled it and tasted it.

The chocolate was fine; she was almost positive. It was just a chocolate, right? She placed it in her mouth and the taste was wonderful. The moment she swallowed it down there was a knock on the door, followed by a distant scream.

She wondered if eating the chocolate was a bad idea.

Perhaps it was.

2

To say that Stephenie ran towards the door, unlocked it, and threw it open would be a lie. What she did was stand there with chocolate in her teeth and her mouth agape, looking at the door like she had never seen one before. The scream she heard was an adult scream, not one from a child. Whether the voice was male or female, she did not know.

Seconds rolled by; they felt slower than most.

She made her way towards the door. When she arrived she hesitated, placed her ear against the wood and listened.

Nothing.

She wondered what to do but her choices were simple. Either she opened the door now or she'd wait a while, and then open the door. Entering the tunnel of rats was a third option, she supposed, but it wasn't really worth considering.

After the better part of a minute slipped past she tapped her finger on the wood and said, "Hello?"

There was no response.

"Is anybody there?"

She waited another half minute before she unlocked the latch and put her hand on the doorknob, thinking about that classic scene in the movie *Psycho*: the shower scene. She wondered if she was about to enjoy her own personal version of something similar.

Her eyes closed and she inhaled a deep breath.

"I can do this," she whispered. She turned her wrist and opened the door slowly, peeking through the crack.

Norman Bates was not there. Neither was Freddy Krueger, Jason Voorhees, Michael Myers, Hannibal Lector, or Chucky the killer doll. Instead, there was a hallway running left and right. It was long, bright and painted white; it seemed to go on for a considerable distance no matter which way she looked. There was nothing hanging off the walls or cluttering up the floor. No carpets; no chairs. There were a bunch of doors, but nothing else as far as she could tell.

She looked left. On the far end of the hallway, there seemed to be a juncture. The path may have turned left or right; it was hard to say from the place she was standing.

She looked right. Same deal.

There was nobody in the hallway. The person that knocked was gone. The person that screamed was gone too; perhaps they stepped through one of the doors.

Stephenie reflected.

As a child, little Stephenie Paige—with her big dimples, hearty laugh, and her bright sparkling eyes—had played a fair amount of baseball. She was good at it; might have been the best on the team. One of her favorite aspects of the sport was stealing a base. Children tend to be lousy throwers and questionable catchers but the art of running is something they can manage. So when it came to stealing second or third, Stephenie was more successful than most because she knew that whoever was holding the ball would probably throw it at the wrong angle and whoever was catching the ball would likely miss. While playing baseball Stephenie spent a fair amount of time standing between two bases, willing to leave the security of one place, eager to arrive at another, worried tragedy would strike between the two.

She felt the same way now.

Stephenie was willing to leave her sanctuary, eager to find Carrie, and worried that tragedy would strike before she did. She stumbled upon a little slice of heaven. Everything else was a big serving of hell. Leaving the room felt risky and dangerous, so the idea of moving on made her feel nauseous.

But she had to go; same reason as always: Carrie.

As Stephenie stepped away from the room the door closed behind her. She checked to see if it would open. The answer was yes. She wasn't locked out.

She turned right and made her way down the hall, limping worse now than before. This wasn't because she was in poorer condition, but because she had time to limp properly. Zombies weren't chasing her and that changed everything.

She came to a door on the left side of the hallway. Like the walls, the door was painted white. It had a knob but no window. She put her hand on the knob and tried to open it. The door wouldn't open.

She moved on.

After a few more feet she came to a door on the right side of the hallway. It looked the same as the last one. She put her hand upon the knob and tried her luck again.

The door wouldn't open.

Not wanting to lose track of the door she had come from, Stephenie turned back. Upon arriving at the original door, which she considered a gateway to her sanctuary, Stephenie stuck her hand into her pocket and pulled out her one-and-only stick of gum. She unwrapped it and chewed it and threw the wrapper on the floor. When she thought the gum was soft enough, she bit it into two separate pieces. She put one half on the door at eye level, marking it like a *Hansel and Gretel* breadcrumb. The other half she left in her mouth; she liked the taste.

Stephenie continued on, walking beneath the florescent lights (always florescent, the contractors in these parts loved florescent). She walked along the concrete-block walls until she came to something attached to one of the blocks.

It was a photograph of Carrie, held in place by a line of scotch tape.

At first Stephenie thought the photo had been snagged from the photo album in the car. It wasn't. The photo was new, one she had never seen before. It showed Carrie sitting on a chair in a big empty room. She looked sad. She looked frightened. Her knees were together, her bottom lip was out and both of her hands were wrapped in a white towel. The towel had a dark spot.

The spot was red; it looked a lot like blood.

3

Stephenie stood there for a while before she released a breath she didn't know she was holding. She felt pain in her hands and when she finally pulled her eyes away from the image, she discovered that her fingernails were biting into her palms. She felt like asking a bunch of questions to the empty hallway, questions like: *what's going on?* And—*who's responsible for this?* But there wasn't any point. She was in hell. That's what was going on. She was in hell and her daughter was too.

Stephenie pulled the photograph from the wall. After looking at it for a few more seconds, she slid it into her back pocket and continued her journey.

She came across three more doors. They were all locked. After that, she came across four more. They were locked too.

Stephenie arrived at an intersection she hadn't noticed until she was a few feet away from it. Now she had choices. She could turn left or right or walk in a straight line. One choice looked the same as the other. The hallways were long and filled with doors.

Stephenie decided to continue walking in a straight line; it seemed like the smartest thing to do. She was rewarded with another photograph of Carrie.

Carrie seemed to be sitting in the same chair as before. Her head was tilted to one side and her body was slumped in a comparable pose. A cloth was wrapped around her hands; it had a dark spot in the middle.

The spot seemed bigger now, darker too.

Carrie looked sad and scared, just like in the first photograph, but with a vacant expression that Stephenie didn't like assessing; it made her feel like she had failed miserably in the department of parenting. In the first photograph Stephenie could see every last inch of her daughter, from the top of her head to the bottom of her shoes. In this photo, Carrie's shoes were just out of frame.

Stephenie peeled the image off the wall and slid it into her back pocket, next to the other.

She walked a straight line; her shoulders sagged.

The hallway seemed to get longer, rather than shorter. And when Stephenie turned around she couldn't see the distance she covered. Everything looked the same. After she hobbled a few more feet Stephenie considered yelling something out. Something like, "Carrie! Are you in here?" Was yelling a smart move? Maybe, maybe not; but she was afraid now—afraid *still*, in fact. And for that reason and that reason alone, she decided against yelling. She didn't want to draw attention to herself, she just wanted...

Stephenie paused.

God, she didn't even know what she wanted.

Stephenie checked more doors. They were locked. She came to another intersection. It looked the same as the first. She walked a straight line because she was afraid she'd become lost. But she was already lost, wasn't she?

Well, no actually—not really.

Stephenie could always turn around and go back to the change room, travel the tunnel with the rats and...

Ah, but there lies the dilemma. She may not have been lost exactly, but she was trapped. Even if she was brave enough (or *stupid* enough, her thoughts insisted) to return to the tunnel of the rats, the door that led her into the tunnel originally was locked, not on this side, but on the other. So she *couldn't* return the way she came. She may not have been lost but she was ensnared and the result was essentially the same.

She walked, checking doorknobs as she came to them. None would open. The rooms were probably empty anyhow, right?

Deep inside, she didn't think so. There were *things* inside those rooms, lots and lots of things. Some of the things she wanted to see, others she didn't. There were things that could fix everything and things that would make matters worse. How they could possibly *get* worse, she did not know.

She placed her hand on a knob, might have been the eleventh or twelfth one she tried. The knob felt warm. And when she turned her wrist the knob turned with it.

She had found a door that would open.

4

Stephenie stood in the open doorway, seeing but not believing, comprehending on some levels but not on all. The room was an average size, fifteen by fifteen, maybe a little less. There were no windows and only one door: the one Stephenie just opened. The room was empty with the exception of a single chair, which was sitting against the far wall. Sitting on the chair was a girl. She had her head down. Her hair was in pigtails and her hands were resting on her lap, covered in a white cloth. The cloth had a dark spot. The spot looked like blood.

Stephenie's feet started moving. She took three quick steps and was afraid to take a forth. The hairs on the back of her neck tingled, like she had been granted a moment of Peter Parker's Spidey-sense. Something was wrong here; something was off. She didn't know what was wrong but she sure as hell knew it was *something*.

"Carrie," she whispered. And it *was* a whisper. She hardly heard the word herself.

Behind her, the door began closing. It was *creeeeeeeeaking* shut.

And although she didn't want the door closing on her, she let it happen. Her mind was elsewhere, on the goosebumps cultivating her flesh, but mostly on the girl in front of her. And when the girl in the chair lifted her head Stephenie stepped away, thinking: *Oh shit; I might actually die.*

It wasn't Carrie.

It wasn't Carrie, *but it was.*

The girl was dressed the same and for the most part she looked the same, although her mouth and her eyes were completely different, not like in the photographs. Oh heavens no. Her eyes were large, and not a normal kind of large. They weren't large in a *'my-oh-my, your daughter sure does have some big beautiful eyes, Missis Paige, don't you think?'* kind of way. Oh no. Her eyes bulged from her head like they belonged on an insect that devoured its partner after mating. They were *large*, and the way they sat above her nose, high on her head—almost nearing her hairline—they looked *really* large. And when the girl that *was* Carrie but was *not Carrie* smiled *(oh man, oh man—she was* not *Carrie)*, her face looked so unnatural that Stephenie thought she might fall onto her knees and be sick on the floor.

Her mouth, oh sweet Jesus her mouth—it was upside-down; there's no other way to describe it. When the Carrie-monster grinned her lips curled the wrong direction—and yes, Stephenie was well aware that in most cases people accept this expression as a frown. But this *wasn't* a frown. It was a *grin*, sitting on the girl's face horribly wrong, like someone had figured out a way to remove her mouth, flip it around, and plunk it back into her skull without killing her.

Stephenie put her fingers to her chin and stepped away.

The child thing in the corner leaned forward. Her upside-down grin grew fatter and longer until the lips hung right off the sides of her face. Her mouth opened then; it opened just as the child's lips drooped towards the floor like big meaty whiskers. Pale baggy flesh *sagged.* Thick white liquid streamed from the wrinkled flesh; swimming in circles as it hit the floor.

She chuckled and drooled, and said, "Mommy?"

Stephenie could see three rows of teeth. Each tooth looked like it belonged inside the mouth of a baby shark. Upon seeing them, Stephenie whined. She was terrified beyond her wildest dreams.

The child-monster lifted her hands and the white cloth fell to the ground. It landed between her feet with the red spot facing up. Now the child-monster's hands were exposed. The fingers were gone, every last one. Thumbs too. All ten digits had been lopped off somewhere near the knuckle leaving ten bleeding nubs that were less than a half-inch long.

The thing that looked like Carrie stood up.

"Mommy, we need to talk." The voice was just right. It sounded like it belonged to a child, like it belonged to Carrie. The only difference was the tone, which was a little deeper, a little graver.

Stephenie screamed and spun around wildly. Her hand shot out like a bullet and wrapped around the doorknob. The knob felt extra cold. *A cold day in hell*, she thought strangely, and she knew the door was locked before she even turned her wrist.

"Mommy," the *thing* said again. "Oh mommy, look at my fingers. They're all bleedy, mom. Can't you see? Don't you care? Look at my hands. They got bleedy all over them."

Stephenie limped into the corner with her eyes facing the floor, locked on nothing, open but trying not to see. She began shivering.

The Carrie-monster said, "Where are you going? Talk to me, mommy; talk to me."

"What do you want from me?" Stephenie spat. She turned, and wedged her back against the wall. Then her knees gave out and she fell onto her ass with her arms held high. Her knees curled towards her chest. She put her fingers together in a make-shift cross, like she was attempting to ward off evil spirits. It didn't work though, and soon enough Stephenie knew it.

"I want to talk to you about your medication."

"My what?" Stephenie's hands dropped and her eyes shifted.

"You heard me," Carrie's doppelganger said. "Your medication. You know, Lithizine, Mesoridazine, Oxazepam, Thorazine … you understand what I'm talking about, right? How does it make you feel? Have the doctors discovered the right doses yet? Are you having hallucinations?"

For a moment Stephenie looked up at this creature like she didn't understand what had been said.

The creature looked awful, so awful in fact that Stephenie's eyes found new things to look at soon after.

A wonderful thought came: maybe she was dreaming, or at the very least, having a 'bad trip.' What if all the dreadful things were inside her mind? It was a comforting thought, real comforting, super-duper encouraging—at first. Then she started wondering what life would be like if she stayed this way forever. Suddenly the notion of *things being wrong inside your mind* didn't seem so fantastic. What if this wasn't a bad trip that would end soon, but one that turned her into a full-blown crazy woman? What if she was locked inside this nightmare until the day she died? What would she do then?

She looked up, eyes wide.

"Mommy?"

"Yes," Stephenie said, her voice pleading. "I'm having hallucinations."

"Really?"

"Oh God, yes I am!"

"Can you describe them to me?"

"I don't know what to say. Everything's so... bad."

The Carrie-monster's voice was changing, losing its childlike charm, becoming more direct and to the point. "Start from the beginning."

"The beginning?"

"Yes. I want you to tell me."

"Tell you what?"

"Everything. Hurry. Do it; do it now."

Stephenie nodded a couple times. "Okay," she said. "Okay, okay." She closed her eyes and tried to pinpoint the beginning. "There was a restaurant."

"Yes."

"And everybody inside the restaurant was dead."

"How?"

Stephenie slapped her hands on her face and shook her head like she didn't want to articulate her thoughts. She said, "Oh shit, I don't know."

"Yes you do. Tell us."

Stephenie's eyes peeked above her fingers, curious about the 'us' comment. Maybe she was in a hospital surrounded by doctors. That would explain the clean looking rooms and the long hallways, wouldn't it? Sure it would.

The thing that looked like Carrie—with its upside-down grin and big monstrous eyes—moved closer. With its voice growing deeper and meaner, it said, "Answer us, mommy. Answer us! Tell us about the restaurant."

"Don't call me mommy."

"What do you want to be called?"

"Stephenie."

"Fine. Stephenie, tell us about that fucking restaurant or I'll tear your head off your body and swallow your bones one at a time."

Shocked, Stephenie barked, "Don't say things like that!"

"Tell us about the restaurant, Stephenie! Tell us!"

"I don't know what to say! I went inside and everyone was dead! The people looked like they had been ripped apart by a grizzly bear!"

"Yes! They did, didn't they?"

"Yes!"

"And you killed them."

"What? No I didn't!"

"Yes you did."

"No! They were dead when we arrived!"

"No they weren't. You chopped them apart with an axe."

"Are you crazy?"

"Are you?"

Stephenie stumbled on that one, recognizing at once that it was a damn good question. Was she crazy? Yes, perhaps she was. With her voice losing its authority she said, "Leave me alone."

The Carrie-thing grinned its terrible upside-down grin, clicked her bony, bleeding, finger-nubs together and said, "I don't think so, you worthless, evil bitch. I'm not going to leave you alone. You don't deserve to be left alone. You deserve everything you get. Oh yes you do. And you'll get plenty, *mommy*. We'll give you plenty."

Stephenie pulled her hands away from her face. They were trembling so much she looked like she was having a seizure. But she had an idea, and hoped it would work. She said, "There's a sanctuary." Her voice had never sounded so desperate.

"What are you saying?"

"A sanctuary!" Stephenie looked up at monster with the big bug eyes and the upside-down grin. She pushed her half-stick of chewing gum from one side her mouth to the other, and said, "If this is a nightmare, which I think it is, I can go back to my sanctuary. I can stay in there, you know? I don't have to come out. Not ever. I don't have to be out here with you! I can go back to my sanctuary! I know exactly where it is! I marked it!"

"Oh really?"

"Yes… really! I don't have to be here with you. I don't have to be here *at all*. My medications are fucking with me; that's all. This is just a problem with my medications! Nothing more. This is all just one big misunderstanding!"

The Carrie thing sniggered. "And what will you do for food, locked inside a change room with a toilet, huh? Eat your own shit?"

"Ah ha!" Stephenie pointed her trembling finger at the thing hanging over her, the creature that looked like it wanted to swallow her whole. She took several deep breaths and thought she might hyperventilate; then she wiped a tear from her eye, and said, "I didn't tell you it was a change room! That proves what I'm saying! That proves it! You're confirming my words; that's what you're doing! I didn't tell you my sanctuary was a change room, and I didn't tell that fucked up family in the farmhouse what my name was. Blair knew things because he wasn't real. And you know things because *you're* not real. *Oh God*, you're not real!"

"Tell me mommy—"

"And there *is* food in there. I have *chocolates*."

"I hope you didn't eat them, you stupid bitch. I hope for your sake you left those chocolates alone, otherwise you'll be sorry."

"Why?"

"Oh, I'll never tell. I'll never tell you what's impregnating you now, mommy—"

Stephenie cut into the monster's words, saying, "Stop calling me that! Don't you *dare* call me that! You're not my daughter! You're just a problem with my medication!"

"Tell me, *babe*, what is real?"

"I don't know!"

"Then tell me, you stupid, worthless, whiny whore… what do you think of this?"

5

The thing that looked like Carrie stuck her bleeding-nub fingers inside her upside-down mouth and began tearing her face apart.

Stephenie shrieked and squealed and tried to shield her eyes by burying her face in her hands. When she looked up again, Carrie's distorted features were hanging off the child-monster like a mask. But the child-monster wasn't a child any longer. It had doubled in size and sprouted a second set of legs. The legs were long and green and growing from the hips. They looked like they belonged on the back end of the world's biggest grasshopper.

The giant Carrie-monster started laughing. Its bulging eyes grew thicker and fatter and somehow deeper. Then, with a voice that didn't sound human, the monster said, "What's the last thing you remember? Do you remember driving? Do you remember parking your car close to the pump? Do you remember that old KING'S DINER sign? Here's a new thought, you selfish, psycho, blood-loving slut: you and Carrie pulled into the gas station. You filled your tank and brought Carrie inside. Somebody came into the restaurant and killed everyone with a fucking axe, including *you* and *your daughter.* And because you've been such a rotten, miserable bitch all your life, you died and went to hell. And this is it. You're here! *Welcome, cunt! Welcome!*"

The monster laughed again.

Carrie's features dropped to the floor in a pile. A new face was revealed. It was a bubbling mound of puss-covered lumps, a nest of misplaced hair and knots of bone that seemed to change shape at random.

"Do you know *why* you can't find your daughter," the creature went on to say. "Do you, Stephenie Paige, husband killer? It's because she isn't here! She went to heaven, but not until after she had her arms and legs chopped off by a psychopath. She went to heaven and you went to hell!"

"Stop it!"

"Stop what, Stephenie? I'm just telling you the way it is! Someone chopped off your daughter's arms and legs, Stephenie. And she was alive and screaming until the very end."

"Shut up!"

"This is hell, and you'll be here forever. And every day will last a hundred years. And every hour will be worse than the last!"

"NO!"

"You haven't seen the really hellish things yet, because we haven't shown them to you. This is day *one* Stephenie. *DAY ONE!* Wait until you've been here a couple million years. You have no idea how bad this world gets. We're just getting started."

"FUCK OFF!"

"I'm going to cut your throat with a hacksaw, which is a better fate than you deserve! But that won't kill you Stephenie. Nothing can kill you here. I'll cut your throat a thousand times a day!"

"LEAVE ME ALONE!" Stephenie screamed. She crawled out of the corner and forced herself onto her feet. She grabbed the doorknob and shouted: "YOU'RE GOING TO OPEN FOR ME BECAUSE THIS IS JUST A DREAM! I'M THE ONE IN CHARGE HERE! ME! SO OPEN FOR ME, *GOD-DAMN YOU*, OPEN!!"

She twisted her wrist and the doorknob turned. She flung the door wide and exploded into the hall. She started running. It hurt like hell—no pun intended—but she ran all the same. She ran past doors and hallway crossroads. She turned left down one corridor, right down another, then left down a third. At one point she saw a photograph taped to the wall and she pulled it off without slowing her pace. When she came to a hallway juncture, she stopped long enough to look at the image.

It was Carrie.

She was lying on the floor in the restaurant. Her arms and legs were gone; they had been amputated with an axe. Her mouth was open and her eyes were blank. Looking into her face was like looking into the eyes of a dead cat.

Stephenie dropped the photograph and kept running. But she was lost now. She had no idea where her sanctuary was hiding or how she was going to get there. Everything looked the same. Every hallway was identical. She ran and cursed and ran some more. Then she turned a corner a felt her heart drop into her feet.

She was face to face with a woman that looked just like her.

No, that wasn't right. The woman didn't *look* like her.

It *was* her—it was Stephenie.

The woman was dressed the same. She was hobbling; her foot had been wounded in the exact same spot. She had her hair pulled into a ponytail and her shirt was still wet from having washed it.

There were differences too. For one, this new Stephenie had a face that was really, really pale. Not a little pale, *white*. Blood was pouring from two separate places: a wound on her hand and a wound on her arm. The blood was all over her shirt and face. It was in her hair. It was dripping onto the floor in bright red bunches.

Looking at herself, Stephenie felt the air fall out of her, like her lungs had just gotten a flat. She couldn't *believe* what she was seeing; *she couldn't believe it!*

But the *other* Stephenie was even *more* freaked out—the *other* Stephenie, not her.

The other Stephenie smacked her gory hands against the sides of her head. Blood speckled the wall in a line. Slurring her words this new Stephenie screamed, "Oh my God! Oh my God!

This can't be right! Look at what's fucking happening!" Her hands became red fists, shaking in the air like mad. Blood splashed in generous amounts around her. She punched herself in the head and she spit whatever was in her mouth right in Stephenie's face. She said, "*Now* do you understand, huh? Do you? Fuck!" Then she turned and ran off, speeding around the first corner she found.

Stephenie couldn't take it any more. She needed out. She needed to escape.

She slapped a hand on a doorknob and turned it.

The door was locked.

There was another door beside the first, plus two more on the far side of the hall. She tried her luck a second time and came up lucky. The door opened wide. The knob slipped from her fingers. And when she saw a full-sized wolf standing in the center of room, looking at her like it had found its next meal, she nearly fell over.

6

The wolf was easily half the size of a mountain lion. It was big and brown. Its eyes were icy and blue. When it growled, the damn thing sounded like a chainsaw chopping down a tree.

Stephenie backed away, across the hall, wondering what she was supposed to do. After all, how do you fight a hungry wolf?

A question came: how do you know its hungry?

The answer came right after: the wolf licked its muzzle and stepped forward. Its snout curled into wrinkles and Stephenie got a first-rate look at teeth that could chew through steel.

In desperation, she closed her eyes and said, "I never opened that fucking door. The door is closed. Oh please Lord; the door is closed! I never opened it! It's closed! And this is just a dream, or some fucked up medication. I never opened the door! I never *touched* that door!"

Stephenie opened her eyes cringing, only to find the door hadn't moved.

The wolf stepped into the hall.

Stephenie spun around. She grabbed a doorknob, praying for a miracle. The knob turned beneath her fingers and she counted herself lucky.

The wolf growled.

She pushed on the door as the animal made its move.

She felt paws crashing into her back and she fell forward. Her ankle crunched beneath her and she let out a squeal. Her body slammed against the floor and the animal went past, snapping its teeth in the air. She felt its breath on the back of her neck and she braced for the worst. A fraction of a second slipped by and when she looked up, the beast was landing on it paws and sliding forward.

She swallowed back a scream, figuring her next scream would be her last. She thought she'd be dead inside of two minutes with her throat ripped out and blood rolling across the floor in a thick, hot wave unless she found a better plan than screaming. But what was that plan? Fact was, she didn't know.

Getting her throat ripped out didn't happen.

What happened was this: the wolf snapped its head in a different direction, then it started growling and barking and its hair stood high upon its back.

There was something else in the room, something Stephenie couldn't see.

The wolf didn't like it.

Stephenie figured the thing, whatever it was—and she really couldn't see it, unless she wanted to step into the room and snatch a look—might be some type of monster. She wasn't sure if this was good news or bad. Either way, it gave her a little breathing room, which she quickly squandered like someone without five cents worth of brains rattling inside her empty head.

She watched the wolf growl. She watched it show its teeth. She watched it move towards the thing that was making it upset.

Then she wondered, *what the hell am I doing, waiting in line to be eaten?*

She pushed herself away from the door and out of the wolf's view. Her face was masked in grave fear. Her eyebrows were lifted. She stood, biting her bottom lip, trying to suck up the pain in her foot. She needed to close the door and contain the beast but was unable to find the courage to do so. She started limping, walking—trying to keep her feet quiet. Walking became running. Running became pain. Pain became screaming. At one point her ankle twisted the wrong way and she went sprawling to the floor. She cried out loudly. And when she pulled herself to her feet her ankle hurt more than it had since the injury occurred. For a moment she thought it was broken. It wasn't; she kept moving. She tried a door and found it locked. And when she turned around to see if she was being followed, the wolf was standing about seventy feet away, looking at her with its lips pulling away from its teeth and its ears pointing straight up. Its eyes gleamed; they grew wide and bulged from its head like a pair of full moons. Its tail was tucked down between its legs, nervous like. But it wasn't nervous. Stephenie was the nervous one. She was quite literally ready to wet her pants in fear.

"Oh shit," she said.

Then she ran a few feet, slapped her hand on another doorknob and tried her luck again. The door wouldn't open. Across the hall was another door. She grabbed the knob and hoped for the best. Locked.

The wolf was trotting now, soon it would be on top of her, eating her alive, drinking her blood, chewing the meat from her bones. She didn't want that. Oh sweet merciful hamburgers, she *really* didn't want that.

She ran another fifteen feet and came to another door. She slammed her hand upon the knob and turned it. The door was unlocked.

Thank God. It was opening for her.

The wolf ran faster. It was close, less than a few feet away. It growled and barked and when it leapt into the air, its mouth was wide open.

Stephenie could see the wolf from the corner of her eye. Screaming, she pushed on the door and blasted through the doorway like a bullet. And before she knew whether she was in a safe place or not, she slammed the door shut.

7

There was a moment of total confusion, followed by a large pair of hands grabbing Stephenie by the shoulders.

"Come now, my Lady," the man grabbing her said. His accent was one Stephenie didn't recognize. It sounded like old English, maybe Scottish, or maybe a bastardized version of both together.

Stephenie said, "What?"

He pushed her forward and she found herself walking. Beneath her feet was a dirt path. On her left there were hundreds of people. On her right there were hundreds more. They looked like villagers from a time long forgotten. Most were dirty and sick and dressed in rags. Some looked mean enough to fistfight a kitten.

Stephenie, still finding her bearings, focused on a single man. The man was tall and slim and was dressed in big, baggy everything. He had a two-inch beard that looked more itchy than attractive, and he was eating an ear of corn, raw, straight from a cob that still had dry husks hanging off the handle.

She focused on another, a woman.

The woman had long grey hair that hung down to her waist and whiskers on her chin. She might have been as young as fifty but her face was so weathered and wrinkled that she looked a hundred or more. She wore no shoes. Her entire ensemble consisted of something that looked like a dirty toga that had been dragged through the mud and kicked down a mountain.

Stephenie lifted her head and looked to the sky.

Her mouth dropped open.

She was in a village. Vultures circled in the winds, high above. The sky wasn't dark, but overcast. Raindrops were small enough to seem like mist. It wasn't raining yet, but soon enough it would be.

Above the crowd on her left, Stephenie could see a bell tower, a bunch of dead trees and a row of houses that seemed ready to fall over. Most of the homes were no better than a shack. Behind the crowd on her right there was a graveyard and a church that was big and gothic and undeniably creepy. It loomed over the street like a sickle over the Grim Reaper.

The people standing along the path stepped away, parting like Stephenie carried the bubonic plague on her lips. Some were yelling. Some were waving their fists and shouting obscenities.

Stephenie saw a woman that looked like a witch, standing next to a broken fence. She had a wart on her nose, another on her chin, and a hump the size of a soccer ball growing on her back. Her eyebrows were thick enough to keep her face warm at night. She wore a black dress and black boots that went up to her knees. She had a leash wrapped around a hand that looked like a talon. The leash wasn't attached to a dog, but to a baby pig that kicked and squealed and tried to escape.

" *'Member me?'* "The witch said with a cackle. *"Did ya lookin the baffroom, dearie? Did ya? Did ya find ya daughter with 'er throat cut open and 'er eyes scooped out? Was she in da killin' box? Are ya havin' a good time?"*

Before Stephenie had a chance to place the voice (but she knew that voice; oh yes she did) she was shoved ahead.

Still eyeing the crowd, she saw a man that was missing a handful of teeth. The few Chiclets that remained were blacker than the witch's boots. The man had one hand on his hip, and an arm wrapped around the nastiest woman Stephenie had ever seen.

The woman's face was bloated and blotchy and covered in bright red pimples. Her hair was so wild that an eagle could have nested in it and invited friends over for dinner. She wore noth-

189

ing on her top half; her fat and unsightly breasts hung to her ample belly for all the world to see. They were streaked with veins and filth; her nipples were the size of pancakes.

Stephenie turned away.

She watched a man with a long beard punch a child in the face. The child was skinny and naked and went down in a hurry. Blood gushed from his nose and mouth; he couldn't have been older than five.

A man with a leg lopped off at the knee threw a rotten tomato, and screamed as it soared from his fingers. His aim was true. The projectile caught Stephenie in the chin and exploded on impact. She stumbled back, more surprised than hurt.

Howls of laughter mixed with shrieks of approval erupted from the crowd.

The man behind Stephenie pushed her forward. He mumbled something under his breath that sounded like a curse.

Stephenie tried to wipe the foul smelling vegetable from her skin. Only then did she discover that her hands were bound together and tied to her waist with rope. She said, "What's happening to me?"

Rotten tomato juice dripped from her chin.

The big man grunted, pushed her again.

And a boy—not much older than Carrie—pulled away from his mother and came running; he had no shoes on his feet. Instead, he wore sacks designed to hold grain. They were tied at the knee with twine. When he arrived at Stephenie's side he kicked her in the shin with his sack and the crowd roared with appreciation.

Stephenie was shocked. She was outraged. She looked into the horde and saw one man raise a bottle to his lips and another snatch it from his hand.

The boy's mother came stomping towards her with both hands on her hips. She was dressed in a cloth so dirty and chocked full of holes it wasn't fit to be worn by a rabid dog with an advanced case of leprosy. She grabbed the child by the ear and dragged him away. The child meowed like a wildcat in heat and the crowd roared once again, this time in amusement.

On the heels of that, a goat ran onto the path bleating. The owner nabbed it and dragged the goat away, never for a moment looking in Stephenie's direction.

The place was a madhouse; that much was obvious. But why was she here?

Stephenie followed the path with her eyes. She looked through the people and saw where she was headed; her throat felt unexpectedly dry.

The gallows.

Oh God, they were taking her to the gallows pole.

Fear gripped Stephenie completely. She twisted and turned and tried to break free.

The man with the large hands wouldn't allow it. He wrapped his fingers around her neck and choked her until she couldn't see. And when he released his hands she was walking up a staircase, wincing in pain.

Before she could voice a complaint or construct a plan for escape, she was looking down at the townsfolk with a noose around her neck. She felt it tighten; felt it tighten again. She could see a windmill in the distance; its blades moved slowly. The setting sun behind the structure was almost beautiful. The vultures circling above the gallows were not.

A voice came and she snapped her head towards the sound.

There was a priest standing to her right, telling her to be strong, telling her to cast Satan from her heart and beg the Lord's everlasting forgiveness. If only she would denounce Satan, she would find eternal peace. He begged it of her.

She said, "You don't understand. I shouldn't be here. I'm innocent."

"Innocent," the priest said, nodding his head and pursing his lips. "Yes, innocent." Apparently he had heard that one before.

Stephenie lowered her eyes.

Another voice came. It was male. "Hello Stephenie. They got you too, huh? Whatcha do, kill somebody?"

She looked left, towards the man's hands first; they were tied together. And when she looked up she saw an old man with a flat nose, small lips, and a scar that started at his chin and went all the way to his ear. His teeth were small and sharp. He had a nest of white hair bunched on top of his head like Albert Einstein. Oh shit. It was Grandpa Ray, the man she had seen in the painting, the one she considered a madman.

"Grandpa?" Stephenie said.

"Yes darlin'," the man said. His eyes seemed to be filled with shame. "It's me. I guess it don't matter much if ya killed somebody or not. You're here now... here with the rest of us. Reasons aren't really important, I suppose. Perhaps they never are."

Stephenie's mouth fell open. She didn't know what to say.

There was a man standing in front of Stephenie and Grandpa Ray. He was talking to the crowd, getting them excited. He looked and sounded like a politician and was saying something about responsibility and Satan and the difference between right and wrong. His voice was loud and firm. It chilled Stephenie to the bone.

Stephenie didn't care what the man was saying.

And Grandpa Ray cared less than that.

The look in his eyes suggested he heard it all before.

He said, "Don't believe the stuff they've told you over the years, okay? I tried, darlin'. I'm not a bad man... and if I am, well then, I never meant to be. I tried to be good. I tried to be the best man I could, but I guess you could say I wasn't always in control. It was like... oh, I don't know... like I had someone whisperin' in my ear half my life, telling me what to do, what to think. The voice kept telling me that the bastards shouldn't get away with it, you know? The voices were tellin' me to do things I *knew* was wrong. But at the time, they didn't seem wrong, not *really* wrong anyhow. They seemed like, oh... like I was *supposed* to do them, if you can dig it. I guess sometimes life blows in your direction; sometimes it blows against. And sometimes a man like me finds himself doing things, even when he knows he shouldn't be doin' them. I did some terrible things in my life, darlin'. I know I have, and from the look in your eyes you know it too. If I could take back my mistakes I would, you better believe it. I'd take 'em back in a heartbeat. I can't though; Lord knows it's too late for that now. He turned his back on me." The old man nodded. "On us, I guess. He turned his back on *us*, Stephenie. I've always loved you though, darlin'. I hope ya know that. I still love ya. Maybe now you'll forgive your grandpa for being the way he was created, the way God made 'em. Maybe now you'll understand."

Grandpa Ray looked at the crowd. He pushed his shoulders out and lifted his chin, like he had unloaded a great burden that had been on his mind for a hundred years. He almost looked proud then, proud and strong, like he was happy to admit the things he'd done hadn't been perfect.

A sack was placed over Stephenie's head as she was looking at Grandpa Ray, wondering what to say. The sack was not unlike the one the boy had been wearing on his feet. It smelled like a barnyard.

The crowd roared once the sack was in place, sounding like sports fans at a championship game.

She heard a man say, "Untie their hands."

A moment later someone was working the rope. Might have been the priest; she did not know. Once her hands were untied, the countdown began.

Five. Four. Three. Two. One.

The crowd roared. Some of them broke into song.

Stephenie whispered, "I denounce Satan."

Then she was falling.

8

Stephenie fell with her hands in the air and the grain sack blocking her vision. She was about to scream when her feet smashed against something very solid. Screams came, nearly loud enough to mask the sound of her ankle snapping—nearly, but not quite. She heard the SNAP, fell onto her side, and shrieked like mad woman. Blood sprayed across both legs, into the air and across the sack before it poured from her ankle and created a pond deep enough for kids to play in. Light danced in front of her eyes, blood rushed to her head and she thought she might faint. Her mouth became drier now than before. The world was spinning, not that she could see it spin. She couldn't. All she could see was the blurry weave of the barnyard sack, which light penetrated with ease.

Once she was able, she yanked the sack off of her head with a shaky hand and threw it in front of her. She cried out—in pain, and in fear.

She was in the hallway again. God help her, she was in that same fucking hallway.

Screams came from her throat, followed by shrieks, moans, whines, whimpers and cursing. Tears rolled down her face. She no longer wanted this nightmare to end. She *needed* it to end. Things were fucked up beyond all realms of logic. This was a level of insanity she didn't know existed.

After ten minutes of whimpering and crying and cursing out loud, she heard a voice. "Listen to me, Stephenie," the voice said. "Listen."

Stephenie flinched at the sound.

What now? she thought.

Still sitting in the hall, holding her bloated and broken ankle like she thought it might fall from her leg, she turned around and found Christina. She was dressed the same as before: in her little brown and white, retro, polka-dot dress.

Stephenie said, "You!"

"Yes, me." Christina sat down next to Stephenie looking like she was extremely disappointed. Using the palm of her hand, she wiped the wrinkles from her dress. She said, "What did I tell you?"

Stephenie raised both shoulders. "Huh?"

"Don't give me that bullshit. What did I tell you, Stephenie?"

"I don't know. What the fuck is wrong with you? I'm hurt! Can't you tell?"

"I don't care if you're hurt. In fact, you might want to get used to it; it's going to happen again and again."

"What? But why?"

"I told you not to go into the basement, remember? I warned you, but did you listen? No."

"Well, I'm sorry. Does that make it better?"

"Sorry?" Christina huffed like bull and flattened the wrinkles on her dress again. "What the hell is sorry going to do for you? Nothing. That's what. It's not going to do anything at all. You're in deep now, Stephenie; you're in way over your head. You had the opportunity to get in your car and drive away. You had a chance to leave all this behind. And you almost made it! You were smart enough to get into your car and drive, but not smart enough to leave. God, you're so stupid and you don't even know it."

"What was I suppose to do, leave Carrie behind?"

Christina's eyes widened and she lifted her hands in the air. "Yes! That's exactly what you should have done! But did you? *No*. Why? *Too stupid*, that's why. Instead of leaving you came back and entered the one place you weren't supposed to go. You entered the *basement*, sealing your fate—probably forever."

Stephenie felt the tears rolling down her face and she pushed them away with a bloody hand. Her ankle throbbed, so she held her other hand against the wound, trying to stop the bleeding. She said, "I want to get out of here."

"Of course you do. Jesus lady, you think I don't know that?"

"I don't know."

"You don't know much, do you? You've become one sorry piece of work, I must say."

"I'm sorry."

"Sorry, sorry, sorry... again with the sorry. That's awfully sad. You're stupid and sad; did you know that? You are. If I could slit your throat and be done with you, I'd do it—but you and I both know killing doesn't work in these parts, isn't that right?"

Stephenie shook her head, confused. "I guess."

"You guess? My God girl, that's worse than saying *sorry* again."

"What do you want from me? I don't understand what's happening."

"I don't want *anything* from you," Christina said. "I don't want anything, but I can help you... if you're smart enough to listen."

"Okay."

"Okay what?"

"Okay, I'll listen."

"Are you going to do what I say?"

"Yes."

"Are you sure? The last time I offered you advice you spat it back in my face the first chance you could."

"I'll listen this time! I'll listen!"

"Promise?"

"Yes, I promise."

"Okay, fine." Christina took a deep breath, and said, "There are doors down here that'll set you on fire as soon as you touch the knob. There are doors down here that will turn you into a lizard, or a snake, or a wasp, or about a million other things you don't want to be. There are doors that'll make you scream and doors that'll melt the arms off your body. They are doors that are capable of biting your hand and doors that'll impregnate you with monsters that will spew from your mouth for all of eternity. There are too many doors for you to comprehend. There are billions upon billions. But not all of the doors are bad. In fact, some lead to places that are amazing, like tropical beaches and beautiful countryside. Not many, but some. We're meant to know about these good doors, we're meant to know they exist. Knowing about them makes eternity here worse. And if you find one, if you step into a paradise room, you'll get nice and comfortable. They'll let you be happy. Then after a dozen years or so it's over and back you come, suffering worse than ever. There is also one door—and one door *only*—that will bring you back to the place you started."

"There is?"

"Yes."

"Which one?"

"What am I supposed to do, describe it? It's a white door that looks like all the others, but I can show it to you."

"Really?"

"Yes, really."

"Where will the door take me, back to my sanctuary? Is that where the door leads?"

"No. It will take you to the outside, to the parking lot."

Now it was Stephenie's turn to huff like a bull. She said, "But there are things out there, too. Don't you get it?"

"Not if you take this door. This one door is special. It'll lead you to the moment before you lost Carrie, before all this happened."

Stephenie opened her mouth but nothing came out. She couldn't believe what she was hearing.

There was a door that led to her old life.

The very idea of being tucked away in the safety of her old world seemed like heaven. In her regular life, she never knew how good she had it. But it was good, *very* good. If she could go back, why then, oh God… the notion of escaping was too good to be true.

Christina said, "Stephenie? Hello? Are you with me?"

Stephenie nodded. "Yes, yes. I'm with you. Where is Carrie? Do you know where she is?"

"I don't know."

"Is she alright? Is she alive?"

"Again, I don't know."

"Oh." Stephenie tapped her knuckles against her knee. She said, "If I go through this door you're talking about—"

Christina interrupted. "If you go through the door you'll find yourself in the parking lot before all of this stuff happened. Carrie will be fine, you'll be fine, your ankle will be as good as new."

"Well, what are we waiting for? Take me."

"I'm not finished talking to you. When you go back, Carrie will be in the parking lot, inches away from entering the restaurant, inches away from stepping out of one world and into another. If she goes through that door, everything starts again."

"What?! But why?"

"This isn't *my* world Stephenie, this is your world now. I'm only trying to help."

"But why would it start again?"

"Technically it wouldn't. Things would simply continue. You're in hell, Stephenie. I'm not sure if you figured that out yet or not, but you are. You found yourself in the wrong place at the wrong time, and now you're in hell."

"But I didn't die… or did I? Did I die?"

"No, you did not."

"Then why me?"

"Why not you? There are cracks in the universe that lead from one world into another. People slip through the cracks; it happens all the time. It happens every day. There are billions of people on earth, you know? Sometimes they get misplaced, as I'm sure you can recognize. And when someone goes missing, it doesn't always mean they've run away from home, or fell off a boat, or found themselves buried in the desert... get it? Sometimes they end up here." Christina shook her head and her eyes slipped closed. She said, "*A lot of times* they end up here. You have no idea. The Lords of this place snatch people away every day."

Silence came.

Stephenie wiped away more tears, and said, "I'm not sure how well I can walk, but I'm ready to leave now."

Christina nodded. "One more thing."

"What's that?"

"There's an axe leaning against the side of the restaurant. Did you see it?"

Stephenie shook her head almost solemnly. "No."

"It's there, probably leaning against the woodpile. Did you see *that?*"

"Yeah, I saw the woodpile, but I didn't see an axe."

"Well you might want to look. If Carrie gets into the restaurant, get the axe. Defend yourself. Remember, when you go through that special door you'll be in great condition. Your ankle will be as good as new; your cuts and scratches will be gone. Don't let the dead stab you again. And whatever you do, don't trust them. Once Carrie gets through that door, just remember, you're still in hell. But if you can stop Carrie from entering, you can drive away, home free. You and your daughter can lead a normal life, live happily ever after."

A few seconds rolled past.

Stephenie said, "Thank you, Christina."

Christina stood up, extended Stephenie a hand and helped her to her feet.

She said, "No worries, *babe*. Anything I can do to help." Then she turned away from Stephenie, grinning like a woman that poisoned the children's candy on Halloween Night.

9

They walked, slowly. Stephenie could barely stand but she walked anyway, leaving a trail of blood in her wake. She didn't complain. Occasionally a whine or a whimper escaped her lips, but not on purpose. She was trying harder than ever to stay strong. And it hurt. Her ankle felt like it was dipped in acid.

After ten minutes Christina put her hand on a knob, turned her wrist and opened a door. She said, "There are short cuts."

"Short cuts? How do you know where they are?"

They stepped through the doorway and were in a different hallway. They crossed the hall, opened another door and stepped through again. Now they were in a hallway that looked just like the last two.

Christina said, "We all have our crosses to bear Stephenie, every last one of us. If you don't escape today you'll learn my tricks again and again. We learn things as we go. We also get taught. We get schooled. We get forced to do things we don't want to do, and are required to give hope to those who seek it. The Lords of this place inflict darkness upon our hearts by showing us the light, time and time again. Nothing here is a constant. We are the damned. And the damned cannot dread what they are currently enduring, as I'm sure you can understand. They punish us endlessly, but part of that punishment includes time away from the screaming, so we can heal, so we can wait, so we can fear the future and dread which lies ahead."

They continued walking.

Stephenie bled, biting back her tears.

In time, they stepped into a hall sticky with old blood. There were chunks of meat on the floor and bones stacked in piles. There were eyeballs, intestines and clumps of flesh big enough to sink a canoe. There were severed hands and feet sitting together in a bucket. There was a pile of human hair so big it resembled a bale of hay.

They walked past the carnage without speaking.

A little further along they saw a frog hopping away from them.

Stephenie wondered if the frog had once been a man, and which door the man had opened. They walked past it, and she said, "Why are you helping me?"

"I'm being forced to do it."

"So, this is a trick of some kind; is it? I can't really escape… you're just setting me up so you can knock me down."

"No Stephenie, listen to me and hear my words. Stop thinking egotistically. Everything in this place isn't about you. I'm showing you an exit that I can never take. By showing it to you my existence grows worse. If you are lucky enough to gain freedom it will augment the pain and suffering, not only for me but for others as well. Those who dwell here will recognize your escape from the nightmare they must tolerate. Others will be shown. They will be told. They will be taunted and haunted. The Lords of this world want you to escape so the ill fated will know how unfortunate they are. The suffering in this place does not begin and end with physical pain. It has no limits. They torture the mind as well as the body, in spiteful and malicious ways. And if you are unlucky—if escape eludes you, you will remember this moment again and again for all eternity, which I assure you is a very long time. The freedom you failed to seize today will be a flavor upon your lips forever, and forever the taste will be bitter."

They stepped through another door, entered another hallway. They heard a man bust into a bout of screaming like he'd lost his mind. Who knows, maybe he did. The screaming ended abruptly. After that, a door swung open.

Christina held a hand in front of Stephenie's chest and said, "Wait."

Stephenie stopped walking, looked at Christina and saw fear in her eyes that wasn't there before.

Something stepped into the hallway not thirty feet in front of them. It looked like it crept from the script of a science fiction movie. It had multiple arms and multiple legs and its head was shaped like a shovel. Its skin was yellow and brown and covered in long scales. Teeth the size of knives stuck out of its mouth in all directions. In some ways, the thing resembled an alligator.

Christina stepped away, saying, "Don't move."

The creature looked them, but only for a moment. It didn't seem interested. It shuffled side to side, reached into the room with one of its arms and dragged a fresh corpse into the hallway, holding it by the face. After sniffing the air, the creature walked in the opposite direction, moving slowly, dragging the body and leaving a trail of blood two feet wide.

It was Christina that finally broke the silence. She said, "Lets go back. I know a different way."

Stephenie nodded. "Okay."

They walked the way they came, turned several corners. Stephenie's ankle was throbbing insanely but she didn't complain. She was worried Christina would get fed up and leave her stranded.

Ten minutes later they arrived at a door. Sure enough, it looked like all the rest.

Christina said, "This is it. Are you ready?"

Stephenie nodded. "Yes. I think so."

"Remember what I told you. If Carrie makes it into the restaurant, nothing changes. Don't believe what you see."

"Okay."

"You only get one chance at this… I think. If you somehow managed a second, I'd be very surprised."

"Thanks again Christina."

"Like I said, there's no reason to thank me. I'm being forced to show you this door."

Stephenie considered her words. She said, "How are they forcing you?"

"You don't really want to know, do you?"

"No, I suppose not." Stephenie eyed the floor for a moment; then said, "Can I ask you something? Do you want me to succeed?"

Christina's eyes wavered. She shrugged and said, "Honestly, I don't know. Mostly, I wish it would end."

Stephenie nodded, almost understanding. She took a deep breath, put her hand on the doorknob, turned her wrist and opened the door.

What she saw was blinding; it hurt the eyes to look.

Things were fuzzy and ill defined, like a swooshing, swirling, swimmy kind of static that boiled and swelled, moving back and forth, left and right, up and down.

"What's this?"

"You need to step through," Christina said.

"You're setting me up."

"No, Stephenie. This is your chance. If I were in your place I'd be through that door in a heartbeat, before it slammed in my face." Christina considered her words. "And soon enough, the door *will* slam in your face. You better believe it."

Stephenie squinted her eyes and forced herself to be brave. She said, "Okay. Here I go. Wish me luck."

Christina smiled insincerely.

And Stephenie stepped into the whirlwind.

10

No sound. No light. No taste, smell, or feelings inside her body. Just darkness, an empty void, a vacant shell, a hollow abyss that drained all thoughts and emotions away, nothing, nothing—then it came back. Light crept like static. Sound did too. Her mental self returned, bringing her fear, grief, desires and concerns. The physical self returned too, causing aches and pains throughout her body.

"Oh God," Stephenie whispered, stumbling in this new place. But the place didn't look new, and maybe it wasn't.

She was in a hallway. It looked the same as the last—and the one before that, and the one before that, and the one before that. *I'm getting the royal screw-job*, she thought before her vision had returned completely. And when it did return, it seemed as though she was right. She *was* in a hallway, and that wasn't where she was supposed to be. Because being lost in the bowels of hell's corridors is a whole lot different than being set free.

She turned around, angry and confused, tired and annoyed.

Her eyes widened.

Looking at the door she had come through, Stephenie gasped. Because what she was looking at, well… it wasn't right.

It wasn't… *fair.*

That's the word she clung to: fair. But nothing was fair in this place. Nothing was honest.

The door had a stick of gum attached at eye level. There was an empty wrapper sitting on the floor.

This was the door she had originally come from, her sanctuary.

Or was it just pretending to be that way?

Stephenie tried to open the door, just to see. Because maybe, somehow, her sanctuary would be on the other side, or the parking lot would be on the other side, or something good would be there, right?

The door was locked.

"Of course," she said, with tears forming in her eyes.

A moment slipped past; she wiped tears away and took a deep breath. Her chin started shaking and her nostrils flared. Her hands turned into fists and her teeth clenched together. Suddenly her heart was racing. Suddenly her knuckles were becoming red and her fists were pounding against the wood. "OF COURSE! YOU BITCH, CHRISTINA... YOU FUCKING BITCH!! I'LL *KILL* YOU! I SWEAR IT, I WILL!"

She cursed into the door, hating everything about everything. POUND, POUND, POUND. Her fists grew tired and sore.

She rested her head against the wood for a minute, maybe more, huffing and panting, swallowing back her rage. She looked at the door feeling angry, misled, toyed with, and mistreated. She wondered what she was going to do, where she was going to go. Nothing resembling a solution showed itself. She was alone. In every way that mattered, she was alone. And she didn't have a clue what she was going to do about it.

A noise came from behind her; sounded like a growl. Stephenie didn't want to spin around, oh no. She wanted to slink away and never return. But she did turn around. Slowly. Just in time to watch a door open.

Her last breath of hope escaped her then, as unlikely as it may seem. Yes, she still had some optimism kicking around inside her thinking; a little piece of her mind actually thought something good might creep through that door. *Something good*, can you believe it? Isn't that a laugh riot? Needless to say, she was wrong. Nothing good stepped through the door. In fact, nothing in the same ballpark as 'good' stepped through the door.

What shuffled through the opening was a living corpse, a zombie—the walking dead.

Stephenie felt her stomach flip.

She said, "No, please. No more."

The zombie was a man. His face was pale and shiny and tinted green with mold. He had bugs crawling on his skin and worms crawling beneath it. In life he lived less than twenty years; Stephenie could see his youth hiding beneath the decomposed flesh in a way that made her feel sad and empty as well as terrified.

The zombie wore jeans and a t-shirt. The jeans were tight. The shirt said *MAD MAGAZINE* at the top, *WHAT, ME WORRY?* at the bottom, and had a picture of *Alfred E. Neuman* somewhere in the middle. The zombie's hair was glued to his head with a thick layer of yeast and mildew. Both of his arms were broken and twisted in ways that reminded Stephenie of pretzels.

She stepped back.

Another door opened, followed by another.

Doors were opening on her left and right. Zombies started slumping their withered and rotting bodies into the hallway. Some were just children. Some were old enough to be pals with *Jesse James* and *Billy the Kid.*

Stephenie saw a woman with no hands, a man with a chunk of metal rammed through his throat, and youngster with his guts swinging from his belly. She saw an Asian man that had been burned to a crisp in a fire and a Spanish lady that had been run over by a bus. She saw a doctor and a cop, dead and rotting but still in uniform. She saw a black man that had been strung up at the gallows pole. (Seeing the man brought back memories, oh yes sir, and Stephenie wasted no time suppressing them.) There were zombies dressed in suits and zombies ready for a day at the beach. There were zombies that looked like thugs and zombies that seemed ready to jump on stage and play guitar in a metal band. There was a naked zombie and a zombie wearing mittens and a toque. There was a group of teenagers that looked like they died in a car accident together. One had a chuck of windshield embedded in his face and neck. She saw a corpse dressed like a baseball player and a corpse dressed like a soldier. The soldier had a hole in his chest big enough for a pigeon to fly through. She saw a mother with no teeth holding a dead baby in her thin, wilted arms. The baby's cold, lazy eyes shifted. Looking at Stephenie, the baby grinned like it had a secret it wanted to share. And Stephenie, looking at the slimy child-monster, heard herself scream.

11

She ran down the hallway, knocking the dead over before they had a chance to descend upon her. Her ankle burned but she didn't care. She needed to get away. Besides, the pain in her ankle had become such a constant and relentless thing it was becoming a non-issue. She just hoped it wouldn't give out on her, wouldn't twist and send her falling on her ass... again. Because it could, sure it could. The damn thing was broken and stabbed and swollen and bleeding all over the place.

A zombie with long, wormy hair grabbed Stephenie by the shoulder. It grunted, and something that looked like dirt fell from its open mouth in a writhing wad. She punched the creature in the chin. The chin exploded and Stephenie and kept moving. She *had* to keep moving; she had no choice.

She dodged and weaved, avoiding what she could.

A zombie threw an arm around Stephenie's neck and opened its mouth, attacking. The corpse was so old and putrid that its pants were hanging around its ankles and its shirt was nothing more than ribbons. The corpse had gone beyond worms and bugs. It was in that mummy stage that made Stephenie wonder how the damn thing was able to get around.

She elbowed it in the stomach.

The zombie toppled over like a stick of beef jerky.

Stephenie kept running, merging between zombies like a go-cart on a jam-packed track. She punched a couple, rammed a couple, and poked an old zombie-lady in the eye. Blood, mold, and brains, covered her finger all the way to the knuckle. The zombie-lady howled, spun her old-lady purse in a circle and fell onto her bone-petal ass.

A zombie that looked like it worked in a fast-food joint—before it took a pair of bullets in the forehead, that is—grabbed Stephenie by the arm. Stephenie tried to pull away but wasn't fast enough. The corpse gnawed a giant piece from her bicep before Stephenie had a chance to react.

Blood squirted.

A flap of skin flopped open.

Stephenie screamed, grabbing the torn flap with her hand.

Her eyes blurred. Seeing stars and swirling colors, she thought she might fall over. Blood poured from the wound and down her arm, running across her fingers in a dark river before splashing puddles on the floor.

A zombie stuck its fingernails into her shoulder, then tore a strip from her back. Stephenie howled again. She felt overwhelmed, like she was drowning in zombies. They were all around her, inundating her. Teeth snapped the air next to her ear. Hands groped her chest. More hands pulled on her hair. She was getting pushed and shoved. She was getting scratched and scraped.

She swatted a zombie with her elbow—the same zombie that was eating a piece of her arm (mmmm, yum!). Her fingers tightened around her abrasion, concealing her bubbling wound the best she could, but it wasn't enough. She was bleeding all over the place, and the bite mark wasn't small. It was *huge*. It seemed like she had lost enough meat to make a sandwich.

She tripped; she stumbled. She faltered and cried, wondering if this was the end.

The zombie chewing on Stephenie's arm licked its lips, smacking its gums. A zombie with a blonde afro grabbed her by the shirt, and when she pushed the zombie away, her middle finger slid into the creature's mouth.

The zombie stumbled and swayed and bit down hard.

The finger was severed.

Blood shot from the digit, spraying the zombie in the face before speckling the wall.

Stephenie screamed again. She pushed the zombie a second time, making it fall onto its back. And when she looked at her hand, her finger was gone. Just gone. All that remained was a nub that reminded her of Carrie. Blood spurted into the air, onto her chin. It was squirting in every direction she faced.

Stomach churning, she became dizzy. She thought she might fall over.

A zombie slapped its hand on her face and grabbed her bottom lip.

She pushed it and the monster fell.

Then she turned a corner and ran down a hallway, limping and crying as blood poured from several different places. She was leaving the majority of zombies behind. The few that remained seemed slow, uninterested. Perhaps they thought she was one of them. She had that look about her.

Stephenie turned another corner. And that's when she came face to face with something terrible. Something she didn't want to see, something that had her thinking she had gone absolutely mad-crazy-cuckoo-loco.

Standing a few feet from where she was standing—frightened and confused—was another Stephenie.

Before this horrific imposter had a chance to say anything, Stephenie, dizzy and bleeding and ready to fall over, said: "Oh my God! Oh my God! This can't be right! Look at what's fucking happening!" With the loss of blood, her words slurred like she was drunk. Her hands became fists and she raised them in the air, shaking them like mad, splashing blood where it fell. She punched herself in the head, hoping to snap herself free of the nightmare she was in. When that didn't work, she spit her gum into the imposter's face and said, "*Now* do you understand, huh? Do you? Fuck!" It was all she could think to say.

Unable to look at her own terrified image another moment she turned and ran off, speeding around the first corner she found.

The hall she entered was empty, save two children kneeing on the floor in a prayer's pose. They had their knees down and their hands in front of their faces. Two boys, wearing their Sunday best—dress pants, dress shirt, combed hair, hand-me-down Sunday shoes, clean as a whistle. Looked about eight, no older than ten.

The boys turned towards Stephenie in unison; they began chanting, *"Girly, girly, what you drinkin'? What the hell have you been thinkin'? Cut your throat. Drink your blood. Bury your corpse in graveyard mud! Girly, girly, where you goin'? Took Carrie without you knowin'! Cut her throat. Drank her blood. Buried her corpse in graveyard mud!"*

The children laughed and giggled and made stupid faces that were more disturbing than amusing. Their eyes seemed to be flat, without a trace of sparkle or shine. They disrupted their heavenly façade and reached their hands between their knees with movements that almost seemed syncopated. And when they lifted their hands, Stephenie could see each child was holding a gun, a big one—a gun big enough to take down Bigfoot and Chewbacca together in a single shot.

They pointed the weapons at Stephenie.

Stephenie's mouth popped open as she stepped back. With blood running from her arm, hand, ankle and back, she mumbled, "Wait!"

They didn't. Little fingers pulled big triggers; the guns fired.

Stephenie flinched; blasts shocked her eardrums. One bullet caught her in the stomach. The other caught her in the chest, next to her heart. Guts splashed in all directions, and she tumbled against the wall with two giant holes in her back, smearing the concrete blocks red. Somehow she managed to keep standing. Her mouth opened and closed; her body turned hot all over. She was burning up. Her heart pounded a hiccup beat; her nose started bleeding something that was black. She looked at the children in total shock, eyes wide and wet, hands extended, wondering why, drowning in her internal juices. She tried to say something but couldn't; couldn't breathe either. Her lungs felt crushed. Blood bubbled from mouth and boiled from her chest.

The children laughed again.

They sang, *"Girly, girly, are you dying? Burn in hell with body frying. Cut your throat. Drink you blood. Bury your corpse in graveyard blood!"*

Stephenie's legs trembled. She watched in horror as the children turned the guns on themselves. She only had time to think about what they were doing; then a second bullet was fired from each weapon. Blood, brains and bone fragments splashed into the air and against the wall as their heads blew apart. The children flopped onto the floor, one after another, quivering and twitching as a river of gore poured from their eyes, nose, ears and temples.

Stephenie turned, tumbled, grabbed a random doorknob with her mangled hand and twisted the knob. The door opened. She placed her other hand on her chest and felt her body's heat pouring over it. The bones between her breasts had been pushed into strange shapes; the muscles in her chest contracted. Eyes closed, she toppled from the hallway into the strange new room.

Gasping.

She was gasping, she was—

CHAPTER EIGHT:
RETURN TO KING'S DINER

1

—sitting in her car with her hands resting on the steering wheel. For a moment she didn't move, perhaps *couldn't* move. She felt something resembling shock, but the sensation had come so many times now. How many times can a person be shocked within a single day? Once? Twice? Five times?

But how could she not be shocked? One moment she was being murdered by a pair of creepy children in a place she believed was hell, the next, she was sitting in her car, tapping her fingers against the steering wheel.

"Oh God," she whispered; this was it.

She found the door to her old life, a way to escape the nightmare. She was outside. Healthy. Safe.

She lifted her hands and looked at them. Her hands were clean, which is to say she had all ten digits wiggling in front of her eyes and they weren't covered in blood. They should have been. Oh yes. Blood had been spewing from her severed finger in a hot stream. Not only that, but she had been dying. She *knew* it. She could tell. She had a bullet in her chest and a bullet in her gut, her body was hot in some places and cold in others, her vision was beginning to fade, parts of her spine was smeared against the wall… that's what dying is, right? Sure, but it wasn't happening now. Now she was sitting in her car.

She looked at her arms. The cuts and bruises were gone, the zombie bite was gone; the rat bites were gone too. She no longer had pain throughout her body. Her ankle…

Oh shit, she thought, excited and terrified at the same time. *What about my ankle?*

She lifted her foot towards her knee, but she knew—oh man, she knew. There was positive news waiting; her ankle was in fine condition. No, not *fine* condition… *great* condition! She was good! Her ankle was great! This was amazing!

This was—

A moment of panic came, followed by another. She needed to do something important, something that was… what? Uh? *Time sensitive*, that's what. And she knew what it was, sure she did. It was, umm… Carrie! Find Carrie!

No, not find her, because Carrie should be…

Stephenie looked at the restaurant with her bottom lip between her teeth and her eyebrows raised.

Carrie was outside, back turned, pulling the restaurant's front door open with her little hands, straining her tiny muscles, wedging her body through the restaurant doorway.

Stephenie screamed, "No!"

She grabbed the car's door handle and tried to open it. Locked. It was locked and she was yanking on the handle like she didn't have time to unlock it. But yanking on the handle wasn't working no matter how many times she tried. And she was trying, that was the worst part somehow. She was trying and trying, yanking on the handle harder and faster as her daughter stepped into the restaurant.

Stephenie said, "No! No! No!"

And she yanked on the handle some more.

Finally she stopped yanking on the door handle and put her hands in the air.

"What the hell?!" she screamed. Drool dripped down her chin; she didn't notice. She didn't know what the problem was, but then she knew. She knew! It was so obvious; she was being stupid. The door was locked; it was fucking locked. All she had to do was unlock the goddamn mother-fuckin' door and it would open right up. Sure it would. It would open up as easy as pie if she simply unlocked the door. So that's what she did— with her hands scrambling beside the lock, and around the lock, and over the lock—she found what she was looking for and she unlocked the door. Then she threw the door open and tried to leap out of the car.

Her seatbelt was on, her *goddamn* seatbelt.

Her *goddamn mother-fuckin' ass-licking dick-wagging bitch-slapping time-wasting cock-gobbling fuck, fuck, fucking* seatbelt was on.

Her hands scrambled, both of them, together—like unlocking the seatbelt would be accomplished faster if she tossed eight jittery fingers and two twitching thumbs into the project. But it wasn't making anything faster. It was slowing her down. Way down. Unlocking a seatbelt had never taken so much time in her life. She screamed, *"COME ON!"*

A finger found the button and pushed on the button and the belt was unlocked. It was unlocked and sliding across her lap and the car door was open. She tried to make the seatbelt slide faster by grabbing it and pulling on it.

And the restaurant door was closing. Oh shit, it was *closing!*

And Carrie was… inside.

The restaurant door clicked shut.

Stephenie said, "No, oh-no, oh-no, no, no!"

She threw herself out of the car and started running. Dust clouded the air beneath her feet, which were fine now; her ankle was in great shape. It felt awesome! Her ankle felt FUCKIN' AWESOME! And even though she was freaking out and in terrible danger her ankle felt so fine she almost smiled.

Stephenie arrived at the restaurant door. She snagged the handle and pulled the door open, listening to those Christmas bells sing. She crashed through the door, bounced against the doorframe and screamed: "CARRIE!"

And everyone in the restaurant turned towards her.

2

Little Carrie spun around with her eyes wide, her shoulders raised and her teeth clenched together. She said, "What the matter mom? I've got to go pee-pee really bad or I'll make an uh-oh in my pants! You know that! Don't be mad!"

Stephenie froze. A bead of sweat rolled along her face next to her ear. Her heart was racing and every pair of eyes in the restaurant was on her, analyzing her, watching her every move. Maybe they thought she lost her mind; maybe they thought she was being over protective. She didn't know. Didn't want to know. She just wanted to get the hell out of the restaurant, into the car, and away from the diner. She just wanted her old life back.

Was that too much to ask?

No. Of course it wasn't. It was only logical.

Stephenie looked a Carrie for a second, maybe two. Her eyes shifted and her shoulders lifted. She resembled a cobra that had been backed into the corner, ready to lash out, ready to strike.

There were two people sitting together at a table on her right: Karen Peel and Denise Renton. Stephenie recognized Karen as the corpse that was outside; slumped against the yellow school bus with her jaw smashed apart and her hands covered in blood. And Denise—why, that was the zombie from Jacob's front yard, the one that lifted its finger and said, *'Quoove beanbade,'* with a phlegm-soaked voice and a head shaped like a smashed cantaloupe.

Stephenie cringed, pulling away from the woman.

She said, "Stay away from me! All of you! Just get the hell away, you hear me? STAY BACK!"

She snatched Carrie by the hand and pulled her tight against her body.

"Mommy," Carrie complained.

But Stephenie wasn't having it. She considered allowing the girl to use the washroom for less than a half-moment, and even that was too long. Carrie wasn't going into the bathroom in this place! No way. Hanging out in this hell-trap was a ridiculous idea; it wasn't going to happen. No chance. Not on her watch. She wasn't risking an eternity in hell so Carrie could take a god-damn piss.

She said, "Carrie, that's enough so be quiet. I know some-thing you don't, babe. Okay? Don't be frightened; don't be scared. I've got you. Oh yes. Mommy's right here. Don't worry about a thing."

"But I'm not worried, mommy. I just need the bathroom!"

"Enough!" Stephenie backed towards the door, pulling Carrie along with her.

She looked at the person standing closest: Susan Trigg.

Susan was wearing her yellow waitress uniform with the loose button shirt. She had a pencil in her hand that said *EMPIRE PENCIL CORP* on one side and 2 HB on the other. Her nametag sat just above her right breast. And when Stephenie glanced at it, she could envision Susan lying on the floor in a pool of blood with her skull cracked apart like an egg, her brains covered in bone fragments, and that stupid nametag sitting on her bloodstained shirt for all the world to see.

Susan stepped away nervously, and that was good. Stephenie didn't want her around anyhow, especially when she was carrying that fucking pencil in her hand.

Stephenie's eyes shifted towards Craig Smyth. Like Susan, he was also standing. Craig looked nice, dressed in his clean white shirt, leaning against the counter, in the place he'd fall if someone were kind enough to slam an axe into his chest and split his ribcage apart.

Craig swallowed loud enough for the entire room to hear, and placed a hand on his throat right after.

Stephenie looked past Craig to Jennifer Boyle, who was standing behind the counter, in front of the storage room.

Jennifer looked frightened. She also looked different. She had two arms now; both were attached and seemed to be in fine working condition. Stephenie wondered if Jennifer knew she could wind up sitting on the floor behind the counter, exposing her little pink underwear as blood dribbled from the place her arm had once been.

Stephenie looked away from Jennifer.

Her eyes found Angela Mezzo.

Angela was sitting in a booth across from her husband Alan, next to her son Mark. She was holding her happy-face mug in her hand like it didn't mean a thing. The mug was smiling, just smiling. And in the booth, behind the family, Stephenie could see Lee Courtney sitting with David Gayle.

Oh, she didn't like David. She remembered him sitting beneath the painting with his face locked in terror. She remembered the way his eyes rolled open when she stepped out of the bathroom.

She looked away from David, who looked so nice in his light-pink shirt. Her eyes swept across the room. They were all here, it seemed. All the would-be monsters were accounted for.

She could see Julie Brooks, the woman that had been sitting in her car.

Julie was talking with Gary Wright, the cook that had lost his legs. Strange enough, he had legs now. Oh yes he did. He had a pair of legs that were big and fat and could use a little exercise.

On the right side of the restaurant, Eric Wilde sat alone in a booth near the restaurant's big front window. He was dressed in a cheap blue suit that made him look like a used car salesman. Apparently Eric—*wanna buy a used car?*—Wilde was in the middle of ordering something to eat. He had a menu in his hand and a waitress standing beside him, holding a glass of water.

The waitress was Dee-Anne Adkins. She was the bitch with the broken nametag that tried to bite Stephenie when Stephenie was getting a pencil rammed into her ankle by that other bitch, Susan Trigg.

Dee-Anne's nametag wasn't broken now, Stephenie noticed. It looked just right.

Stephenie looked at the last person she could see: Wayne Auburn.

Wayne was sitting in a booth, dining alone. He sat next to a window that wasn't too far from where Stephenie was standing. He seemed more handsome now that his skull wasn't opened up like a Venus flytrap and his brains weren't wedged into the gap between his eyes. Shame he was wearing a red-checkered shirt that looked like a tablecloth and a pair of jeans that were two sizes too tight. Wasn't doing a thing for him.

Susan lifted her pencil and waved it at Stephenie. She said, "Lady, are you all right?"

Stephenie pulled away. "Yeah. I'm fine. Just stay away from me and you'll be fine too."

Susan gave her a strange look, lifting a hand and raising an eyebrow. "What's that supposed to mean?"

"It means stay away from me or I'll fucking kill you."

Susan's mouth fell open; she seemed both shocked and insulted.

Stephenie didn't care. She turned around and made for the door, dragging Carrie unhappily along.

3

As Stephenie pulled Carrie towards the car, Carrie said, "Mommy? What are you doing? Why are you being mean? I have to go to the bathroom, mom! Let me go back inside!"

"Carrie, enough! We've got to get out of here!"

Stephenie opened the passenger door, escorted Carrie into the car and slammed the door shut. Then, as she was making her way to the driver's side of the car, she heard a voice and nearly jumped right out of her shoes.

"Fill 'er up?"

Stephenie spun around quickly.

It was the gas attendant, dressed in his blue overalls.

Stephenie remembered seeing the man lying on the floor with his head split open. She remembered the enormous amount of blood that had leaked out of his skull and onto the cheap linoleum tiles, not to mention his left eyeball sitting on his cheek, smashed apart and looking like apple flavored Jell-O. He looked so different now. He looked so... alive. And not only that, he had the aura of a nice guy. He had a warm smile and a gentle face. His dark skin made him look handsome—not in a rugged way, in a clean-cut way. He looked like the type of guy you could take to your parents and they'd say he was a keeper.

Stephenie said, "What?" It was a reflex. She might have meant it in a 'what do you want' kind of way, but the attendant took it in a 'pardon me' kind of way.

He said, "How much gas do you need, Miss? Do you want me to fill 'er up?"

"No." Stephenie plunked herself into the car, slammed the door and said, "No gas."

"Oh," the attendant said, looking rightfully confused. After all, she was parked beside the pump and most people that park beside a pump need fuel. "Well, what can I do for you? Want me to check the oil or something?"

Stephenie got into the car. She looked at the gas gauge.

EMPTY.

She eyed the restaurant. Nobody was coming outside. Nobody was sneaking out the side door either. The people inside had gone back to their meals. No doubt, they were talking about the crazy woman that had come into the restaurant with the little girl. They probably felt sorry for the girl and wondered if she was being mistreated. Oh well; that was all right. Let 'em wonder. They didn't know what Stephenie had been going through. They didn't know what was at stake. Those idiots didn't know anything. Let 'em fuckin' wonder. Let 'em fuckin' think whatever they—

"Miss?"

Stephenie looked at the gas attendant. Then her eyes snapped towards the gas gauge again, wondering how far she'd get on an empty tank. Not far, that was the truth of the matter. A couple miles, tops.

Reluctantly, she said, "Okay, fill it. And make it fast. Real fast."

The attendant looked at her strangely. "Sure thing," he said, with an undertone that screamed: *Get a life, lady.* "Regular?"

"Yeah. That's fine."

The attendant unscrewed the gas cap and lifted the nozzle from the gas pump. He put the nozzle into the neck of the fuel tank and pumped gas.

Carrie said, "Mommy, what's wrong?"

Stephenie took Carrie by the hand and said, "Nothing babe. Nothing's wrong. Not now. Everything is going to be just fine. You'll see."

"I have to go pee-pee mommy."

"Carrie, do you love me?"

Carrie's eyes narrowed. "Yes."

"Then trust me, okay? We need to get out of here right away. You can pee in two minutes at the side of the road or the next place we come across."

"Awww," Carrie whined, uncharacteristically. She wasn't like most children in the protest department. Not now. Hal's death, for better or for worse, made her grow up in a real hurry. She didn't cry about the little things these days, meaning the whine wasn't spoiled brat behavior but a result of her being physically uncomfortable.

Stephenie knew; it broke her heart to hear Carrie sound that way.

She said, "How does this sound, babe? Tomorrow I'll make it up to you, *big time*. We can go to the toy store and buy whatever you want."

"Really?"

"Oh yes," Stephenie said with a smile. And she meant every word. If they could get out of this nightmare in one piece she'd be more than happy spend the day at *Toys 'R' Us,* spending every last cent she had. "I'll buy you whatever you want. We can go to the movies too, if there's anything good playing. But please, don't give me a hard time, okay babe? I love you so much, but please, we have to get going as soon as we can."

Carrie wanted to agree, but it was hard. She wasn't putting on an act. The coke she had begged for and drank (against her mother's better judgment) had gone right through her. She said, "But I hafta go pee, mommy. It's going to come out in my pants soon. Honest it will. I don't know if I *can* hold it!"

Stephenie looked at the restaurant, wondering.

The attendant removed the nozzle from the car and returned it to the gas pump holster. He approached the window and said, "That's comes to $53.50."

Stephenie dismissed the idea of entering the restaurant (she couldn't really believe she was even *considering* it), gazed up at the attendant and said, "Okay."

She turned and looked into the backseat. The purse was there, lying on its side. The contents were spilled across the cushion.

Stephenie stopped what she was doing. Slowly, her eyes grew large and her hands tightened into balls. She wondered *why* her contents were lying across the cushion.

She thought, *I threw my purse into the backseat in a huff.*

When?

When I was looking for my phone.

And when was that?

After I saw that everybody was dead.

And what does that mean?

Stephenie turned her head slowly, cautiously. She looked at the attendant.

He smiled.

Stephenie smiled back, trying to hide her fears. But they were back. Oh yes sir, they were back and making her skin crawl. This little scenario wasn't adding up. It wasn't adding up at all. How could her purse be knocked over if she had returned to a time before she knocked the damn thing over? How could *that* have happened?

And what did Christina say to her?

Once Carrie gets through that door, just remember, you're still in hell. But if you can stop Carrie from entering, you can drive away, home free. You and your daughter can lead a normal life, live happily ever after.

But Carrie did step through the door, didn't she?

The attendant said, "Uh, Miss? That's $53.50."

A hot flash came, followed by a deep, shaky breath. Stephenie said, "Just a moment." She lifted her wallet, which was lying on the seat, four inches from the purse. (And oh God, it shouldn't have been there. It should have been inside the purse. *Inside*—not *outside*.) She opened the wallet and looked for cash.

225

She only had two twenties. "Shit," she whispered. Then she said, "Do you take Visa?"

"Sure do," the attendant said with a grin. "Visa, MasterCard, American Express... we take most everything."

Stephenie handed the man her Visa card, wishing she had enough cash. If she had had enough money, she would have handed it over and told the man to keep the change. Now she had to wait.

The attendant walked across the lot and into the gas station, strolling along like he didn't have a care in the world.

"Mommy," Carrie said.

"Babe, please. I don't want to hear it."

"But—"

"Yes, I know. You have to go to the bathroom. Just hold it for two minutes."

"I don't know if I can."

"Just... I don't know. Stand beside the car and go."

"What? No mommy. Please! I don't want to go pee-pee in the parking lot!"

"Then do it in your pants, you're not going inside."

Carrie started crying. "Mommy, this isn't fair! I hafta go really bad and I don't wanna make an uh-oh in my pants!"

Stephenie said, "Carrie... "

But Carrie wasn't having it. With her hand between her legs and body crouched over, she cried harder and louder and kicked her feet wildly. She even let out a couple of high-pitched shrieks. And when the attendant stepped outside with an evil grin decorating his face, he had a long butcher knife in his hand. Stephenie never noticed. Neither did Carrie. In fact, neither of them realized the man had returned from his duties until after he rammed the blade into Stephenie's body.

4

The attendant waited for the right moment, just inside the gas station door. When the moment came, he stepped outside quickly, holding the butcher knife low. His feet moved fast. Once he arrived at Stephenie's open window, he raised the knife up. Stephenie was facing Carrie, so she didn't see the man approaching, and didn't know he was there. He stabbed her three times in the upper back within a single second.

Stephenie screamed once; then she lunged forward with her chest pushed out. After that, there seemed to be no air in her lungs and screaming became impossible.

Carrie's crying came to an abrupt halt. She looked at her mother's horrific expression: eyes wide, mouth open, face seemingly turned to wax. She could see blood on her mother's chest, but didn't know where it came from. She didn't know what happened, but she understood that something *did* happen, something bad. She also realized why her mother had been acting so strangely and controlling. Her mother was worried about their physical safety, and she was *right* to be worried about it. They should have driven away when they had the chance.

The attendant stepped away from the open window, leaving the knife imbedded in Stephenie's frame. He walked to the front of the car slowly, like he was enjoying himself. When he slapped an open hand on the car's hood, Carrie jumped.

Stephenie's eyes watered; she could hardly breath. She tasted blood in her mouth and looked at her daughter's terrified face, knowing how vulnerable she had become. She couldn't help Carrie, not in this situation, not with a knife rammed into her back. One of her lungs felt like it had been deflated. Without a doubt she was bleeding internally. In desperation, she tried to reach around and grab the knife, tried to find it with her fingers so she could pull it out. It didn't happen. The knife was imbedded into a place she couldn't reach.

Carrie watched her mother's face turn white as a trickle of red colored spittle rolled over her bottom lip. She turned her head; looked out the front window.

The attendant was swashbuckling towards her like a cowboy in a spaghetti western. Wasn't dressed that way though. He wore a blue, one-piece jumper-suit with little drops of blood on it.

Carrie knew the blood had come from her mother.

She screamed then, but not like before. This wasn't protest screaming. No, this screaming came from deep down; this screaming was based on fear and anxiety, on things she didn't understand, on things she didn't want to endure.

The attendant opened Carrie's door and said, "Hello, darling."

He reached into the car and grabbed hold of Carrie, handling her with ease. Yes, she kicked and slapped and did what she was able, but it didn't matter. He lifted her off the seat, turned her around and wrapped an arm around her neck. He squeezed her, just hard enough to stop her from screaming.

Carrie's eyes blasted open and her bladder let go. Hot urine poured down her legs. She hardly noticed. What she *did* notice was the fact that she was getting dragged out of the car, away from her mother, away from all feelings of safety, away from the place she wanted to be.

She didn't want to be with *this* man—no, not at all.

There was something *wrong* with him.

With hazy eyes and unfocused vision, Stephenie watched the man (who seemed so nice a moment before) drag Carrie towards the restaurant. She turned away from the abduction and opened the car door. Little black spots appeared in front of her eyes and all at once she felt like fainting. The car door wasn't locked this time; for that she was grateful. She stepped outside, black spots growing larger, stumbling, feeling like a butterfly that had been pinned to a piece of corkboard for some kid's science project, and had fallen off the board.

She leaned forward.

Dark blood poured from her mouth, splashing against her legs and feet. She felt more blood running down her back, getting inside her pants. She coughed twice, thinking she'd fall over. Wasn't getting enough air. Pain in her chest was intense, so intense. It felt different than the pain that had burned her ankle. That pain was extreme (of course) but it wasn't attached to her breathing, her heart, her life. She never thought the pain in her ankle would kill her. But this pain—this pain was different. It *would* kill her. In fact, it seemed to be happening already. She felt like she was dying—with good reason. Those little black spots were the lights going out.

Christmas bells rang and Stephenie managed to look up. She watched Carrie release one last scream before she was hauled inside the restaurant, kicking her feet and waving her arms.

The restaurant door closed.

Stephenie staggered a few feet and fell on one knee. One knee became two. Hands dropped to the ground. Now she was crawling towards the restaurant. More blood ran from her mouth. Her stomach cramped and her face hit the dirt. She pushed onto her hands and knees, crawled several more feet, caught a glimpse of the wooden patio swing and made her way to it. Using the swing for leverage, she pulled herself into a standing position. The little black dots in her eyes faded, becoming big white dots. It didn't seem like a step in the right direction. It seemed like different shades of dying. She staggered to the restaurant door and placed her hand on her chest. The tip of the knife was sticking through her skin.

Eyes watered more.

The world faded completely, but only briefly; she was standing. Just. She grabbed the door and pulled it open. Christmas bells rang as she tumbled inside, wondering what she was going to do next.

5

Craig Smyth said, "There she is! Grab her!"

Stephenie looked up in a daze. She was expecting to see a zombie but didn't. Craig looked the same as he had a few minutes ago, like a normal guy wearing a nice white shirt, only now he wasn't acting nervous; he was showing his true colors.

Craig grabbed Stephenie by one arm. Lee Courtney swooped in and grabbed her by the other. They dragged her towards the counter and Stephenie felt her knees letting go. She wasn't fighting them. She couldn't; didn't have the strength.

Karen Peel stepped behind the trio. She slapped a hand on the butcher knife handle that was embedded in Stephenie's back and yanked the blade from her body.

Pain came first, followed by a fresh batch of blood. It boiled from Stephenie's back, splashing on the floor in three separate piles. She coughed twice quickly and her heart started bumping around inside her chest in a way she had never felt before. It was racing and stopping, racing and stopping. The whites spots in her eyes became black spots once again and for a moment she faded into oblivion. When her eyes reopened, she was lying on the countertop, facing the ceiling, watching the blades of the ceiling fan spin around in a slow moving circle.

She tilted her head left; she tilted her head right.

There were people standing all around her: Susan Trigg, Angela Mezzo, Craig Smyth, Jennifer Boyle, David Gayle, Lee Courtney, Alan Mezzo, Karen Peel... there might have been more, she couldn't tell. Her vision was coming and going.

She said, "Where's Carrie?"

"Oh, don't worry Stephenie," Alan Mezzo said. "Don't you worry your pretty little head, we've taken good care of her."

Stephenie coughed out, "What have you done?"

Craig Smyth stuck his face above Stephenie's line of vision, grinning psychotically. "You shouldn't worry about her, oh no. You see... it's not about what we've done. It's about what we're about to do."

"Absolutely," Lee Courtney said, licking his lips. "Let's look to the future, not the past."

"The future," Karen Peel agreed, tapping her pencil against her chin. "It's all about the future. Lets start with the arms, shall we?"

Jennifer Boyle lifted an electric carving knife and grinned. The carving knife had a white handle and two saw-like blades attached to each other. They were eight inches long and would move back and forth when powered. Jennifer said, "Oh yes. The arms! Lets start with the arms! I love that idea. It sounds perfect; don't you think, Stephenie? Starting with the arms?"

Stephenie looked at Jennifer, registering that fact that the girl had been sitting behind the counter, short one arm, not long ago. For some reason it struck Stephenie as ironic that Jennifer wanted to start with the arms. With blood invading her mouth, she said, "I don't know what you mean. I don't understand what you want!"

"You're a smart lady," Alan said, nodding his head with an excited looking grin. "I think you'll figure it out."

Stephenie looked at the carving knife, just as Jennifer clicked it on.

The knife buzzed, reminding Stephenie of the electric hedge-clippers Hal had purchased the summer before last.

When powered, the knife made a sound not completely un-like an electric razor. And when Jennifer brought the blade down, towards Stephenie's elbow, she realized for the first time what they were planning on doing.

Stephenie said, "Don't!"

"But why not?" Karen Peel said, before the blade touched the skin. "This is fun! Don't you think?" Karen raised the knife that had been embedded in Stephenie's back and licked the blood off the blade, mockingly.

"I think it's fun," Lee agreed. "Do you think it's fun?"

Craig nodded, "Oh yes! I think it's fun too! In fact, this is one of my favorite things to do!"

Jennifer said, "Are you ready Stephenie?"

Stephenie said, "No…" She tried to pull away, but couldn't do it. They were securing her tightly.

"Great! Here we go!" Jennifer brought the oscillating blades down hard. They connected with Stephenie's flesh.

Blood splashed into the air and Stephenie heard herself screaming. Hot, melting misery tore threw her body. Her quirky heart rate increased; she tasted acid in her mouth and thought she might be sick. The room spun. Her vision blurred more now than before and the black dots in front of her eyes grew larger and larger. She convulsed. She heard the metal blades grinding against her bone. She saw a line of blood shoot into the air. Her vision faltered. Karen Peel lifted the butcher knife up, flashed it in front of Stephenie's face and put the blade to Stephenie's throat. Stephenie felt the blade cutting her open and the air rushing into her neck. Her vision faded. It was gone. Someone laughed. Somebody said, "Let me try." She felt her body getting pushed into a different position, like she was a slab of meat and they were a pack of butchers. Chewing noises came; sound washed away, concern dissipated, pain dulled…

Nothing.

Nothing more.

CHAPTER NINE:
DIFFERENT PRINCIPLES

1

Stephenie opened her eyes; she stretched her shoulders and back. She couldn't see anything; everything was dark. She wondered where she was and how she arrived, because whatever she was laying on, it wasn't her bed. It felt hard, like a floor, like a rock. But why would she be laying on something like that?

The palms of her hands found her eyelids. She rubbed them like she was coming out of a deep sleep. When she pulled her hands away, there was no light. Everything was dark, beyond dark. There were no shapes, no shades of darkness and no tints of grey. The term *pitch black* seemed appropriate, and for a moment she wondered if she was dead.

But why would I be dead? she thought.

What's the last thing I remember?

She remembered driving, stopping for gas; the restaurant...

Stephenie's eyes blasted open (not that it changed anything; it was still blacker than a pot of coffee in this strange new place), and she pushed herself to her elbows, mumbling, "What is this?"

She couldn't remember the last thing that happened, not right away. There were too many things to consider and they all came junking into her mind at once—not as complete thoughts, but as fragmented images. She recalled zombies, Carrie, her grandpa being executed at the gallows pole. She remembered her wounded ankle, the white hallway with the endless amount of doors, getting shot by a pair of creepy children and being chased by a wolf.

But did that all really happen?

She wanted to think the answer was 'no' but she didn't.

Stephenie took several deep, stabilizing breaths as she wrapped her head around her predicament. *Okay*, she thought. *Okay, okay, okay. Assuming this isn't some crazy, fucked-up hallucination, what's the last thing that happened? How did I get here?*

Stephenie felt something the size of saltshaker scuttling across her arm and she sat up straight. The thing, which felt light, fuzzy, and quite possibly loaded with legs, stopped scurrying and gripped her skin. She swatted it away.

It fluttered.

Only then did she become slightly in-tune with her surroundings.

She heard things moving around, low grumbles, and tiny squeaks. She heard something sliding from one place to another. She heard something making a *fitt-fitt-fitt* sound.

She remembered the rats, and the way they crawled across her body by the hundreds.

Once again, she wondered where she was.

Thinking she had returned to the tunnel of the rats, she reached a hand above her head. There was no ceiling there. She waved her hand left and right. There was nothing around her, no walls anyhow.

This wasn't the tunnel. So, where was she?

Outside?

Looking up, there was nothing that resembled a sky. Just darkness. And the air, she now realized, was unmoving. There was no draft or breeze, no airflow of any kind. The air was warm and still. Dirty. Stale. And there was a smell. Oh God, the fact that she overlooked it before was a phenomenon. The air smelled awful. Not like rotting meat, but like worms, like damp fabric and reptiles, like animal fur and rodent shit, like earth and stagnant water, all mixed together in a bucket of mule piss.

Something lively landed on her face and she swatted it away. It was a bug of some kind—more June bug than butterfly. Perhaps it was a dragonfly or a moth.

Now the memories came—

She had entered a room, and unexpectedly found herself in a time before the nightmare began.

She remembered the parking lot.

She remembered Carrie going inside the restaurant, alone.

Stephenie tried to stop her. But failed. The people inside the restaurant weren't dead; they were alive, seemed normal. She left the restaurant with Carrie, taking her by the hand. The gas attendant came, he pumped gas and...

Stephenie's mouth opened.

She gripped the sides of her body, searching for the knife in her back. There wasn't one. The knife was gone; the wound was gone too.

"What happened?" she said.

She remembered getting dragged into the restaurant...

No wait! That wasn't right. She didn't get *dragged* into the restaurant. Carrie did. And she crawled in after, on her hands and knees, bleeding and dying, trying to defend her daughter. But the people inside the building attacked her. They pulled out an electric knife. Her arm was getting—

Stephenie grabbed both elbows with her hands. She still had two arms, still had both hands too. The last thing she remembered was losing an arm. And darkness...

That's because I died, she thought. *And you can't die here.*

Once you die, you start over...

She felt something crawl over her fingers that was big enough to wear boots; felt like a tarantula.

She released a little squeal. "I'm surrounded by bugs," she said.

Just like that, she felt them on her body. Bugs were crawling on her legs, back, and neck. They were everywhere.

Stephenie flinched twice and scrambled to her knees. She swatted insects and God-only-knows what else from her clothing. She shook her head back and forth like a dog at the beach, lost her balance and dropped a hand onto the floor. It landed on something that squished and popped. She pulled her hand away and forced herself to her feet. Once she was standing, she rubbed her arms and legs with her hands, knocking dozens of creepy-crawlies away. Oh shit, she was covered in bugs: big ones, wet ones, long ones, hairy ones, bugs with dozens of legs, bugs with wings, bugs with antennae longer than her fingers, bugs with sharp mandibles and black, bugling, obsidian eyes.

Something slithered across her throat.

Something crept into her pants.

Bugs the size of grapes clung to her hair, pinching her skin, nipping at her body. Her lips parted and she shrieked. Something flew into her mouth and fluttered against her tongue. She bit down. Now she was spitting. Now she was kicking. Now she was dancing around in a circle like a cracked-out hippie at a rave, high on too many uppers and not enough downers.

She wanted the bugs *off*.

She *needed* them off.

"Oh yuck!" she screamed, but that barely scratched the surface of her thinking. This was awful!

She spit twice more, flapped her shirt around and felt something clinging to her left breast, her nipple. She knocked it away and rubbed her hands across her thighs, chest and ass. Then she wedged her pinkies into her ears. One ear was empty. The other wasn't. It had a yellow-back, orb weaver spider in it.

Squishing the spider into paste, she released another squeal. The sound of the spider mashing into her skin was loud and sickening. She cleaned her ear the best she could, and when she was finished she heard something that was *not* bugs, something that *rattled* and *hissed*.

She only knew one creature in the whole world that sounded that way.

A rattlesnake.

Stephenie stepped away from the rattling sound, cringing when things crunched beneath her shoes.

"Oh crap," she said.

A heavy pair of wings flapped in front of her face. At first she thought the wings belonged to a butterfly. But when she knocked the mammal with the back of her hand, she knew that it wasn't a butterfly, wasn't a bird either. It was a bat—heavy and woolly and nothing at all like a bird or an insect.

She took another step away from the rattle, followed by two more.

But what could she do?

It was dark, very dark. She couldn't see anything. Imagining a nest of rattlesnakes in the next place she stepped was easy. She wanted to run, but forced herself not to. She forced herself to stay calm, stay strong. Running in the dark was a bad idea. She needed light. If she had light, she could run from this place, try to find somewhere to hide, somewhere to go. But she didn't have light. She didn't have anything.

She thought about the flashlight.

No, strike that. Flash*lights.*

Blair gave her one, and there was another on the shelf in the restaurant storage room. Hell, she probably had one rolling around inside the trunk of her car too. Lot of good it was doing her now, though. She didn't even have a lighter, or matches.

Or did she?

2

Stephenie checked her pockets. She had a small amount of pocket-change and a book of matches.

Perfect, she thought.

But this wasn't perfect. This was the *opposite* of perfect, wasn't it? Calling this situation perfect was like going over Niagara Falls in a canoe and being happy you brought a towel.

She opened the pack, pulled a match free and lit it.

For a second, the match was bright enough for her to see two feet of nothing in every direction. Then the flame died down and all she saw was the top half of her hand. She said, "Uh," bringing the match near her knees. The flame flickered. A bug swooped past the flame and the match went out.

This isn't going to work, she thought.

She lit another match. Same thing: bright for a small amount of time then the flame diminished and became damn near useless. This flame lasted a bit longer though, and she worked the match a little better, getting the maximum amount of light she could. Once the flame crept too close to her fingers she let the match fall. Using her fingers she counted matches in the dark. She had seven. Seven matches weren't going to do much unless she found something to burn, but what?

The matchbook. Okay, yes, she had that.

What else?

She checked her pockets again. Nothing. She had nothing else.

She put a hand to her chest and knocked a bug away. She considered burning an article of clothing but quickly dismissed the idea.

A loud rattling sound swelled from the darkness. She moved away from the sound and lit another match. With the flame burning, the rattling came to a halt. She took another step and bumped into something solid. The object was waist high. She brought the match down a few inches to heighten her visuals. She could see a shape, almost looked like a table. Moving the flame left and right, she could see that the object was four feet by two and a half feet, give or take a little. The top of the table was flat, but the sides were cut at strange angles. It almost looked like an old fashioned... *coffin.*

A child's coffin...

The match flickered and went out.

Stephenie snagged another match. She tried to light it but the match wouldn't ignite. She tried again, and again. Still wasn't working. She tried twice more without any luck. At this point she figured she rubbed all of the phosphorus off the matchstick, which she had. She tossed the match on the ground and heard another rattlesnake shaking its tail. She tried a new match. It ignited, and something fluttered past her face and landed in her hair. She shook her head left and right, hoping to rid herself of the intruder.

Yes, yes—now she could see it. The object in front of her *was* a coffin. It didn't look modern; it didn't have a rounded top and a glossy finish. It was a flattop, wood grain with no polish. But what was a coffin doing here?

Where was *here?*

She looked over her shoulder, nothing but darkness.

A coffin, she thought. *Why a coffin?*

The easiest answer seemed to be: *because she was in hell.* However, that wasn't the answer Stephenie was looking for. The answer she was seeking presented itself in a question: *Where do you find coffins?*

In graveyards, yes… but where else can you find them? And with that, the answer came: she was inside a mausoleum.

Stephenie stepped away from the casket, thinking about escape. Mausoleums had doors, right? There had to be a door somewhere.

She took a couple quick steps away from the rattling sounds, protecting the flame in her hand. There was a slight reflection; then it was gone.

The match went out.

She lit another, moved towards the reflection and found a wall made of stone. She put a finger against the gritty surface and began walking. As she dragged her finger across the rock, a bug crawled over her hand. She ignored it.

The match flickered.

She heard rattles—not one. Not two or three: a bunch of them. Sounded like a samba dance party. Clearly, there was a family of rattlesnakes hanging out in the corner she was approaching. And she could see it *was* a corner. The flame allowed that much. Just.

"Okay," she whispered, and she moved the other way.

The match burned her finger and she dropped it; the fire went out. She walked a couple feet in darkness before she decided to light another match.

A thought came: I'm almost out of matches, why not light the matchbook and have a moment of real fire?

At first she thought it was risky move, but it wasn't really. She was losing her fire anyhow, and after counting the matches by touch, she knew she only had three left. A moment slipped past while she considered the alternative, which seemed to be having three little fires that were next to useless anyhow.

"Screw it," she said.

Without pulling the matchstick from the booklet, she bent the match around its package, rubbed the phosphorus end against the striking surface and ignited the match.

"Yes," she whispered, reveling in a moment of success.

She pushed the flame against the two fresh matches and they ignited too.

For a brief moment the fire was significant. She could see the ceiling, the floor, two of the walls and the outline of the coffin all at the same time. And in that moment she also found what she was looking for: the door. Relieved as she was at finding the door, it wasn't what captured her attention. The ceiling was a living blanket of bats, hanging by their feet, clinging to the rafters. Dark, leathery wings wrapped their bodies like jackets.

She made a quick assessment; her estimate was two hundred creatures. Maybe more. *Probably more*, she thought. She put a hand to her mouth, holding back a chuckle. Not that something funny was happening, heaven no. Seeing a ceiling loaded with hundreds of bats was both startling and terrifying at the same time. But Stephenie felt so nervous and on edge she thought she might laugh anyhow, just to keep sane.

She lowered the flame, and her stare. Looked at the floor.

With no snakes slithering in her direction, she approached the door, touched it, found a handle and pushed.

Nothing happened.

She pulled.

The door opened and light entered the tomb. Not sunlight, moonlight.

Stephenie grinned once again, this time feeling a good-sized touch of relief. She thought she was home free.

Of course, she wasn't.

There was an iron gate blocking her way. She grabbed it with her free hand and discovered that the gate was locked, or at the very least, secured. But this was still good, all things considered. She had found the exit. Now she had light—things were going in the right direction. If she could get out of the mausoleum without getting chomped by a rattlesnake or attacked by a swarm of bats, things would be a whole lot better still.

Stephenie dropped the book of matches, even though the fire still burned. She didn't need it. The moonlight was quite bright; she could see its bloated curves above a sea of tombstones, a few scattered trees and the roll of several hills.

"Please," she whispered, with her spirits rising slightly. "Time to get out of here."

She heard something creak and she felt her stomach tighten. As she turned around, her eyes found the coffin.

At first there was nothing to see. Then there was.

The coffin lid was lifting.

And something was getting out.

3

Stephenie's shoulders sagged as her bottom lip trembled. She watched a small hand push the coffin lid open like it didn't weigh a thing. Once the lid was in place the hand lowered. The body in the casket sat up, but not quickly. The thing inside the box wasn't in a hurry. Dead things don't hurry.

The thing was a child, as Stephenie assumed it would be. And this child had a poise and composure that chilled Stephenie to the bone; it moved like it had all the time in the world. It moved like it was...

It was Carrie.

Stephenie swallowed back the lump in her throat.

Carrie's head tilted from one side to the other, breeding a twisted grin. Her eyes glowed, rolling in their sockets like slow moving spheres. They seemed to grow larger and rounder as they focused on Stephenie's petrified face. But the rest of her face was empty, expressionless—hollow. Even her smirk seemed to be without depth or meaning. She held the ultimate poker face: deadpan, pinched, and somehow not altogether there. Carrie's arid encompassing eyes were nearly vacant too, but there was something inside, something terrible hiding behind the dull glare, something that didn't seem like Carrie one bit.

A cold and tiny hand, pale beyond description, gripped the side of the box. Knees lifted, pallid and dehydrated. Carrie leaned forward, making evaluations and judgments with her gaze. She almost seemed to be floating, almost but not quite. There was a skillful grace that came with her movements, an un-spoken elegance that whispered dire refinement.

Stephenie felt the black-iron gate behind her. Her fingers circled a picket for support. She thought about the gate. If the gate was locked she was in trouble. If it was merely latched she could unhook the handle, push the door open, and be free of this monster—if she found the courage.

But this wasn't a monster. It was Carrie, wasn't it?

The child crept free of her box, legs pouring over the edge of the coffin, bare toes curled inward like a talons on a stick. Her body drifted towards the ground gracefully, elegantly. Stephenie heard the exposed feet touching the earth and stone, and she realized how quiet everything had become. The bugs weren't chirping or squeaking, the snakes weren't rattling their tails; the bats, flies, and moths, were no longer flapping their wings. Everything was quiet. Everything was still. Perhaps the insects and the animals were demonstrating their admiration for the greater being. Or maybe they were showing their fear. Or maybe, just maybe, the child was controlling them.

Carrie, dressed in her favorite nightgown, the one she wore every night before bed, placed one foot in front of the other, licked her lips, held out her hands, and moved towards Stephenie—grinning, more now than before; her long sharp fangs sat exaggerated inside her tiny mouth.

Vampire's teeth...

Stephenie's heart pounded her chest like a mallet on a drum and her fingers tightened around the picket, but the rest of her body didn't move. Part of her mind was thinking, *run!* But a bigger part—the component being dominated by the vampire's yearning—was thinking: *Stay in the tomb, get down on your knees, extend your neck, let it happen!*

The child's eyes glowed a little brighter as she crept across the ancient vault. Eyes gleamed inside dark shells hauntingly.

Stephenie's legs shook; her teeth chattered. She felt cold now, like she was dying.

She wasn't. The icy chill was coming from Carrie's skin, cooling Stephenie's blood.

Carrie said, *"Mother."* But her voice was not her own. There was no soul in that voice, no compassion, just an empty space; an impassive hate that dwelled from a time long past. *"Mother, not only to me. But to the world."*

Stephenie dropped to her knees. She heard herself saying, "Yes. I'm yours."

A feeling of dread came. Stephenie didn't want to say those words; Lord knows she didn't mean them. But she did say them. It seemed she had no choice. The vampire's will was dominant and she was powerless against it. She wondered what would happen next and was afraid to search for answers.

Carrie opened her mouth slightly; she leaned closer than before. A pause. *"Do you remember me?"*

Stephenie nodded. "Of course."

"No," the thing whispered. *"Not my shell. Of course you recognize the image of your daughter. But do you know who I am? Do you remember me?"*

Stephenie wasn't being forced into specific answers, not now. Maybe she never was. Maybe she was just so overwhelmed her mind snapped. Was it feasible? Oh yes, it definitely was. But now her will had returned (and maybe it never left); she could answer the question as she wished. She could lie or speak the truth. But what *was* the truth? If this wasn't Carrie, what was it? Another trick? Another hallucination? Some creature dressed in Carrie's skin?

"I don't know," she said as tears leaked from her eyes. "I don't who you are."

"Yes you do, Stephenie. Think."

Stephenie shook her head. "No, I don't know. I don't remember." But she did, a little. She knew that voice, she just didn't know why.

The thing that looked like Carrie, said: *"I told you Stephenie— that night inside your room, the night you still revisit in your dreams, that you... you're the one. The dead will rise for you. It will be the beginning of the end, the beginning of the apocalypse. No one will hear you scream. No one will hear your voice. They won't believe your words no matter how much you try to convince them. They will discredit you and your actions. They will call you names behind your back and say you're the one at fault; you're the one responsible, never once thinking you might be their savior, you might be the one they should fall upon their knees and praise!"*

Stephenie's eyes grew large. She remembered those words, those terrible and confounded words. She whispered "no" once again, but this time there was no truth in her voice. Oh God. Oh dear God. What was happening?

What did it all mean?

"Stephenie," the thing wearing Carrie's husk said.

"No."

"Listen to me."

"I don't want this. I don't want *any* of this!"

"You don't understand this, that's the truth. You don't understand the gift that you have been given, but soon enough you will. Soon you'll understand everything and more. You will fulfill your destiny, and all the world will bow before you. You are the chosen one. You are the savior."

"This is crazy. I want my old life back."

The child's eyes shifted—saddened, if it was possible. *"Your old life is gone, Stephenie. It is gone forever. Let it go. Embrace the future. That is what you have now."*

"Maybe I don't want to let the past go. Maybe I don't want the future."

"But you need to let the past lie, and you will. For what it's worth Stephenie Paige, mother to the world, savior of us all, I'm sorry they mistreated you. They didn't know how dear you really are. They didn't know your true merit. But I do, Stephenie. I do. And sooner than you think, others will know your true significance as well."

"Who? Who doesn't know how dear I am?"

Carrie lifted her hand and her fingers fluttered. With obvious distaste, she said, *"You know of whom I speak: them."*

Stephenie looked at the fluttering fingers. All of Carrie's fingers were attached and accounted for. She wasn't sure if this was good news or bad. She wasn't sure if there was any Carrie inside this monster or not. Everything was so confusing. Nothing was stable or everlasting. Nothing was consistent. With her eyes closed, she asked, "What are you?"

A smile. *"Soon, I shall be your servant. I shall be the Renfield to your Dracula."*

Still on her knees, Stephenie opened her eyes. *"My* Dracula? What does that mean?"

"Yes Stephenie, your *Dracula. You know about literature, don't you? Of course you do. But first, before that is to happen, before I am to be the servant at your side, I am to be your host. The giver to your eternal life, the hand which is to feed—and for that I am both honored and grateful."*

"I don't understand any of this!"

Moving closer. *"Again, I must say it. Soon you will understand everything and more. All will be explained, in time. You have one more death in this realm, Stephenie. Just one. And my hand shall be the hand that delivers your death and seals your fate. After that, you and I shall return to the place in which you desire—you and I, almost together. You first... alone; then after a short while I shall join you. Soon, everything begins."*

"But I don't—"

The vampire clutched Stephenie's wrist with one hand. Her fingers felt like ice. With her other hand, she tapped her index finger against her temple. *"Remember this, and you will understand, Stephenie. Just one more death in this realm, and you will!"*

She tapped her finger against her temple again and again.

And Stephenie didn't know why.

4

The vampire opened her mouth, and leaned forward.

Stephenie pulled back, but she had nowhere to go. She felt her neck extending despite what she wanted. Fangs penetrated her skin. Muscles contracted. Sharp frightful pain shocked her neck and spine and rolled through her body like an arctic current. She released a high-pitched squeal; her eyes watered and her lips pressed together. She could feel the child-thing sucking the blood from her body by the mouthful. The vampire's cold lips and tongue grew warmer as her own body turned to frost. She wanted to draw away, escape the vampire's embrace. She couldn't. She felt like a fly caught in a spider's web, wrapped in silk and being devoured. She remembered the vampire's words: *One more death in this realm; my hand shall be the hand that delivers your death and seals your fate...*

She thought, *Oh please, no more.*

Then something changed—everything changed.

The pain increased. She felt an unexpected hot flash rip through her body. An overwhelming amount of ecstasy came rushing in, submerging her, drowning her, erasing the pain and engulfing her. It was a heavy wave of delight and bliss, a sexual pleasure that rippled through her thighs and made the moonlight in her eyes sparkle. Her nipples hardened and her pussy turned hot and wet. Her hands grasped at nothing before they found the child's shoulders. Feet kicked. Then she found herself pushing her neck *into* the bite, trying to make it happen, wanting it to happen. If she could bottle the feeling and save it for later she would. If she could spend the rest of eternity in that moment, she would do that too. She loved what was happening, loved the way it felt, the way it made her feel. She never wanted it to end.

Something in her body exploded and her eyes rivered.

"Ooooh God," she whispered, knowing now that the explosion was her first massive orgasm, unlike anything she had experienced before. "Oh God, oh God."

But this wasn't about God. This was adjacent to God. This act of flesh, blood, and lust, was an abomination that stood defiant against all things good and pure. Stephenie knew it; she knew it as soon as the dead child's lips fouled her skin. This had *nothing* to do with God. It had to do with something else, something primitive and evil. Satanic.

Stephenie felt a second enormous orgasm taking her and her body began to quake. Her eyes grew blurry and her fingers curled tight. She fell back against the iron gate, moaning, writhing, pushing her hips and her chest out as her toes tingled.

The vampire continued feeding. It licked its lips and drank her blood.

A splash of hot juices escaped, rolled down Stephenie's chest and belly; it dripped to the floor. She closed her eyes; her heart clunked inside her chest.

It slowed; she was dying, dying...

Dead.

The thing that looked like Carrie pulled away and wiped the blood from her face. She looked at Stephenie, her Master—the selected one. A smile came, brimming with twisted delight.

Time passed.

Stephenie's heart was useless now, a dead muscle inside her chest. It wasn't beating. It was still. It was still, yet her eyes fluttered and her body shifted. Her mouth opened and she expelled her last breath from the time before, the realm before.

She said, *"Where am I?"* Her voice was different now. It was empty and hollow; like Carrie's voice.

"Sit up Stephenie," the child-thing responded. *"Sit up; tell me how you feel."*

Stephenie sat up, dizzy and disoriented. *"I feel hungry."*

The child-thing grinned. *"That's good. And what do you see?"*

Stephenie looked away from the vampire child; she eyed the mausoleum walls around her. Everything seemed different now; she could see so much. The casket was gleaming. The dark corners shimmered. The darkness inside the tomb was gone, replaced with a brilliant, colorless glow. It was like seeing everything in black and white—only it was perfectly luminous and shimmering with radiance. The colors were desiccated, not dull exactly, but dreary. Things glittered with a lifeless hue that was toned down and immaculate at the same time.

She could see the world like never before.

She looked up.

Bats hung from the ceiling, standing together and facing her. Their bodies danced and quivered.

On the floor, snakes had curled in the corners of the tomb and mice scurried beneath the casket. Seeing the snakes and the mice together was as strange as it was amazing. They cared not about each other now; all eyes were on Stephenie.

Stephenie's focus modified again. She could see spiders, crickets, moths, ants, millipedes and flies. Everything living inside the tomb, she could see them all.

And she liked it.

"It's beautiful," Stephenie whispered.

The vampire child lifted her wrist and offered it to her Master.

She said, *"Drink from me. Let me be the first to feed you. But I beg, do not drink too much, for it will be the end of both of us if you do."*

Stephenie considered the vampire child's words, but only for a moment. Then she wrapped her fingers around the wrist. The little one's skin felt warmer now than before. After running her tongue across her teeth, Stephenie realized they felt sharper, different—more powerful.

The vampire child spoke words that were contradictory to Stephenie's thoughts. She said, *"The teeth—they do not grow at once,*

251

Master... but over time. Taste me, for it is what you want. I know this to be true. Taste me now and rest; then it shall begin."

Stephenie grinned before she bit into the vampire's flesh, not knowing if she was biting Carrie or if it was just another trick. At that moment, she didn't care. She drank the child's blood by the mouthful regardless, but not for very long. When she was finished her wicked and immoral act of debauchery the vampire child stood up with blood flowing along her hand and off her fingers. Drops of blood trickled like rain. Her body was colder now. Not as cold as it was before she had taken Stephenie's life, but close. She did not mind, and if she did, she did not show it.

Carrie unhooked the gate's latch and led Stephenie outside, but before she did, Stephenie asked a question.

"Do you have a name?"

The vampire nodded. "My birth name is Cameron. I come from a town called Cloven Rock. It burned to the ground, not long ago."

"Cameron."

"Cameron English. But you can call me Carrie if you wish."

They stepped outside. The first thing Stephenie noticed was an old maple tree. It was huge and completely devoid of leaves. The branches hung over the mausoleum like giant fingers. Past the tree, she saw that the graveyard was enormous, beyond enormous—titanic. Tombstones were laid out in every direction. Some were large and some were small. Some were rounded and simple while others were huge monstrosities with stone demons sitting upon great mantles. There were stones shaped like winged cherubs and stones that had turned green with age. They littered every roll of every hill... every roll, but one. And in that one direction—at the foot of a grassy knoll, behind a fifteen-foot, cast iron gate—was a single village.

Stephenie perceived the community to be a small settlement of no more than a few thousand souls. Light inside the district was negligible. She gazed at the town and the graves before it like she had never seen anything so beautiful in her life.

This wasn't life, however, this was death, or un-death—where everything old was new again.

The vampire child stood close by while Stephenie took it all in. She held Stephenie's hand. Together they walked across an acre of the necropolis. Stephenie turned back only once, eyeing the tomb she had come from and the tree that hung over it. Hand in hand, they entered another crypt, this one, larger than the first. A coffin sat in the center of the space. It was open and empty, clean and waiting for its occupant to arrive. There were no bats, no bugs, no vermin nor snakes. The vault was kept empty as if by magic.

The vampire child said, *"This is yours, valued one. Nothing will bother you here. Sleep now, for the sun will rise too soon. Sleep now, and tomorrow night we'll feed. You and I together, we'll feed."*

Stephenie took the vampire child in her arms, and gave her a little kiss. *Yes,"* she said. *"Tomorrow night we'll feed."*

The vampire child smiled a creepy, twisted smile.

She couldn't have seemed happier.

5

Stephenie's eyes opened. She pushed the coffin's lid away and sat up. The mausoleum was dark but she had no problem seeing. The nighttime was her time, her *only* time. Things were clear and easy to define.

She crept from the casket and away from her tomb.

The graveyard was stunning. She had never seen such a gorgeous landscape.

She glanced at the other vault, the one that held the vampire child beneath the tree with no leaves. She remembered what the little one had said: *Tomorrow night we'll feed. You and I together, we'll feed.*

Upon awaking Stephenie saw this statement in a new light. Without a doubt, the child *was* waiting for her inside her mausoleum. The little one, she now understood, truly was her servant——the Renfield to Stephenie's Dracula. And knowing this, or perhaps *because* of this, Stephenie felt nothing for the girl. The girl could sit in her tomb and wait; Stephenie did not care what the girl did, or if she did anything at all. The vampire child spoke of feeding together, not as a teacher showing a student how something was to be accomplished, but as the weak hoping to tag along with the strong. There was much that Stephenie didn't know, and truth be told, many things the vampire child could teach her. But these things were of minor importance. These things could be discussed at a later time, at Stephenie's leisure, not at the vampire child's request. Dealing with them now would only confuse matters. Going to the child now, a precedent would be set, one that would later need to be un-set. Stephenie was the

Master. The vampire child was the servant. How this came to be, she did not know. Perhaps the vampire child could explain, perhaps not. Perhaps the answers would never be revealed.

Mother to the world.

Savior to them all.

She walked.

Over the hills, through the graves, towards the town, she walked. Alone.

Upon arriving at the gates that separated the village from the land of the dead, she paused. This was a great night, her first night—a night to be remembered.

She looked at the gate.

There was a sign on the gate that read: BLEEDINGTON NECROPOLIS.

Stephenie grinned.

Bleedington, she thought. *What a fitting name for the town.*

Her thoughts shifted to the vampire child sitting alone in her tomb.

Stephenie made a decision: she would not be selfish on this night; she would be generous, giving—masterful. For this was a night of significance, a night all others would be weighed against and Stephenie wanted her servant to know she could be benevolent and compassionate as well as cruel. Her night of celebratory consumptions would be one of teaching, of playing both sides of the deck, of articulating her skills as the ascendant one.

She closed her eyes and inhaled and exhaled a deep, exaggerated breath into lungs that would otherwise remain motionless. The breath was not for respiration purposes, for breathing was no longer an obligation. Stephenie inhaled to consume the scents and aromas of the community at her feet. She could smell and taste them, all of them. Like rats in a pen, they were. She took a moment, filtering one fragrance from the next. There were so many choices, so many tastes to choose from. Most were old and souring. Some were vibrant and lush. A few were exotic;

many were bland. There were also children, fresh and delightful and brimming with a sweet pleasant scent.

A trio of flavors caught her attention. And even though this was Stephenie's first night as the *thing* she had become, she knew what a rarity she had found. Her lips curled and her eyes gleamed. Luck was finally on her side.

She walked along a dirt path and onto a cobblestone road.

There were no cars on the road, no motorcycles either. For she was in a time before mechanical invention had turned the world on its head, a time when travel meant horses and wagons, and electricity was not yet conceived.

The roads of Bleedington did have lampposts however, though they were few and far between. As Stephenie made her way to the nearest post she smirked. There was a candle sitting inside four walls of thin glass. There was not enough light coming from the contraption to illuminate five feet in any direction, even though the top of the post was barely four feet from the ground. She wondered why the villagers had even bothered.

She entered an alley to avoid a pub, not to suggest that the pub was overly busy. It wasn't. Still, on her first night she didn't want any unexpected surprises, and there were a few too many patrons inside that one establishment for her liking. In many ways, she was still finding her feet and she was smart enough to know it.

She moved on, peeking in windows and watching villagers from the safety of darkness. She saw a drunken man staggering down the road and two women talking about children. She saw a couple getting friendly on a park bench, kissing and hugging and carrying on in ways only new lovers do. She saw a pair of dogs tied to a post and she kept well away from them, for animals have a keen sense of smell and intuition beyond those who are human. Often times they are not afraid of combat. Stephenie knew this instinctually.

She walked on. In time, she came to her destination.

It was a house, big and grand and without a doubt, furnished with expensive things. She stepped through an open gate and made her way to the side of the building. High above was a shuttered window. It was open, not that it mattered.

Stephenie listened.

Not trusting the things she heard, she waited. After an hour had passed Stephenie walked away from the great building. She was mildly frustrated, but mostly she was excited. Timing was everything and at that particular moment, the timing wasn't right. Soon though, soon it would be. And things would be grand.

She explored the village: the alleys and back roads, the parks and farmland. She kept her distance from the animals, although several dogs along the way caught her scent and barked in fear and agitation. They did this despite her concerns and vigilance.

She was hungry but she did not eat. The first meal of her new existence was not to be something she consumed at random, but a delicacy worth waiting for, worth remembering. It was special. And as time marched on she came to understand how perfect her selection was, how no other choice would do. Her feast would be one she remembered for an eternity, a feast to recall with great fondness, the choice of a Master.

She returned to the home of her choosing. Listened. Grinned.

She placed her hands on the stone-rock wall and began to climb. She climbed quickly and with great ease, like a spider, like a bug. When she arrived at the window and peeked inside, she found what she desired; three baby girls—triplets, less than forty days old. Each child was lying inside her own crib. They were asleep now. They were asleep and without supervision.

The girls were a true rarity.

Stephenie's first night would be a night to remember.

6

The room was large, lavishly furnished and meticulously hygienic. Not the work of an exhausted mother, but that of a staff of devoted and talented servants. There were several candles attached to each wall, but only two of them were lit. There were also several paintings of jesters, landscapes, and smiling children.

Stephenie crawled through the window.

The floor creaked beneath her feet.

On her right, a dresser sat next to a closet door. She knew it was a closet by the slender design of the doorframe. Beyond the dresser sat a single crib; the headboard faced the wall. On her left there was a shelf tastefully decorated with knickknacks and ornaments, ceramic mostly. A plant sat next to it on a small table. On the other side of the plant there were two more cribs. Again, the headboards faced the wall.

She approached the nearest crib, which was the first one on her left. A smirk crept from ear to ear. Looking down at the child she felt herself drool. She was hungry, so hungry. The need to feed had never been so great. Still, Stephenie controlled herself. She would not be a slave to her own desires, but the architect of her choices.

She listened.

The house was quiet but not everyone was sleeping. Someone was awake, however Stephenie had a feeling that someone was *always* awake inside this particular home.

If the community were larger, Stephenie figured the house would be secured behind fences and gates that most would find difficult to encroach. But the community wasn't larger, and the gate she had stepped through wasn't locked. In fact, it wasn't even closed. The doorway was an open invitation to the entire village. Perhaps the people who lived inside the home ruled the town. Perhaps they knew each person by name. Perhaps, perhaps... still, someone was awake, probably not for security reasons, but rather to keep an eye (and an ear) open for the needs of the children. Yes, that seemed about right. That seemed to fit.

The child before Stephenie had rosy pink skin. She was lost in the deepest kingdoms of sleep and buried beneath a pair of white sheets that were clean and fresh. All Stephenie could see was the baby's head, neck, and one little hand, poking out between the linen. The fingers were so tiny they were frightening. If they were any smaller they would have looked like swollen grains of rice.

Looking away from the child, Stephenie noticed the artistic design of the wooden crib for the first time. The crib was custom made by a skilled hand and loaded with subtle detail. Engraved on the headboard between a wealth of inventive swirls was a name, carved in delicate script. It read: Paisley Rae.

Paisley Rae, she thought. *That's a yummy name.*

She looked at the other two cribs—the one in front of her and the one against the opposite wall. The two other cribs were evidently the work of the same carpenter, or carpenters—for the workmanship was similar, not exact, but definitely comparable. The other two cribs were also garnished with corresponding headboards.

One read: Mandy.

The other: Cynthia.

Stephenie wet her lips and her eyes returned to the child before her, Paisley Rae.

Paisley Rae looked so innocent and beautiful that she made the heart feel weak. She was a gift to the world; it was easy to see.

Stephenie reached into the crib, rubbed a cold knuckle against the child's face and watched the baby cringe. Carefully, oh so carefully, she pulled the blankets off the child. Paisley Rae was naked, save a thick cloth that had been wrapped around her midsection for a diaper. Stephenie lifted the child and the child squirmed. She tilted Paisley Rae to one side, sniffed her like a wolf and licked the child. Then her eyes narrowed and she tore into the infant's neck.

Paisley Rae's mouth blasted open and her feet started kicking. Her eyes watered and her arms reached out. They were no longer than a pair of candlesticks. Her tiny rice-fingers stretched apart. A line of blood shot across Stephenie's cheek and the baby's body began to convulse.

Stephenie sucked harder, draining the baby of every drop she could.

Paisley Rae began to deflate like a beach ball with a hole in it. Her eyeballs drew into her skull and her lungs folded shut. Her nose compressed and her cheeks sucked in. Lips turned white, then blue. Wrinkles were formed in places that no wrinkles should have been.

Stephenie consumed the infant until there was nothing more to swallow. She dumped the empty shell into the crib and stormed across the room with her back arched, her hands grasping and her eyes shining like fire.

The floor thumped beneath her feet.

She reached into the next crib, Mandy's crib.

She grabbed the baby by the face, yanked her from the bedding and rammed the tiny body against her lips. Her teeth bit down twice, three times. She chewed on the child ravenously. The slightest cry escaped the Mandy's lips; then Stephenie's teeth (not fangs, oh no—she didn't have fangs, not yet) tore a mouthful of flesh away.

Stephenie spat the meat out as blood poured on the floor. Attaching her lips to the wound, she sucked the blood fiercely. She sucked harder now than she did with the first child. She sucked with all the strength she had. The baby's limbs curled like a bug held above a flame. Intestines contracted and veins tore into pieces. Her eyes popped into her skull. Bones snapped, cracked and crunched. They sounded like twigs beneath a foot, like a campfire crackle.

Stephenie was lost inside her own world, her own time. She was in love with the moment; the children tasted so good, so pure—so true.

An orgasm came, taking her, washing over her, overwhelming her.

She sucked Mandy more and more, draining her completely. She squeezed Mandy's face in her hand and Mandy's skull caved in. A spider web of splits appeared in the child's pink skin and her skull cracked apart like a hardboiled egg. Bones smashed together and the girl's tiny brain squished out, fell between Stephenie's fingers and dropped onto the floor. Stephenie tossed the shriveled, empty infant into the crib. The withered and mangled corpse banged against the posh wooden pickets.

One more child, she thought. *One more, and I'll surely come again.*

Before she had arrived at the home, Stephenie thought she would take the third infant back to the graveyard and offer it to the vampire child that lived behind Carrie's façade. Now she knew that doing such a thing was impossible. She couldn't share these gifts—these three wonderful gifts—any more than she could command herself to leave the third child alone. Drinking the children's blood was a pleasure beyond anything she had ever hoped to experience. This was a feeding frenzy—nothing more, nothing less.

She spun around, grinning as blood dripped from her chin. Her eyes were shining impossibly bright. She looked at the third child, Cynthia.

Then she heard it.

Something that was—

7

The bedroom door blasted open.

Tiffany White, a housemaid and servant to the children, stood in the doorway. She had light skin and long brown hair. She held a fireplace poker in one hand and a lantern in the other. She heard the ruckus and thought there was a wolf in the room.

In many ways, she was right.

Tiffany saw Stephenie's outline in the glow the moonlight, courtesy of the open window. She saw a flickering of features from the light of the candles. She saw the fire in the vampire's eyes and felt her heart drop into her feet.

Stephenie hissed at the woman—she actually hissed, like the rattlesnakes in the crypt.

Tiffany gasped and flinched. She stumbled back; then she forced herself to step forward, stand tall; defend the children.

She shouted, "What are you doing here!? You're not welcome here! Get out! Now!"

Her words were strapping but there was terror in that voice. Real terror. Deep down, emerging from her soul, childlike, terror. Tiffany was not the smartest woman in the village but she was not dumb either, and she was well aware that eyes were not meant to glow in the dark. Not ever. Wasn't right; it wasn't natural. If she lived to tell the tale she'd be plagued with nightmares for years. Those eyes were wrong. Those eyes were immoral.

The third infant, Cynthia, released a weak sounding wail.

Stephenie hissed a second time and moved towards the housemaid with her blood stained teeth exposed.

Tiffany screamed, "Mister and Misses McCullagan! We have an intruder here! Doctor McCullagan!" She was about to say more but then she caught a better glimpse of Stephenie's ghoulish features and her mouth snapped shut. She felt a tremble in her knees and wondered if she might fall over.

This *thing* that stood before her 'twas the devil, plain and simple.

Stephenie heard the rumble of feet coming down the hallway; her time was short. After a slight pause, her eyes shifted towards the last remaining newborn and she licked her lips.

Cynthia McCullagan, currently weighing fourteen pounds, three ounces—who had just been robbed of her two sisters—opened her mouth wide and released her first boisterous cry of the night.

Tiffany snapped her head into the hallway and saw Mister and Misses McCullagan running before being promptly shoved aside.

Mister and Misses McCullagan exploded in the room.

Tiffany's lantern bounced up and down erratically. Shadows bounced across the walls at random.

Seeing the babies' parents, Stephenie knew her time had run out. She took one large step towards Tiffany with anger mashed into her features. She tightened her fingers into rakes and lashed out, tearing Tiffany's throat apart.

Blood speckled the air and splashed against the shadowy wall in a thick L-shaped splotch.

Tiffany fell to her knees as gore dropped from her neck in lumps. The fireplace poker slipped from her fingers and landed with a CLANG. The lantern fell onto its side and the fire beneath the glass burned brighter.

Misses Marion McCullagan, mother of the children, screamed.

Bruce McCullagan, who was the town's chief doctor, sounded a bit like a stage actor in a play when he said, "Oh my goodness! What's happening here?"

Bruce didn't know it, but his tone didn't fit the moment. He sounded like he discovered the neighbor's kids stealing apples from his tree. But this wasn't apple-theft; this was a triple murder and two of the victims were his children.

In the man's defense—assuming Doctor McCullagan deserved one—he didn't have a clue what was happening. He didn't know Paisley Rae and Mandy had been drained of their fluids and discarded like trash. He didn't know his favorite servant (and if he was to be honest with himself, his good friend) was literally dying at his feet. He didn't know what the problem was or what might have caused it. He just stepped through the door. One minute earlier he had been lost in sleep, dreaming about horses. Point is, Doctor McCullagan didn't know anything and his lack of authority was proof.

As blood ran from Stephenie's claw-like hand, she spun around, made a quick dash towards the third crib and snatched Cynthia by the throat. She yanked the child from the bed with a high-pitched screech.

Cynthia's face, shoulder and arm slammed against footboard.

A terrible newborn cry was heard throughout the room.

Tiffany, gagging and bleeding, lost consciousness. She fell onto her face, breaking her nose and smashing several teeth free. Didn't matter. She didn't need the teeth anyhow. In another thirty seconds she'd be dead.

With the child gripped between her fingers, Stephenie made for the window.

Marion McCullagan clipped her scream and rubbed her eyes. Staggering forward she managed to shout, "What are you doing with *MY BABY? My baby! My baby!* What are you doing with *MY BABY?*" Her words echoed through the house.

Doctor McCullagan—a man that had once fasted for eleven days because God willed it (how's that for doctoring?)—looked at his wife, considering her words. He was taken back by how upset she had become, and was yet to put the pieces of the puzzle together. "Oh my goodness," he said, more firmly this time than before. "What's happening here?" He was like a broken record, a needle skipping over the same phrase. "Oh my goodness," he said for a third time. "What's happening here?" It was almost funny.

Stephenie grabbed the window's ledge with her free hand and tossed herself through the opening. She fell twenty-eight feet, still holding Cynthia by the throat. Upon landing, Stephenie tumbled onto her back and the child slipped from her grasp.

Little baby Cynthia slammed into the earth headfirst; her miniature body crunched.

Stephenie leapt onto her feet. She grabbed the little one by the leg and started running, sprinting.

Missis Marion McCullagan ran to the window and watched Stephenie go. She couldn't help noticing that her child never screamed. But *she* did. She opened her mouth wide and screamed loud enough for both of them. And beneath her cries she could hear her husband's voice.

He said, "Oh my goodness! What's happening here?"

At that moment, the man was an idiot.

8

Stephenie ran across the lawn and through the open gate. She ran down the street and into an alley. She could hear shouts and cries and screaming and cursing. Upon turning a corner, she came face to face with an old man that had one too many at the 'ole watering hole. The man's name was Bill Wessington. He had a red nose, starry eyes, and was as bald as a freshly picked peach.

Bill burped, stumbled, and said, "Uh-ha... Pardon me, my lady!" His voice was loud and his words sounded like they were overflowing with the letter 's.'

Stephenie grabbed the old drunk by the hair, yanked his head back and snapped open her mouth. Before he even knew it was coming she bit into his greasy neck and blood splashed in three separate directions. Gurgles, burbles, bubbles and babbles—all this, followed by Bill's hands shooting into the air and his left knee buckling. He fell onto himself, bleeding from the throat and nose, smelling like a barstool, dying where she left him.

Someone screamed and Stephenie kept running, still holding Cynthia by the leg. The child was hanging upside down with her head clipping off Stephenie's leg with every stride she took. Bruises formed and blood drained from both ears.

More screams were heard.

Someone blew a whistle.

Stephenie turned a corner, and a man stepped in front of her. He was tall, skinny, and missing several teeth. Without a moments hesitation Stephenie smashed the man in the face, using the child as a club.

The man fell onto his back as the bones inside Cynthia's body snapped.

Dogs barked and alley cats found shelter where they could. Birds took flight from a nearby fence.

Stephenie ran and ran. When things turned quiet she headed for home, which is to say she made for the graveyard. Upon arriving she went straight to the vampire child's tomb. She plowed her way inside and the vampire child was there, sitting against the wall, next to the family of snakes.

As Stephenie's eyes fell upon her, the vampire child said, *"Hello Master. Did you have a nice night without me?"*

Stephenie, still holding Cynthia like a bag of trash, could hear the contempt in the vampire's voice. She said, *"You ungrateful bitch! Don't you ever speak to me that way! Understand?"*

The vampire child looked to the floor, disgraced.

Stephenie was right, of course. It wasn't her place to flaunt such a scornful display of disdain. *"I apologize, Master. It's just that… I thought you and I would enter the town together. Last night you showed such affection, I thought things were different than they are. Now I know the truth, honest I do. I won't make the same mistake twice. You have my word."*

Stephenie flung the baby across the tomb like a playing card; Cynthia's tiny, battered frame spun around in a circle and crashed into the vampire child's chest.

"I brought you this, didn't I? Is the prize of Bleedington not enough?"

The vampire child lifted Cynthia by an arm. She was about to say the baby was dead, and drinking blood that no longer flowed was something neither of them should do. Then she saw that little Cynthia *wasn't* dead. She was alive. She was horribly bruised and swollen. Her bones were broken and her eyes were black, but she was breathing. Not much, but some. The vampire child said, *"Thank you Master. You are both wise and kind. I shall never doubt you again."* She bit into Cynthia's neck, devouring the baby fluids ravenously. When she was finished, she tossed the baby's corpse in the snakes.

267

Time passed. The two vampires spent their minutes brooding.

After twenty minutes had passed, Stephenie said, *"I made a mess down there, in town."*

The vampire child nodded. *"I know. I heard."*

"Do you think they will come?"

"Did you leave evidence of what we are?"

Stephenie's eyes fell to the floor. She considered lying but decided against it. *"Yes. Quite a bit of evidence, I'm afraid."*

The vampire child seemed to know this already. She said, *"Then yes. They will come. They will hunt us like dogs. Maybe not today, but soon."*

Stephenie's brow furrowed. She walked to the door, looked across the graveyard and at the town that sat below it. The view was still beautiful, but now everything was tainted. Bleedington seemed to have grown teeth in the last few hours, if only in her mind. She said, *"What should we do? Is there anywhere we can go?"*

The vampire child shook her head. *"The night is almost over. Soon the sun will rise. There is nowhere for us to go tonight."*

"Are there no other tombs?"

The vampire child masked a tone that bordered on condescending, and spoke as if she had already considered the situation. *"The graveyard is massive, but there are only thirteen crypts in all. Is one safer than the next? I think not. When they come, they will check each vault systematically. If they come today, they will find us."*

"Well… what shall we do?"

"We will do the only thing we can do. We will sleep, and if tomorrow night comes, we shall enter the town once again. We shall take residence and feed from within."

"Take residence inside the town? That's madness!"

"No Master. It's not madness, if you don't mind me saying so. We shall exterminate a family, maybe two, but nobody of significance… the act should go unnoticed easy enough. We shall dwell inside the family's home. No one will search for us there. No one will enter the residence unannounced and uninvited. By the time the villagers realize the family is missing, we will

have moved on to another family. We shall travel from place to place, feeding voraciously on those with little value to the town. We shall stay one step ahead of those who oppose us. It won't be easy, but it's our best plan, perhaps our only plan. You see Master, it won't be long before they check the tombs, not if you left ample confirmation of our existence."

"Maybe we should go into the village now. Find a place…"

The vampire child shook her head. *"We don't have time Master… not to find the right place. Not to make us safe. In twenty minutes the sun will rise. Twenty minutes, that's not long at all. Entering the town now will work against us, not for us. It is in our best interest to stay where we are."*

Stephenie opened her mouth but she did not speak.

A few minutes later she returned to her crypt, wondering how dire her mistakes truly were. Slept came easy enough though, and her sleep felt wonderful—for a while. She woke earlier than expected.

Much earlier.

9

Arthur McNeill was a simple man, a good man. He didn't learn much in the way of schooling, and when it came to being employed, he took what he could get. Often times, he was jobless. Other times he worked inside town's only sewer. And sometimes, when luck was upon him, he was a gravedigger.

Arthur liked being a gravedigger. Working with a shovel in Bleedington's necropolis was hard, objectionable work—of course. But he endured it, and over time he began to enjoy the vocation. He wasn't the graveyard *caretaker*, Lord no. *That* job was actually pleasant, and it belonged to a man named Ed Patch. If Patch stepped down and the position was offered to Arthur, he'd take it in a heartbeat. Why? Well for one, the job was yard-work mostly. Yard-work was good work. For two, yard-work came with a steady paycheck. And for three—and this is the big one, kiddies—the job was *a job*. A job that was too good for Ed Patch, who wasn't anything like the trade he sustained, which is to say he wasn't pleasant. Patch was a grumpy old fart that wouldn't sell a glass of water to a man with his pants on fire.

No, Arthur McNeill wasn't the graveyard caretaker; he was a *gravedigger*.

He dug holes that needed to be dug.

And money came slowly, if it came at all.

∞∞∞Θ∞∞∞

The morning after Stephenie introduced herself to the town, Arthur woke up learning that two new graves were needed.

Patch had dropped by and told him the news, saying—in a guarded, *don't say anything* kind of way—that the two graves might soon become three. Doctor McCullagan's newborn children had suffered some type of illness.

News of this kind always struck Arthur in opposing ways. He was glad to have more work; denying it would be a lie because earning a paycheck was always welcome. But he also felt sad to hear that someone died. Arthur had a big heart, and because of it, today's news pushed all kinds of strange buttons.

A dead child was a terrible loss. Not just for Doctor McCullagan and his wife, but for the entire town. Multiply one dead child by two and terrible loss becomes tragedy. Multiply it by three and tragedy becomes disaster. Disasters are never good. But on the other hand, a disaster meant that Arthur might land three jobs in a single day and that was cause for a celebration. Toss in the fact the deceased children came from one of the wealthiest families in the village and that meant that he didn't need to deal with people applying for the underprivileged-discount credit. This was a full-pay contract, people—the big bucks. Plus child graves were smaller than adult graves. This meant the workload got cut in half while the salary stayed the same. *(A grave is a grave, don't ya know?)* And digging a hole for an infant, as sad as it is to do, is the easiest grave to dig.

An hour after Arthur heard the news of the infants deaths, Patch returned. He said two graves had just become four. Not because of the third child, but because Bill Wessington and Tiffany White were also dead. Patch offered no more information than that.

The news was absolutely terrible. Wessington was a good man to drink with and White was a good woman to look at. But four graves, possibly five. Wow. It was the most work Arthur had been offered in years.

Around 1pm, Boyle Scott, the town's Mayor, arrived at Arthur McNeill's front door. Mayor Scott told Arthur a similar story to the one Patch had told, although the Mayor didn't mention Bill Wessington and Tiffany White, at least, not right away. His focus was the children.

As the Mayor spoke, Arthur found himself stunned.

Being asked to dig holes didn't usually come from high up. Being told that two baby-holes might become three *(but keep that under your hat, good man, for the love of the Virgin Mary!)* added to his surprise. Not because of the dead children, and not because he needed to keep it under his hat. (And how *under the hat* can the information be if he heard about it twice before noon? Not very—that was *his* thinking.) The astonishing part came when Mayor Scott told Arthur that the children weren't just dead; they had been *murdered*. Somehow, this part of the story hadn't been shared with him, probably because Patch didn't know.

For fifteen minutes or more the men talked about the horrific tragedy (the deaths, not the killer) in all kinds of ways except one: just why the Mayor was standing at Arthur's front door in the first place. There was a slight pause in the conversation, and both men knew the time for answers had come.

Mayor Scott said, "Arthur, I need your help. Doctor McCullagan needs your help. In fact, the entire *town* needs your help, although most folks in town don't yet know it."

Arthur rubbed a hand across the stubble on his chin. He looked a little like a man yanked from a concession stand and asked to play quarterback at the Super Bowl.

He said, "Anything, you want, Mayor Scott."

The Mayor, who was a nice enough guy with a gigantic belly (that he sometimes referred to it as 'the bucket'), said, "You can call me, Boyle, Arthur. Truth is, I'd prefer it if you do. I might be Mayor Scott, but I'm also just a man. And I'll still be a man after the title of *Mayor* gets handed to someone else."

Arthur nodded. He said, "Okay." But he didn't call the man Boyle. Not once. It didn't seem right. Boyle Scott had been Mayor for twenty-two years and most people figured he'd be Mayor for twenty-two more. He was a man of the people, and it was comments like the one he just unloaded that kept him in charge.

Boyle said, "I didn't come here to talk to you about digging holes, as I'm sure you can imagine." He paused. "Bleedington is not a big place, which is to say the people that live here know everybody. And if you don't know somebody, you've probably seen 'em around. I've seen *you* around, Arthur. Oh yes I have. I know you're a good man that deserves more from life than life has given you." Boyle paused again, looking thoughtful this time, looking the way a Mayor should.

Arthur considered saying something, but he didn't have anything to add and he thought silence was a respectable policy that kept him from getting in trouble.

Boyle put his hands together and looked at them.

He said, "Bruce McCullagan is my friend. I was with the Doc and his family when his wife Marion gave birth. There were *four* children born that night. Not three, *four*. Four girls. Did you know that?" He looked up. "Probably not... I suppose most people don't." He looked down. "After eighteen hours of pushing and screaming Marion gave birth to all four girls within an hour and a half. The forth one came out in a pile of blood. The child was... well, what I'm trying to say is, she wasn't ready yet. She wasn't... *formed*. The poor thing had no arms and no legs, no neck either—she was just a lump, really. She was a lump with a face imbedded in her chest. The face had eyes and the eyes were moving around, real alive-like, although not for very long. The child, if you could call it that, died. Marion took it poorly, very poorly. We tried to tell her to be happy with the three children that survived but she wasn't having it. We buried the lump-child in the McCullagan's backyard that night, under the light of the moon. Marion told us to do it. She didn't want the town to know what had happened."

Arthur felt uncomfortable knowing about all this stuff that was none of his business, and he didn't want to hear any more.

He cleared his throat, and said, "Mayor Scott. You don't—"

Boyle shut him down and raised his voice. "Both Bruce and his wife Marion told me the same thing this morning. They told me some terrible things through more tears than you can imagine." Boyle lifted an eyebrow. "I forgot. The housemaid is dead too. Don't know what her name was, Trisha, or Tiffany... something like that. You can add 'digging Trisha's grave' onto your to-do list. Charge it to the town; it's okay."

Arthur nodded, saying nothing. He already knew about Bill Wessington and Tiffany White and felt there was no reason to make a point of it.

Boyle White continued: "When Bruce says he knows *everyone* in Bleedington, I believe him. Not just because Bruce doesn't need to embellish things, but also because every person in town filters through his office from time to time. He might not be everyone's personal physician, but he oversees everything. I know it. Hell, everyone in town knows it."

Arthur nodded again. His mind began drifting. He was thinking now about the money he was stepping into, and where it was coming from. His economic situation was about to change.

"Bruce told me a wild story; he said a woman broke into his house and killed his daughters. He said she wasn't from around here and I have no choice but to believe him. He also said—*his words, not mine*—that the woman wasn't human."

Arthur's thoughts were suddenly swayed from finances. "Sir?"

"You heard me. Not human. A vampire. That's what Bruce said: *the woman was a vampire.*"

"But—"

Boyle pointed a finger and looked Arthur in the eye. His fat face started turning pink. His shoulders lifted. "Arthur, I like you but I don't want to have a philosophical discussion with you. When I say I need your help I'm thinking about your hands and your eyes and your knowledge concerning the graveyard. Doctor Bruce McCullagan is one of my best friends in the whole entire world, and he has suffered a deep loss and serious mental shock. He said last night's intruder wasn't a woman, but a vampire. He said her eyes were glowing in their sockets like she had candles burning inside her skull. I want to dismiss him and frankly I'm trying as hard as I can, but there's a problem too big for me to ignore. He's a smart man and he's a doctor. He knows what he knows. And he has two baby girls in his home with every last drop of blood drained from their bodies. I've *seen* them Arthur. I've seen their crumpled remains."

Arthur's eyes widened before they dropped to his shoes. He didn't know what to say.

Boyle continued: "This is what I want and this is what I'm offering: I want you to come with us. I guess I should say that Bruce has asked me go into the graveyard and check the mausoleums with him. I told him he was crazy. He told me he'd never seen the woman before in his life. He said she wasn't from around here. He said she killed Paisley Rae and Mandy. He said she grabbed Cynthia by the throat and jumped out a second story window, dragging her along like a handbag. He said the vampire's eyes were glowing like she had candles inside her skull, and she drank his daughters blood straight from their little necks. He said he has *no choice* but to check the vaults no matter how crazy that may seem. And he asked me—*as his friend*—if I would be there in his most desperate hour of need."

Boyle's pink skin started turning lobster-red and line of sweat appeared on his brow. He was getting himself worked up now. The stress he was under was starting to show. His bottom lip trembled. His Adam's apple bobbled up and down.

"Well Arthur, what am I suppose to say to my good friend Bruce? Huh? Should I say no? Maybe? Let me think about it? Should I tell him I'll get back to him some time next week? Heaven help us! I can tell you what I *said*, Mister McNeill— *Arthur*, if you *prefer*. I *said* yes! I told him yes! I said I'd help him! Of *course* I'll help him! He's my best friend! I've known the man for thirty years! Do I think there are vampires in the Bleedington graveyard? I don't know how to answer that. I really don't. The answer that comes to mind is, *No! Of course not! There are no vampires in the graveyard! That's crazy!* And do you know why? Do you know why I'm thinking that way, *Mister McNeill?* Because *VAMPIRES DON'T EXIST!* But there's a problem, Mister, a big barn-sized problem! I've seen the babies! Don't you get it? I've seen their shriveled little broken bodies! They were drained, Arthur! Their bodies are EMPTY!"

"I'm sorry, Mayor Scott," Arthur said, cutting in, looking slightly afraid. "I'm sorry for your loss. I'm sorry for Doctor McCullagan's loss too."

Boyle opened his mouth but stopped himself from speaking by slapping a hand across his lips. He breathed heavily through his fingers, pulled a handkerchief from his back pocket, and wiped sweat from his brow.

"No," he said, ashamed of himself. "It is I who must apologize. I'm upset, but I'm not upset with you. Trust me, I'm not. How could I be? I'm just upset by what I saw, and what has happened." Boyle blew his nose and wiped his eyes. "I was asked to be the children's Godfather, you know. The ceremony is scheduled for next week."

Arthur shrugged; then thought it was the wrong thing to do. He had never seen a man—any man—so upset. And this was his first time talking with the Mayor. 'Strange' didn't begin to explain the way he was feeling. This was a whole new pile of everything.

Boyle said, "I'd like you to join Doctor McCullagan and myself as we search the tombs. You know the cemetery better than we do. If there really is a vampire, or a woman who *thinks* she's a vampire, you might be able to figure out where she's hiding. Assuming we don't find anything, we'll pay you the same rate as digging five graves. If we do find something—that is to say, if we find this abomination hiding inside one of the crypts, or anywhere else you think to look—consider that number doubled. If you kill the bitch, double the number again—understood?"

Arthur nodded; his eyes widened. He wasn't good with numbers, but it occurred to him that he might soon be rich.

Boyle Scott, Bleedington's beloved Mayor, watched Arthur's expression change and his eyes grow thoughtful. He read the man's face the best he could, but he read it wrong. He said, "If you're wondering why I'm coming to you instead of Patch, it's because Patch is an asshole. Simple as that."

10

Doctor Bruce McCullagan, Mayor Boyle Scott, and Arthur 'gravedigger' McNeill, stepped inside a mausoleum and gathered around the coffin solemnly. The coffin had a simple design and sat in the center of the tomb on a concrete block that was a little over waist high.

Arthur stood near the casket's center, holding a stake in one hand and a mallet in the other. The stake was made of wood and nearly fourteen inches long. He said, "I'm ready when you are."

Mayor Scott stood as close to the box as he dared, holding a lantern near his chest. Exhaling a deep breath, he said, "Ready."

Doctor McCullagan put his hand on the lid and without too much hesitation he opened the coffin up.

Just then, two things happened that none of the men expected. First: a big cloud of stinky, ashy, dusty, human remains poofed into the air. Next: the bats that were hanging from the rafters lost their little rodent minds.

A flurry of wings and squeals exploded throughout the crypt.

All three men fled the building in a hurry, waving their hands in the air and screaming like little girls. Once they were outside——beneath the safety of the warm sun—Doctor Bruce cried, Mayor Scott consoled, and Arthur McNeill stood away from the other men feeling like a fool. He had seen the bats; he knew they were there. At least half of the tombs were loaded with them, but he didn't feel it was his place to say.

After a while the condolences ended and the men moved on.

The next crypt they entered didn't have bats clinging to the ceiling but it did have a rattlesnake in the corner, lying in a pile of bones that might have belonged to a cat. All three men saw the reptile and they kept their distance. They opened the casket in a hurry and when they discovered a corpse that looked like a dried prune wearing a stain-yellow dress, they got the hell out before the snake made a meal of them.

Doctor Bruce McCullagan didn't cry this time but he did make an observation. And when he voiced his thoughts he sounded nothing at all like the overwrought, broken record from the night before. *(Oh my goodness! What's happening here?)* He said, "If the vampire had been inside that coffin, we'd be in serious trouble right now, you better believe it. With a vampire attacking our front and a rattlesnake attacking our back, the odds of us leaving the crypt in one piece would be minimal."

Mayor Boyle Scott didn't believe that vampires were real—regardless of what the dead babies looked like and the terror that he felt when Bruce threw open the coffin's lid. He didn't want to say anything though, so he nodded his head and kept his big mouth shut. His best friend needed support and he was planning on giving it to him any way he could.

Arthur McNeill also kept quiet, but for different reasons. Today he was fortunate enough to be working with men that were—by the town's standard—rich, famous, and highly respected. He wasn't going to mess it up. Also, Doctor McCullagan was a smart man, so whatever he was thinking was fine. After all, Doctor McCullagan was a *doctor* while Arthur McNeill was a part-time gravedigger and *not* educated. He was, however, a smart enough man to recognize these truths and modest enough to accept them.

Doctor McCullagan continued with his train of thought; he said, "I'd like to finish the day without incident, so next time, let's drag the coffin outside."

Mayor Scott spoke without thinking. His voice was loud and laced with the beliefs he was trying so hard to keep locked in his belly. He said, "What if people see us? What will they say?"

"I don't care what people see," Doctor McCullagan said. "I don't care what they say either. This isn't something we should be covering up, Boyle. This is bigger than that. And if we have a nest of vampires living in our cemetery the people need to know!"

"But what if... " Boyle trailed off. He said too much already.

"You don't believe me," the doctor said, with the truth of the matter dawning in his eyes. "You saw Mandy and Paisley Rae and you still don't believe me."

"I'm just thinking about your practice, Bruce. And if I'm to be completely honest, I'm thinking about my job as the Mayor. This is going to ruffle some feathers, you know? Do you really think this woman is a vampire?"

Doctor McCullagan turned on his friend with an expression that was close to rage. He said, "You're thinking about your job?! Well I'm thinking about our lives and the lives of the community... about Cynthia! I *know* what we're up against, Boyle! *I saw!* I was there! This is no woman! This is Nosferatu!"

The Doctor snapped his head towards Arthur as if to say: *You understand where I'm coming from, right?*

Then the Mayor looked at Arthur with a similar expression, only his was coming from the other side of the debate. He might as well have said: *You're not believing this nonsense, are you? Tell me you're not as foolish as my best buddy Bruce!*

Arthur swallowed loud enough for both men to hear. A bead of sweat rolled across his skin. Apparently the decision-making was up to him now. He was standing between a doctor and the mayor, and they were looking to *him* for guidance—the part-time gravedigger.

Wonderful.

After a moment of intensive thought, Arthur bundled his courage together with his logic, and said, "If we really think there's nothing living inside those boxes, why bother looking? And if we think there *is* something living inside those boxes, we should probably drag the coffins outside. In all the stories I've heard, vampires hate sunlight. If you're worried about what the people in the town will say, maybe you two gentlemen need a fresh perspective.

"Doctor McCullagan, you're the best doctor in Bleedington and probably the smartest man I know. And Mayor Scott, the people in this town love you and respect you. That's why you're the Mayor. Your jobs are safe. If the people ask why we're looking inside the coffins, tell them the crazy lady that murdered your children *told you* she *lived* in one. How can anyone not understand us looking after hearing *that*? Tell them she was out-of-her-mind mad, and she thought she was a vampire. Then tell them the crypts are filled with bats and snakes, which they are. And we didn't want to end up dying from a snake bite, or rabies. People will understand us checking the coffins and they'll understand us bringing the coffins outside. Don't you know that? Your children are *dead*, Doctor McCullagan. I'm sorry to say it so blunt, but it's true. You have the sympathy of the entire town. Lord knows you have *my* sympathy, every last ounce of it."

He paused.

Then he said, "As for these... " He lifted the hammer and the stake. "Tell 'em they were *my* idea. Tell them I wouldn't walk you through the graveyard without them, being the nervous fool that I am."

Silence came.

Arthur thought he said too much, and cursed himself for saying anything at all. He wished he were home in bed.

Doctor McCullagan began to cry. Through his falling tears, he said, "Thank you, Arthur. That's exactly what I needed to hear."

Mayor Scott followed that up with, "You're a smart man, Arthur. You're thoughtful and considerate."

Arthur, who usually didn't say much to men of such stature, was surprised by the compliments. Sounding embarrassed, he said, "Thank you."

The Mayor said, "No, thank *you*, Arthur. You're a credit to this town, and after today I want you to work for me. Will you? You needn't dig graves any longer, unless of course it's what you like to do."

"Honest?"

The Mayor nodded. "Honest. You're a good man, a truthful man. You're a smarter man than you realize. I'm not sure how I can use a man like you just yet, but I can employ you. That's for sure. I can always employ a man of your quality."

Arthur didn't know what to say.

The three men walked towards the next crypt. Two of them were crying now, but for different reasons. Doctor McCullagan was crying because he was traumatized, Arthur McNeill was crying because he was absolutely astonished by the turn of events. This was the best day of his life.

It was also his last.

11

They entered the next crypt. There were several bats on the ceiling and a pair of rats in the corner but no snakes. They lifted the coffin from its riser—Arthur on one end, Boyle and Bruce on the other. The coffin was heavy but they managed.

Arthur wasn't sure if the other men realized that he dropped the mallet and stake to lift his end, and he didn't say anything because to him it seemed obvious. Once the box was outside he lifted his tools from the lawn and braced himself for war.

Doctor McCullagan lifted the lid; the Mayor watched.

The casket was home to a woman that looked like a dog's chew toy.

They hauled the coffin back inside the tomb and moved on.

Searching the next crypt was a similar adventure. They hauled the box outside and found nothing but bones.

Four crypts down, nine to go.

They entered the fifth crypt.

Doctor McCullagan took one look at the bats on the ceiling and the size of the coffin and said, "Forget it. Lets move on."

Boyle nodded.

Standing at the tomb's door, the gravedigger said, "Wait."

A shiver rolled down Doctor McCullagan spine. "Why? What is it?"

"Something's not right here."

"But Arthur," Mayor Scott said, with a new level of respect in his voice. "The woman we're hunting can't fit inside the box. That's a child's box."

"Vampire," Doctor McCullagan corrected. "Not woman, vampire. And yes, this casket is too small."

"But sir," Arthur ventured bravely, speaking directly to Doctor McCullagan. "That's what bothers me. Assuming there was a vampire in your house last night—"

"There was."

"Yes, well, if that is true... and vampires *do* exist, there is no reason to assume that *your* vampire is the only one in Bleedington."

"Yes, but—"

"And this coffin wasn't here before."

The men became quiet. It was Boyle who broke the silence. He said, "What do you mean?"

"I mean this coffin shouldn't be here. It's new."

"How do you know this?"

"Sometimes, when it's cold or rainy, I use the tombs for shelter. I've been inside all of the mausoleums. It takes a good while to dig a hole, especially in the winter. I'm sure you can understand. This is the first time I've seen a child's casket inside this crypt."

Doctor McCullagan wore an expression that was hard to read, like he was analyzing ten different scenarios at once. Finally he said, "But why would somebody switch coffins? Are there other people involved here? Is this some type of strange conspiracy? Where did the other coffin go, and where did this one come from?"

"I don't know," Arthur said. "But here's another fact: this crypt is colder than the others. Can't you feel it?"

Doctor McCullagan stepped inside the door realizing that Arthur was right: the crypt was unnaturally cold. What did that mean? It meant they found the vampires! They found the monster that killed Paisley Rae and Mandy, the vampire that snatched little Cynthia from her crib.

The Doctor yanked the hammer and stake from Arthur and raced towards the coffin.

Arthur could have challenged him, but didn't.

Mayor Scott shouted, "No!" feeling a flash of horror unlike anything he had ever known. "We have to pull the box outside, remember? Bruce! It's not safe!"

As the Mayor was speaking, Doctor McCullagan grabbed the lid and flung it open, yelling, "Goddamn you!" His eyes were wide and insane.

With the coffin's lid raised, the rafters exploded in a frenzy of wings as hundreds of bats took flight. From the corners of the crypt, rattlesnakes hissed and sprang into an attack position.

Doctor McCullagan screamed, and fell backwards, onto the floor. But he saw something, something—

He turned his head.

Cynthia's corpse was lying in a coil of rattlesnakes.

A snake snapped its jaws and Mayor Scott yelled, "Get out of there!" Scott was standing at the door with both hands on the top of his head and his eyes bulging from his sockets.

Doctor McCullagan flipped onto his belly and crawled towards the door, trying to erase the image that was inside his head. He couldn't. Seeing his baby lying there would burn into his thoughts everyday for all eternity. Bats swirled and swooped. McCullagan crawled. Once he was outside, Arthur slammed the gate shut; the interior door was left open.

Bats circled the tomb in a coiling tornado.

Doctor McCullagan lifted himself to his feet and dusted himself off; his heart pounded his chest. The men watched the winged rodents through the iron pickets in awe.

"What should we do?" Mayor Scott asked.

"We'll come back after they settle," Doctor McCullagan said. "Then we'll drag the coffin outside and kill what we find."

"Did you see anything?" Arthur asked. "Did you see anything inside the casket?"

"Yes," Doctor McCullagan said, with his chin quivering. "I most certainly did."

12

Stephenie's eyes opened to the sound of men talking. Someone was yelling; someone was frantic. She heard someone crying out, saying there was a baby's corpse lying in a heap of snakes. Her coffin got nudged. It seemed that someone wanted to open it and somebody didn't. Someone said something about 'doing it quick' and being done with it. Someone said something about dragging the casket outside and letting the sun fry the abomination to ash. But *she* was the abomination now, wasn't she? Oh yes. The men wanted to snuff out the existence she loved so much. They wanted to destroy a world where everything was beautiful and she was the most powerful creature of them all.

She wasn't having it, wasn't going to allow the fools to drag her outside. She *knew* what the sunlight would do. It would burn her to a crisp.

The coffin was nudged again.

Enough, Stephenie thought. *This ends now.*

She threw the coffin's lid open and sat up straight.

The three men turned towards her. Doctor McCullagan was closest, holding the long, wooden stake at his side. Arthur McNeill was beside him, gripping the hammer tight. Mayor Boyle Scott was several feet away. His hands were empty; a lantern was sitting on the floor behind him.

With a speed nobody expected, Stephenie attacked.

She clawed the left half of Doctor McCullagan's face from his skull before he knew it would happen.

Doctor McCullagan dropped the stake and lifted his hands. He was screaming. Blood poured through his fingers; a flap of skin dangled beneath. His right eye focused on Stephenie with a combination of terror, hatred, and rage, which was so direct it looked like he was putting a hex on her. His left eye dangled from its socket, cracked apart and useless.

Stephenie reached out, bloodlust crazy. She grabbed the Doctor by the collar and hauled him towards the coffin. She knocked away his hands and bit into his neck several times quickly, chewing on it like she was a rabid fox. And after she had hacked into his meat with her teeth, she sucked the fluid out of him. It tasted so good, so fucking good. She loved her new life. She loved it with all her heart, the dead one that failed to beat inside her chest.

Mayor Scott felt his balls pull into his lungs and then he was running. A moment later he was outside, standing in the sunlight, watching the event through the open door. He couldn't believe his eyes. He couldn't believe his best friend Bruce was being eaten alive by something that lived inside a coffin. How could something like this happen? How was something like this possible? It occurred to him then, as strange as it may seem, that the good Doctor was right. This wasn't something to be covered up. It was something people needed to know about. Trivial things like job security and popular opinion didn't matter. What mattered was the safety of the town, the greater good. The truth.

Oh Bruce, he wanted to say. *Oh Bruce, get out of there! Run Bruce; run!* He didn't. His voice, for the moment, was lost.

Arthur, still inside the crypt, took two steps back and watched the assault in horror.

He needed to do something helpful, something that would change the situation, but what? He looked at Mayor Scott, who was standing outside with his mouth hanging open and his bucket-belly shaking in front of him. He looked at Doctor McCullagan's twitching shoulders and at the thin line of blood that was draining onto the floor beneath his feet.

Then he saw the stake.

He had the mallet—the stake was sitting on the floor. Not far. It wasn't far at all.

He dropped onto his knees and snatched the tool in his fingers.

A second later Stephenie tossed the Doctor into the corner like a rag. He landed in a broken pile. Half of his face was white and drained of fluid. The other half was gone. His mouth was open; he had one cold dead eye, locked into place, gleaming white inside its awful black pits. He looked ghastly and terrified. Even in *death*, he looked terrified.

Stephenie leapt out of the coffin with unnatural speed. She was hissing again, hissing and spitting as Doctor McCullagan's blood drooled down her chin. She landed in front of Arthur, legs wide; hands open, looking at him like a meal. She grinned and it was a terrible sight to see. There was no happiness in that grin, only loathing and fury. Only evil.

Arthur, still on his knees, lifted the stake up and slammed it into the vampire's chest. He lifted the mallet high over his right shoulder, steadied his arm and focused his vision. He swung the mallet towards the stake, knowing his life depending on landing a direct hit. The mallet sped through the air. His aim was true.

The hammer—

Stephenie swatted both tools away with her hand and arm. She grabbed Arthur by the shoulders and threw him onto his back. With a quick jump forward, she landed with a leg on each side of his arms. She dropped onto his chest, grabbed his hair and yanked his head left and right several times. She pushed his head to one side and held it in place, exposing the flesh on his neck.

Arthur screamed, not once but a string of times. He thought the vampire's plan was to rip his head from his body.

Stephenie, drooling and insane, tore into his neck like the animal she was. She chewed his flesh, swallowed it down, and drank greedily, like devouring blood was the single most important thing in the world. Her nipples hardened and her body grew warm. She loved killing. Loved it more than anything.

Blood splashed, feet kicked, and arms waved.

Arthur was convulsing. Eyes fluttered.

Mayor Boyle Scott ran into the crypt. He lifted the hammer and stake.

Snarling like a wolf, Stephenie lifted her head. Something had changed. She—

Mayor Scott slapped the stake onto the vampire's back and brought the hammer down hard.

The wooden spear blasted through Stephenie's cold, dead heart.

She screamed, "NOOOOOOOOOOOOO-ooooooooo!"

But it was too late. The damage was done. She could see the stake in between her breasts, covered in black, steaming blood. Her vision faded; light grew dim. Her body convulsed, not unlike Andrew's had.

Twitching and moaning, she tumbled forward.

The Mayor pushed her onto her front, looking down at her with a full portion of disgust in his eyes. His spit on her, cursing her very existence.

"Go back to hell," the Mayor said. "Go back, demon. And don't return. We don't want your kind here."

Stephenie looked up at the Mayor, thinking about hell, and what hell meant to her. She whispered, "No... please no—"

Then the fading lights were fading no more.

CHAPTER TEN:
GROUNDHOG DAY

1

Stephenie opened her eyes. She was sitting in her car with her hands resting on the steering wheel. Again. The diner was in front of her. The passenger's door was wide open. Carrie was making her way towards the front door with her knees squeezed together. She grabbed the door's handle, which seemed to weigh a thousand pounds or more. She pulled with all her might. In the end, Carrie managed to wiggle herself inside. Just.

Stephenie watched it happen. And kept sitting there.

Doing nothing.

The swing between the gas station door and the restaurant door was empty. There was nobody named Christina ready to wave a hand.

Stephenie looked across the parking lot. Empty. Just six cars and a yellow school bus, no attendant, no cars on the highway. Nothing.

Time passed—a minute, maybe less.

The overwhelming amount of—well, everything—didn't matter now. She wasn't shocked. How could she be shocked again? She was numb. That's what she was: NUMB. She didn't care anymore, not about herself, or what happened to her, or what was about to happen to her. She didn't care about Carrie—

Well, that wasn't true.

She still cared about Carrie. She loved Carrie. But Carrie was gone now; nothing was going to change that. She was going to meet Carrie over and over again, in all kinds of new and interesting ways. Ten minutes ago, Carrie was a fucking vampire. Before that, she was some kind of bizarre monster that changed shape and talked about medication. Before that she was, what—an evil voice on the phone? Was that right? Was she missing one? Or two?

God, what was coming next?

Would Carrie be reincarnated as *Frankenstein's Monster? The Wolf-Man? The Creature from the Black* fucking *Lagoon?*

Somehow, Stephenie had slipped through the cracks of what people commonly consider reality and now she was living in hell. It wasn't going to change. It wasn't going to get better. It was only going to get different—and sadly, worse.

She remembered creeping into the bedroom and killing those poor unfortunate babies.

My Lord, she thought. *Help me. This is not right.*

She put her hands to her face and cried. Then she looked up. The parking lot was still empty, of course. It was going to stay that way until she walked into the restaurant bought whatever shit those bastards were selling.

What's it going to be this time? she thought. *What haven't they done to me yet?*

Well, they haven't set me on fire, right? Hell's supposed to be all fire and brimstone, so I've got that to look forward to. And what else? Drowning? Oh yeah, that's a good one. A little bit of drowning will be a real fucking treat, you bet. Oh... I shouldn't forget falling, or have I done that one already? Yeah... no, no... I only thought about falling. Falling 'for real' is still up for grabs, so that's good. Getting eaten by a shark, fuck. That one is so dynamite it should've happened already. Guillotine. Car accident. Poisoning. Oh, and how about getting caught in some kind of nuclear meltdown? It might take 'em a while to get around to that one, but it'll be good when it happens. Maybe my face can melt onto my tits. Oh... speaking of tits, what about rape! How could I forget rape? It's a classic. Maybe they can mix things up—the Wolf-Man can rape my back end while a guillotine lops off my front end.

Stephenie punched the steering wheel. Then she punched it again.

What am I going to do?

Stephenie got out of the car slowly, looking a little like she didn't know where she was. She slammed the door closed, turned around, looked at that fucking bungalow and cursed again.

"I can't do this anymore," she said. Her voice was flat and cold. "I just can't."

She looked at the side of the building; then she remembered...

She started walking fast, with quick moving strides. At the side of the building she saw a woodpile. She approached it. Looked at it.

And there it was: an axe.

She picked it up. It felt good in her hands this time, really good. The hatchet she had earlier was just a toy compared to this bad-boy. This motherfucker was the real deal.

"Okay you dirty cunts," she said, grinning, holding the heavy iron blade in front of her eyes—shaking it back and forth while she prepared her heart and mind for battle. "You want to play. Okay. Lets play."

She turned around, walked away from the woodpile and approached the restaurant's front door. She was grinning. And as she opened the door, she took one final look at the sign that KING'S DINER and listened to the Christmas bells sing.

Halleluiah, she thought. *Halle-fucking-luiah.*

2

The scene was tranquil. Everything was calm. The customers were eating and socializing, the staff were working and everyone was happy. There was no blood on the walls, no bodies slumped over in the booths, no body parts lying amputated on the floor. There was nothing out of the ordinary. Nothing disturbing. Nothing to suggest there was a problem big enough to have people shaking their heads in disbelief. It was a diner, just a simple diner with no strings attached. Florescent lights buzzed in the ceiling and ceiling fans spun below. It smelled like coffee, toast and bacon. The smell alone was enough to get your stomach rumbling and your waistline expanding.

Susan Trigg was closest. She was standing near the door dressed in her yellow waitress uniform, holding an *EMPIRE PENCIL CORP* pencil in her hand. She looked at Stephenie and smiled.

And from there, things happened fast.

Stephenie raised the axe over her head and slammed the blade into Susan's skull. Susan dropped to the floor like a bundle of rags with her eyes wide open, shockingly open, dreadfully open. Her face held an expression of terror so absolute she seemed to have died of fright before the killing blow had been able to claim her. From Stephenie's current point of view, she could see Susan's brain just as clearly as she could see the bone fragments lying on top of it.

Half the restaurant screamed. The other half didn't see it happen.

Stephenie turned towards Craig Smyth and lifted the axe.

Craig's eyes widened and his mouth fell open. Then Stephenie plunged the axe blade into Craig's chest. Craig fell against the counter with blood exploding. Within a blink, Stephenie had raised the weapon again.

Jennifer, who was behind the counter, was reaching for Craig. Her movements suggested that she was trying to catch him.

The axe came down a third time with blistering speed.

Jennifer's arm got caught beneath the blade. Iron slammed into the countertop, and Jennifer's arm was severed at the elbow. She raised her bleeding arm up and blood shot into the ceiling fan. From there, it rained blood eight feet in every direction. Jennifer's legs gave out and she tumbled behind the counter with her arm bouncing after her.

Again, all of this happened fast. The people in the restaurant were still screaming, still releasing their original cry. Some hadn't even had a chance to scream yet. Some were facing the wrong direction and didn't know what was happening. And those that knew—the one's that saw everything—well, hey, they weren't thinking defensively yet. They were in awe with their feet planted on the floor.

Stephenie yanked the blade from the countertop and spun around.

Karen Peel and Denise Renton were sitting at the table on the other side of the door.

Karen had a spoon in her hand and saw what was happening.

Denise was faced the other way and didn't see anything yet, but she knew something was wrong. Everyone was realizing *that*.

Denise turned towards the action just as Stephenie brought the blade down on her skull. The pain she felt was enormous and blood splashed everywhere, but the blow didn't kill her. Not instantly. And in the minutes that followed the assault she managed to make her way out of the restaurant, cross the highway, and die on Jacob's lawn.

But before that happened, Karen opened her mouth and screamed for the first time since she was twelve years old. She had time to think, *I need to get out of here!* Then Stephenie swung the axe like a baseball bat and caught her right in the mouth. Teeth went flying and most of Karen's jaw was gone.

Wayne Auburn was the first one to make it to his feet. Wayne, with his long sideburns and a round potbelly, was the fifty-five year old man that wore a red-checkered shirt that looked like a tablecloth and jeans that were two sizes too tight. He said, "What do you think you're doing, lady? Are you trying to hurt somebody?!" And before he had a chance to realize that he was a complete fucking moron, Stephenie was bringing the axe down again.

She had her rhythm now. She wasn't chopping and hunting. Her enemies were everywhere. All she had to lift the axe and bring it down; lift the axe and bring it down.

So far she was four for four.

And after she cracked Wayne Auburn's head open, making his skull look like a Venus flytrap, she was five for five.

Wayne dropped onto his knees with his squished brain sticking between his eyes. And right around the time he fell over, things started getting real messy.

Dee-Anne was standing two feet away from the place where Wayne fell. In the booth next to her, Eric Wilde had been giving her his order. Eric was the thirty-three years old man that wore a cheap suit that made him look like a used car salesman. He was still holding his menu when Dee-Anne dropped the glass of water that was in her hand. The glass exploded on the floor. Instead of running or screaming or begging for her life, Dee-Anne looked at the floor where the glass had fallen. And before she had time to look up, Stephenie plunked the axe blade into her chest, chopping her nametag in two and puncturing her heart.

At the same moment that Dee-Anne was struck, David Gayle jumped up from his booth; luck was not on his side. He slipped in a splotch of blood. It wasn't surprising. At this point, there was blood all over the place. It was pouring out of Craig, Karen, Wayne, Dee-Anne and Denise. And the ceiling fan made sure that everyone enjoyed a little taste, if nothing more.

As David fell, and Dee-Anne was being chopped with the axe, and Denise was crawling towards the door on her hands and knees, and Karen was holding the place where her jaw had once been, and Jennifer was lifting her severed arm off the floor, and Craig was breathing his final breaths, slumped against the counter with his chest split wide open, Lee Courtney, who had been sitting there with his good pal David, screamed, "OH MY GOD DAVID! DON'T GO OUT THERE!"

Well, if Stephenie didn't know who the next victim was going to be, she did now.

Dee-Anne, who was one minute away from being dead, finally had her knees buckle and she dropped.

Stephenie raised the axe again.

After falling, David landed on his chest. Then he shoved himself away from the floor like he was doing an army push-up.

Stephenie slammed the axe into David's back, shattering his spine.

Lee, still in the booth, watched the blade sink into his buddy. He watched it get raised above Stephenie's head; then he realized that he was next. But what was he going to do? He was still in the booth. He hadn't even started to move his ass yet. He, like everyone else, was in shock. And people who are in shock aren't the world's fastest thinkers.

Moving out of the booth would mean that he had to go *towards* Stephenie. The other side of the booth had a wall, and he sure as shit didn't have time to jump the wall. He only had time to move towards Stephenie and glance at the people in the booth beside him, the Mezzo family: Angela, Alan, and Mark. Then the blade came down. Not once, not twice, but three times. For reasons unknown, Stephenie decided to give this poor chump named Lee three chops while everyone else only received one.

Now there were bodies and blood all over the place. And this was, what—twelve seconds, maybe thirteen seconds after Stephenie walked though the front door? It was only *now* that people were thinking defensively. Now, with nine different people either dead or dying, the wheels started rolling.

Julie Brooks, the third and final waitress, was standing near the back on the restaurant talking with Gary Wright. Gary was the only cook that decided to show up for his shift. He had been explaining to Julie that he had to get going home; he had a scheduled appointment he told them about weeks before. He was saying they should have been prepared; it wasn't his problem; don't fuck with me. Julie was getting her bitch on. She was saying he couldn't leave; they had nobody to cover for him; he'll be fired if he left them like this. Then the shit hit the fan and the blood started spilling. Julie and Gary found themselves holding each other like lovers. They watched in horror and screamed with their arms wrapped around each other's body. At some point Gary pushed Julie's face against his chest and Julie allowed it to happen. Then he pushed her against the wall. That was his defense: stand against the wall. If Julie hadn't been screaming so loudly she might have fired him for having such a worthless plan.

The Mezzo family was thinking a bit more clearly but they were in a worse position. They were sitting in the booth next to David and Lee, enjoying a real front row ticket to the horror show as it played out. And they were next in line. Of course they were. Stephenie was right there, chopping Lee into bits. The only way they wouldn't be next in line, would be if Stephenie turned around again. And she might. There was still a chance it could happen. Eric was right behind her, curled inside his booth like a human cannonball.

David Mezzo, trying to save his family, jumped up from his booth, stood directly in front of Stephenie with his hands in the air and screamed, "Run, Mark! Run!"

Angela Mezzo, still holding the coffee mug with the happy face on it, watched her husband jump up from the booth in awe. She was about to shout something, maybe a *DON'T GO OUT THERE*, or a *STAY WITH ME*, but then David barked his order, Mark complied, and she thought she might faint.

Little Mark, looking like the kid in the Omen movie, was having quite a day. He went to a funeral for the first time in his whole entire life. An uncle he had never met, passed away. Everyone was sad, except him. He pretended he was sad but mostly he was excited. He had never been to a funeral before and he wanted to know what the fuss was about. The funeral was boring. On a scale from one to ten he gave it a zero. He couldn't understand why his parents wanted to go in the first place. After the funeral was over he went to something called a wake, where old people told him how special he was with tears in their eyes. Being called special was all right, and there were a couple of other kids to play with. So the wake, in his opinion, wasn't too bad. But he was in no hurry to go to the next one. Once the wake was finished Mark found a twenty-dollar bill lying on the sidewalk next to something that might have been a dead bird. His mommy and daddy told he could keep the twenty. A few minutes later they went for ice cream and he ordered chocolate mixed with something called tiger's tail. He paid using his newly found money, feeling like a grown up. The ice cream was delicious. After the ice cream was gone they drove for two hours. He had a little snooze. Now he was at King's Diner with a pocket full of cash, watching something he couldn't wrap his head around. And when he heard his daddy shout, "Run Mark! Run!" he did just that. He jumped up from the booth a made a B-line for the bathroom.

Stephenie raised the axe and slammed it into David Mezzo's face. David, who had his hands up like he was expecting someone to pass him a football, didn't even move. He just took it. Hard.

Angela Mezzo released her first scream, her only scream.

Then Stephenie was standing next to her, chopping her apart.

Bones broke and blood spilled.

Stephenie spun around, red gore flowing from the blade. There were three people in the restaurant's main section that Stephenie hadn't gotten to yet. There was Eric, who was still curled up like a cannonball in his booth, and there was Julie and Gary, standing near the bathrooms, holding each other like lovers.

Stephenie made a quick assessment and decided Eric wasn't going anywhere, so she marched past him and headed towards the lovers with the axe held high.

3

Gary Wright was an above average cook and a below average crisis manager. When he saw Stephenie coming at him with a blood-drenched axe he tried to do *something*. But if his actions could be analyzed a million times in slow motion, what that *something* actually was, would be a hard thing to determine. Gary seemed to push Julie away from Stephenie, while trying to pull her closer to him, while turning himself around, while attempting to run, and scream, and hold his position, while he ducked away from the blade.

Julie, with her head planted in Gary's chest, didn't know what was happening. All she managed to do was get dragged around a bit and tilt her head to one side.

Then Stephenie brought the axe blade down.

The blade was intended for Gary, but that's not where it landed. It landed just above Julie's left eye, causing some of the bones in her neck to break while splitting her skull wide open. Julie, without a doubt, would have fallen to the floor if Gary hadn't been holding her. What happened next was in many ways, just a simple continuation of Gary's hopelessly inept line of defense. He pushed on Julie and pulled on Julie and his legs boogied beneath him like he wasn't sure which way to run. And as he danced around in a circle, his partner's blood poured from her skull, onto his chest, arms and legs. Blood poured down her face and fell to the floor. And when Stephenie swung the axe a second time she actually missed her target completely for the first and last time of the day.

Gary ducked low and pushed Julie in a way that started her feet running. And although she was about to die, running is exactly what she did. Julie ran towards the front door, which at that particular moment was open. Why was it open? Because Karen Peel—still holding the place her jaw *should* have been—was making her way outside.

Karen had plans. She was going to jump into her car and go. And that's what she did, sort of. She made her way outside and headed for the car. But on the way there her vision started to fade. The blood loss was catching up with her. She tumbled towards the big yellow school bus not knowing where she was. She fell against the bus face first, smearing her blood where it fell. With the last of her strength she forced herself into a sitting position. Then she died, propped against big yeller with her hands at her sides.

Julie didn't have plans. She had instincts, which directed her in a similar way. Her instincts said, 'Get away from the restaurant any way you can.' So with blood pouring from her skull and some of the bones in her neck broken, she ran to Stephenie's car, threw the driver's door open and plunked herself inside. Five seconds later she died with her face resting against the steering wheel.

But before all that had happened, back in the moment when Julie had started running, Stephenie was missing her mark for the first time. Why? Because Gary the cook had dropped to the floor like a coward; it was his first good move.

And his last—

Stephenie booted Gary in the ass.

Gary screamed and tumbled into a slightly different position. Then Stephenie brought the axe down on left leg. Skin tore. Meat was severed. A bone snapped. Gary screamed and the blade went up. When it came down again it caught Gary on the right leg.

Stephenie looked over her shoulder.

Eric Wilde was still in the booth, curled up like a cannonball. His eyes were peeking above his knees but there was nothing in those eyes that suggested that he was preparing to make a move.

Stephenie hacked on Gary's legs six more times. When she was finished both of his legs had been amputated.

Stephenie walked towards Eric, panting and sweating, dragging the axe along the floor. She could hear crying and moaning but no one was screaming. Not now. The screaming had ended.

Standing at Eric's booth, with Dee-Anne bleeding between her feet, she said, "You're the last one here. You ready?"

Eric shivered and said, "No."

"Good enough."

Stephenie slammed the axe into him a few times and that was the end of his story.

There was a slight pause; then Stephenie looked at the bathroom doors. Knowing from previous experience that the woman's bathroom was empty, she walked towards the men's bathroom and kicked open the door.

Mark was hiding beneath the sink, in a place that impossible for Stephenie not to notice.

"Here we go, kid," she said, and she chopped him four times quickly.

She pushed open a stall door. Empty.

She tried to push open the next one and found that it was locked. With a swift kick the door blasted open and there was Dan Meltzer.

Dan was sitting on the toilet with his pants around his ankles.

He said, "What are you doing? This doesn't have anything to do with me! I don't even know you!"

Stephenie decided to mix it up. She flipped the axe around in her hands and pounded him with the blunt end. The mallet side of the tool was not a whole lot kinder. It mashed his face and crumpled his skull in a way that seemed like it would hurt more.

When she was finished, Dan was still sitting, slumped forward with his back exposed. She chopped it once for pleasure.

Upon stepping out of the bathroom she noticed that David Gayle had somehow managed to crawl several feet with his shattered spine and lean against the wall. Not surprising, there was a framed painting above him. It was the image of a man and his two boys. All three subjects were standing by a tree on what appeared to be a beautiful summer day. The boys looked happy; the man looked proud.

Movement caught Stephenie's eyes. She looked down, and discovered that Dee-Anne was trying to crawl into the lady's bathroom. She gave Dee-Anne one final chop and she marched across the restaurant towards the gas station.

Once she was there she looked the gas attendant in the eyes. The man was holding a greasy rotary phone in his hand.

He said, "It is over now? Is it stopped? I'm calling the police!"

Stephenie lifted the axe, and said, "Remember me, fucker?"

The attendant whispered, "No."

Then Stephenie hammered the blade into his face.

When she yanked it free the attendant fell. An enormous amount of blood poured out of his skull and onto the cheap linoleum tiles. His left eyeball sat on his cheek, smashed apart and looking like apple flavored Jell-O.

It was finished. That was the last of them.

Stephenie walked into the restaurant; the place was a slaughterhouse.

The customers and staff were splattered everywhere. They were slumped over in the booths and in pieces on the floor. Body parts were on the tables and chairs. The walls were soaked with blood. The carnage was nearly immeasurable.

Just like before.

And Stephenie was responsible.

She smiled; then she noticed Carrie.

Carrie had stepped out of the woman's washroom, over Dee-Anne's corpse, and was standing in the heart of the restaurant. Her face looked tremendously frightened.

Stephenie wondered if it was the real Carrie, but she didn't wonder long.

Carrie said, "Mommy, what are you doing?"

And all at once Stephenie realized something awful: she didn't know what she was doing. She didn't have a clue.

CHAPTER ELEVEN:
RETURN TO THE STATION

1

Officer Lynch didn't speak. Officer Quill didn't speak either. The two men just sat there, quietly thinking about all the things she had said.

After a few minutes Stephenie said, "And that's it. The attendant had already called 911. Ten minutes later the cops showed up. End of story." More time passed. Then Stephenie said, "Oh God. I'm so glad I'm back. I didn't want to stay there forever."

Quill cleared his throat. Nervously, he said, "And what did Carrie do?"

"When?"

"Between the time that you, uh... *killed*... all those people."

Stephenie didn't say anything for a moment. She was considering his words. It seemed that even in her version of the story she was guilty of murder. She hadn't realized that until just now. When she was ready, she said, "To be honest, I turned around and walked out the front door. I sat on the patio swing with the axe at my side. I stayed there until the cuffs were around my wrists. Carrie didn't come near me. Maybe she was afraid."

Officer Lynch was sitting at the table with Stephenie and Quill. He had been quiet for a long time. The anger and fury that had been swirling around inside his mind when the interview began was gone. He seemed thoughtful now; in some ways he seemed like a different person. With a voice that sounded almost kind, he said, "I'm sorry."

Officer Quill looked at him curiously.

Stephenie said, "Pardon."

"I said, 'I'm sorry.' Lady, don't go off the handle when I say this but... you need help. Something's not right inside your head."

Stephenie looked Lynch in the eye. "Is that what it is? Am I just crazy? Is it that simple?"

"In my opinion, yes. I think it's just that simple. Before I thought you were, oh, you know... pretending, I guess."

"But you don't think that now?"

"No."

"Do you think it's possible that these things really happened to me?"

"No."

An expression filtered across Stephenie's face. She almost looked insulted. She said, "Why not? I'm not lying to you, you know."

"That's just it," Lynch said. "I don't think you're lying. I think you believe every word you've said. That's why you need help, Miss Paige. You need someone to help you see clearly."

"You believe me because I'm telling you the truth."

Lynch took a moment. He didn't want a yelling match, not at all. Everything was controlled now, everything respectful. He wanted to keep it that way if it was at all possible. He said, "Miss Paige, it's my belief that you *think*... the key word is *think*...that these things happened to you. But these things couldn't have happened."

"Why not?"

Lynch sat back in his chair. He thought, *Where do I begin?*

Quill said, "Miss Paige, while you were telling us your story we've been given a bit of information. Did you notice an officer handing me a folder?" He lifted a few scattered sheets of his desk.

"No," Stephenie said. "I was lost in the story."

Quill nodded. "That's fine. In fact, that's what I thought. Nevertheless, I was given some information. Would you like to hear it?"

"Okay."

Quill pulled his chair a little closer to the table. He said, "The house across the street. That house has been boarded up for a long time. You said that you went in there, but walking through the front door is impossible. There are planks of wood across all of the doors and windows."

"There can't be."

"But there is Stephenie. There is. And if you weren't arrested right now, I'd love to show them to you. Next up, the farm-house."

"Is it boarded too?"

"No, but it's abandoned. It has been since for a while. And here's where your story gets a little weird. The Split family was killed there in August of 1968. Apparently they were murdered with an axe. The killer was never identified."

Stephenie though about this for a moment before saying, "So, you think I saw their ghosts?"

"No Miss Paige. I don't. If your story included a moment where you were chopping up that family, I'd actually start thinking I had fallen into an episode of the *X-files*. But you didn't say that, did you?"

"No."

"Did you chop that family up?"

"No, I didn't."

"Well then," Quill scratched his head. "This is where I get a little confused Stephenie… the family in the farmhouse, back in 1968. Their names were Christina Split, Anne Split and Blair Split. Why do you think that is?"

"I don't know. What do you want me to say?"

"Frankly, I don't know what I want you to say."

"The Split family are a bunch of ghosts; is that what you're suggesting?"

"You wish. What I'm suggesting is… you did your homework. At the beginning of this interview Officer Lynch thought you knew what you were doing. I was the one that thought you were mentally unstable. Now don't get me wrong, I still think you're unstable, but now I'm thinking it was premeditated."

"What?"

"You heard me. How did you come up with those names if you hadn't done your homework?"

"I came up with those names because I'm telling you the truth."

Quill shook his head, becoming slightly angry. "No, you're not."

"How can you say that? What makes you so sure?"

"Because there are holes in your story. Big ones."

"Look," Stephenie said. "I can understand you guys not believing me. Honest, I can. But this stuff happened. It really did."

"You might think that it did," Lynch said.

"And you might be making it up," Quill said, not just to Stephenie but to Lynch as well. "You might be making it up, and I think you are."

"Why would I do that?"

"To get a lighter sentence."

"What? That doesn't make sense. I sat there, waiting to get arrested. Does that sound like the actions of somebody that's aiming for a lighter sentence?"

"Like I said," Lynch mumbled. "I think you *are* crazy. I'm surprised Quill doesn't. Seems like a no-brainer to me."

"And it seems like bullshit to me," Quill said.

"Wait," Stephenie said. "Just wait a minute. Assume for a minute that there was a crack in the earth, in our time, in our reality."

"Like something from *Star Trek*," Lynch said, in a condescending kind of way.

"Yeah," Stephenie said, matching his tone. "Like something from *Star Trek*."

Lynch shrugged. "Okay."

"If there *was* a crack in our reality, I could have really been in a different place. And that would explain why I know about the Split family."

"But Miss Paige," Quill said. "There are holes in your story."

"What holes?"

"Want me to tell you?"

"Yes."

"Okay then. Listen to this—"

2

"First of all," Quill said. "You went back in time?"

"If I fell into a different reality—"

Quill waved her off. "Okay," he said. "Okay, okay. Let me start over." He lifted his notes from in front of him. His eyes scanned the words. "I'm going to start at the beginning. You arrive at the gas station, you go inside—everyone is dead."

"Yeah."

"You're aware that in your version of the story, you're the one who killed them."

Stephenie felt her stomach clench. "Yeah, it's starting to seem that way."

"It's starting to seem that way because it *is that way*, Miss Paige."

Stephenie nodded. "Go on."

Quill expelled a long breath that seemed to be loaded with frustration. "You know what? Lets assume that you did time travel, or whatever. Okay? You said you stopped for gas, you went into the restaurant, and everyone was dead. Right? And from there you looked around for Carrie, you drove away, you came back—then you went into the bungalow across the street. Is that correct?"

"Yes."

"But it's boarded up."

"So you said."

"Why don't you see this clearly," Lynch said. "The woman's crazy."

Quill ignored him. He said, "Then you were chased around by some *zombies* and you went to the farmhouse and talked to *ghosts*."

"I didn't know they were ghosts."

"Okay, fine Stephenie. But you told us—in great detail—that Blair went into the barn and looked at his tools. Hell, you even told us about the old car. How do you know that stuff, Miss Paige? How *can* you know that stuff, if you were sitting in the living room with a pencil rammed into your ankle, which, by the way, isn't there now."

"I explained why it's not there now."

"Oh, I know. You explained away every bit of evidence there is."

"That's not fair."

"No Miss Paige. What's not fair begins and ends with the seventeen dead bodies we found in and around King's Diner."

"I thought they were—"

"Zombies. Yeah, I know. Personally I think you just wanted to find out what it was like to live out a sick fantasy."

"That's not true."

"Fine then. It's not true. You still haven't answered the question. How do you know about Blair's trip to the garage if you weren't there?"

"I don't know."

"Exactly. And in your story, you end up being a vampire, which… uh… don't even get me started on that pile of bullshit. But if, and I mean *if*, that actually happened… why do you know all about…" Quill looked at his notes. "Doctor Bruce McCullagan, Mayor Boyle Scott, and Arthur 'gravedigger' McNeill, huh? Where did that little story come from?"

Stephenie said, "I don't know."

But this time there was concern in her voice. Officer Quill had a good point. Why did she know that stuff? Why did she know *any* of that stuff? Oh God. Maybe she *was* crazy. Maybe she hallucinated everything because there was a problem with her medications. Somehow the idea of walking into that restaurant unprovoked and slaughtering those people was worse than anything else. And let's not kid ourselves; that's what she did. She slaughtered them. She chopped them apart with an axe.

"Is that the best you can do, Miss Paige?" Quill said. "*I don't know?*"

Lynch said, "I don't know why this is hitting you this way, Quill. It still boils down to the same thing. She's crazy."

"But it was premeditated!" Quill exclaimed.

"So she was crazy before she showed up at the restaurant, so what?"

Just then, the door to the interrogation room opened, *creaked* open actually. Stephenie, Lynch, and Quill, all turned to see who was there.

It was Carrie.

Both Lynch and Quill looked at her oddly, wondering what she was doing and where her supervision had gone and how she knew where to find them.

Stephenie pushed away from the girl, afraid.

Very afraid.

Carrie, or perhaps the thing that looked like Carrie, tapped her index finger against her temple.

And with that, the vampire child's words haunted Stephenie's memories: "*Soon you will understand everything and more. All will be explained, in time. You have one more death in this realm, Stephenie. Just one. And my hand shall be the hand that delivers your death and seals your fate. After that, you and I shall return to the place in which you desire—you and I, almost together. You first... alone; then after a short while I shall join you. Soon, everything begins.*"

Stephenie found herself reaching into her back pocket. Her fingers fell upon two photographs. Both showed Carrie sitting on a chair in a big empty room. She looked sad. She looked frightened. Her knees were together, her bottom lip was out and both of her hands were wrapped in a white towel. The towel had a dark spot. The spot was red, looked like blood.

"Oh my God," Stephenie said.

And when she ran her tongue across her teeth, they seemed a little bigger.

October 21/08 - March 31/09

More great titles from
BOOKS OF THE DEAD

BEST NEW ZOMBIE TALES (Vol. 1)
BEST NEW ZOMBIE TALES (Vol. 2)
BEST NEW ZOMBIE TALES (Vol. 3)
JAMES ROY DALEY'S - TERROR TOWN
JAMES ROY DALEY'S - 13 DROPS OF BLOOD
JAMES ROY DALEY'S - THE DEAD PARADE
MATT HULTS - ANYTHING CAN BE DANGEROUS
BEST NEW VAMPIRE TALES (Vol. 1)
MATT HULTS - HUSK
CLASSIC VAMPIRE TALES

BOOKS of the DEAD

CPSIA information can be obtained at www.ICGtesting.com
Printed in the USA
LVOW07s1625130916

504435LV00001B/117/P